# GRIDLOCKED

### A NOVEL BY

### KEVIN FLANDERS

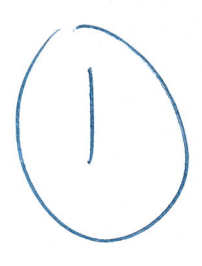

KEVIN FLANDERS

Gridlocked – Copyright © April 2017 by Kevin Flanders

All rights reserved.

This is a work of fiction. All characters, locations, ideas, and related content were either invented by the author or presented fictitiously. Additionally, all organizations, businesses, associations, and other entities featured in this work were presented in a fictitious context.

Excluding reviews, the accounts of this work may not be reproduced, sold, uploaded, disseminated, stored in a retrieval system, or displayed in any form without the written consent of the author.

## ACKNOWLEDGEMENTS

Much thanks to the following folks, who gave selflessly of their time to ensure that this story fulfilled its potential.

Brian Allenberg
Jeremy Bedson
Mike Flanders
Susana Flanders
Dominick Palmucci
Kimmy Palmucci
Mr. Stumbles (a man of few words but great wisdom)

# ALSO FROM KEVIN FLANDERS

Please check out the following novels:

**WELCOME TO HARROW HALL**

**INSIDE THE ORANGE GLOW**

**LASER TAG**

**THE INHABITANTS (trilogy)**

**BLAZE THE GRID (second book in the *Gridlocked* trilogy)**

**BURN, DO NOT READ!**

For more information about upcoming works, visit www.kmflanders.wordpress.com.

# GRIDLOCKED

## Prologue

When it happened, they were advancing along various stretches of Route 49, flanked sternly by deep wilderness, each pair of travelers threading a different skein through the fabric of the night, strangers to each other and to the plans carefully reserved for them.

Ahead of the travelers, disaster lurked in the darkness, ready for the first flashes of their lights. But for now disaster could only wait, an imminent menace, counting the miles and minutes in between. Eagerly, it beckoned.

Nearing the northern terminus of 49 in Spencer, Massachusetts, where the road was straight and the stars plentiful, high school juniors Amelia Valenzuela and Xeke Hamilton held hands and stared up at a familiar firmament, the wind swirling icily against their faces, constellations winking down at them, complicit in their crime. They kissed.

Farther south, in East Brookfield, there was nothing but blackness for Paul Shannon as he walked along, irrelevant that it was night for a man who lived in constant darkness. Paul's hearing, however, had elevated to nearly preternatural heights over the seasons, enabling him to detect distant echoes of gunfire that were, to his guide, Sherman "Steel" Sparks, inaudible above a cold, stiff wind.

In Sturbridge, meanwhile, even farther south, brothers Tommy and Dominick Sims came upon a car stopped in the middle of the road – a black Mustang, baleful with its driver's door partly open and its headlights daggering into the night and its engine rumbling. Dominick looked inside, muttered about the system being down ("goddamn screen's blank, too"), while Tommy, confined to his wheelchair, stared at the Mustang's license plate – **GRDLCK** – trying to remember why it was so familiar to him.

Where had he seen it before?

New thoughts stirred, just out of reach.

The wind snapped and clawed at his face.

He thought he heard a hollow sound somewhere down the road. Footsteps?

For a moment he wondered if he was really awake, stranded on this road with his older brother, or if he was still stuck in–

Suddenly Tommy remembered where he'd seen **GRDLCK** – the middle.

# GRIDLOCKED

## Part I: A Journey

## Chapter 1

"Who won the World Series?" Tommy tried to ask, another set of memories returning to him. Game 6. A walk-off homer. Hernandez had taken Morrison deep on a 2-1 count, the series all tied up at three games. But that must have been five years ago, too; all of Tommy's most recent memories were five years dusty for everyone else.

"Who won–?"

Tommy didn't bother finishing. There was still no way for him to convert his thoughts to intelligible words. When he tried to speak, everything came out gurgled and wrong, as if his mouth were full of water. His arms and legs wouldn't respond, either; from the neck down he was imprisoned in his body.

"Are you hungry?" Mom asked, guessing at what he was trying to communicate.

Tommy managed a feeble shake of the head. His ears rang dully. His mouth was dry, his lips only a little less numb and puffy than yesterday. His head pulsed. They had given him plenty of medications, but what if the meds had actually made him worse?

Tommy could plainly see his family's fear. It blanched their faces to corpse-white complexions, the lines on their foreheads etched solemnly like headstone engravings. Worse, he could almost hear their unspoken prayers for him. Dominick wore a worried half-smile matched by those of their parents, who completed the gathering around Tommy Sims's bed.

# KEVIN FLANDERS

"The World Series!" Tommy's voice lifted nearly to a shout, panicky, desperate, senseless – the voice of a man left lost and destitute. "Who won the World Series?"

A ribbon of unease stretched across the room, frail like wet tissue paper. Glances were exchanged. "It's okay, Tommy. We'll figure it out together," Dad answered softly, taking his son's hand.

Tommy knew he was doing it again. He didn't want to upset his family, but he hated being trapped, hated that hyper-clean hospital smell, hated all the machines, hated the cold prickles that scurried with varying intensity up his arms and legs, hated what the doctors had said – because all of it meant that he really had been in a coma for five years.

Sixty months torn off the calendar, just like that, crumpled up and thrown in the garbage. And now he was back but not the same, never the same.

Tommy suddenly felt like he couldn't breathe, like he might go insane if he couldn't release these thoughts coherently.

If only he could find the strength to break free and articulate what was so clear in his head, then extricate his limbs from the invisible cement that held them.

Mom hugged him yet again, tears freshening.

Tommy was momentarily quiet. After finding an inner calm, he resumed his series of nods or headshakes in response to their questions. He wanted to go home. Most of all, he wanted his mother to stop crying. *A coma*, he thought, recalling in fragments what the doctors had said since he woke up yesterday after one final dream.

*(Comatose and unresponsive. Do you remember anything from the accident, Mr. Sims?)*

# GRIDLOCKED

They'd asked him to blink twice if he could understand them. He'd done so. In time he'd tried to speak, capable only of useless watery sounds. They'd then told him not to overdo it, and that his recovery would take a very long time. But how long was *very long*?

Tommy's helpless gaze made Dominick's stomach twist. Seeking and beseeching, it wrenched Lori Sims's heart. There was nothing she could do for him to make it better, every parent's nightmare. Her son, her beautiful boy, had been confined in the darkness for five years – and what long-term damage had the coma caused? How had he made it out after such an extended period? Would he ever be able to speak again? Would he remain almost fully paralyzed for the remainder of his life?

Raymond Sims hurried from the room, their five minutes alone with Tommy suddenly feeling like a bad idea. Ray wanted Dr. Hagin present, just in case something went catastrophically wrong. He couldn't escape a fear that his son was still walking a tenuous rope, even after multiple encouraging tests. There had been weeks and months and years of squeezing Tommy's hand; begging him to come back to them; talking to Tommy about current events and sports; taking turns reading to Tommy with Lori and Dom; bringing him birthday and Christmas gifts; unwrapping them for his son; placing them in his hands.

After year two, doctors had said improvement was extremely unlikely. During year four, there had been talk of reviewing all options (*no neurological responses whatsoever*).

Tommy is a fighter, they'd kept saying. Prayers had begun to seem pointless, but most mornings had nonetheless found the family at their church, hands joined, faith their only solace.

Tommy's eyes wandered from person to person – Mom and Dad and Dominick and the doctor who'd recently entered, with his square-rimmed glasses and severe brown eyes, none of them able to tell him who'd won the World Series because they couldn't understand him. He had all the details perfectly straight in his head, even after five years (Hernandez's homer had been a line drive over the left field fence, the first homer relinquished by Morrison all year). But these details kept getting botched in translation from thought to language.

Feeling a fresh wave of tiredness – he was as in-and-out as plaid shorts – Tommy took a few moments to focus on his breathing. Among a myriad of other instructions, they'd told him to breathe slowly, deeply.

There wasn't much else he could control.

"The Mariners won it this year? Really? But they were brutal," Tommy said the next morning, though the only halfway understandable word, at least to him, was Mariners.

Dominick had pulled up Mlb.com on his shifter, Tommy nodding in excited approval. Scolding himself for not thinking of this sooner, Dominick had then shown his brother recent baseball headlines, the conclusion of the World Series just days old. He wondered if Tommy understood everything he read; it definitely seemed like he did, and that made Dom close his eyes and offer a prayer of thanks.

"Great idea, Dom," Lori said, her eyes drifting to the window, where a streaky glare of headlights and tail lights pressed softly against the glass, climbing up from the highway.

"The M's finally broke through." Dominick scrolled through a page of playoff scores and received additional nods from his brother. But Tommy's smile looked wooden and fragile, like his lips might crack and bleed. "The year of your accident," Dominick added, "the Yankees won it all that season, I think." He tapped away at the screen, then maximized it fully and held it out for his brother's review. "Yup, Yankees in seven."

"Damn. I thought the Nats had 'em." Tommy sighed, remembering Hernandez being mobbed at the plate, but apparently the Yanks had taken it back to the Stadium and won it nonetheless.

"Mariners sucked for years. Now they're the champs," Dom said.

More questions about the accident ensued, Tommy directed to nod in affirmation or shake his head. Most of the questions were met by shakes. Tommy couldn't remember the accident, only his life before it and his dreams – countless dreams that formed a bridge connecting game six of the 2025 World Series and these last two days with his family in November of 2030.

Tommy had dreamt he was at the side of a road somewhere, voices whispering down to him from steep forested hills, calling his name, his mother's and father's voices? He'd thought those voices sounded like Mom's and Dad's. Another dream had found him inflating like a balloon and rising high above his neighborhood, lifting from darkness toward brilliant light, but it was unreachable white light, Tommy never quite able to access it. In a third memorable dream, Tommy had been shot in the head. He hadn't died right away, though, a few moments of abject knowingness to be had between bullet and final breath, that same blinding white light slowly filling in around him.

The details from his dreams had come back to Tommy like forgotten lyrics returning only upon the playing of their respective songs. When he'd remembered that dark, forlorn road and the alley in which the dream shooting occurred, the accompanying details had surged quickly forth – words, images, emotions – and he'd known precisely where they belonged, able to sort them into the appropriate contexts. Yet still, he sensed, there were many more dreams to be remembered, more details, shadows to be given shape, symbols to be blessed with meaning, a dark and obscure world to be brought into focus like a predawn landscape coming gradually into clarity with the first tinges of sunlight.

Though Tommy's brain hadn't responded to the tests while he was in the coma, it hadn't been completely shut down.

Tommy's recovery was a slow, frustrating process.

Following a week of testing, he was moved to a specialized rehab facility nestled in Boston's Back Bay, an unassuming two-story building where, for an hour every day, a speech therapist helped him rediscover his voice. The rest of the day was dedicated to the attempted rediscovery of other lost basics, though these didn't progress nearly as quickly as his speech.

It was strange, the ability to speak, taken for granted by Tommy until he'd emerged from his coma and spilled out the first gasp of gibberish. The disconnect between thoughts and speech had scared him and begotten sickening dread, but steadily – through seemingly endless exercises – he relearned how to manufacture letters and words and sentences.

Just over a week since transitioning to the rehab facility, Tommy gained partial functionality of his arms and hands…but the internal wires were crossed and dusty. Sometimes, when he wanted to move his right arm, he would instead elicit a twitch of the left arm. On other occasions, an attempted flex of the fingers would result in an achy bend of the wrist. And below his waist there was nothing but sporadically dull throbs and itches.

Equally unpromising, he felt constantly lethargic. His appetite was minimal. Many simple physiological processes were still well beyond him, and the inevitability of sleep brought fear to him. Each time he closed his eyes to the world that had welcomed him back, he worried they wouldn't reopen.

# GRIDLOCKED

But whenever Tommy found himself growing too impatient or afraid, whenever he shook with the need to be free of the tubes and bags and setbacks of circumstance, he tried to remember how lucky he was to be alive. Apparently the wreck had claimed two of the three passengers in the SUV that had veered across the line and struck Tommy's car that foggy night on Route 20 five years ago.

Five years ago. He couldn't believe it. Maybe he would never believe it. So much had changed, both from personal and societal perspectives.

It was a different world than the one he'd left.

"How about I take you out of this place for a while?" Dom said one morning after Tommy completed his speech exercises.

It was the Friday before Thanksgiving. The trees were mostly naked, ready for winter. They were in a bright room overlooking the neatly manicured lawn surrounding the retention pond, sunlight angling cheerfully through the oversized windows and engendering a robust optimism that never could have been achieved on a gray morning.

Tommy was in his wheelchair at a circular table, staring at the smartboard from which he'd just been reading simple sentences and making them sound complex, feeling as he often did, like an invalid, scarcely more self-reliant than an infant. He longed for the day that saw him walk again and tie his own shoes, which he hadn't considered to be blessings on the other side of the bridge, when he'd taught middle school science and jogged two miles a day and led his men's league basketball team in points – a life that sometimes seemed more like a fabrication of his comatose dreams than his actual past. He'd been two years removed from college, the best of life's offerings still ahead, but the accident had shattered him.

One second of one day had changed everything.

(*If only AVA had been in place then*, everyone kept saying in different ways, confusing him. *You missed it by a few years. There are hardly any accidents anymore.*)

"So what do you say, Tommy?" Dom sat across from him, fiddling with a pen left atop a notepad by the therapist. "Are you up for a few days at home? I've been keeping up your aquarium – only a handful of the fish have died, believe it or not. That biosource food works wonders. I'm thinking of eating that stuff myself."

"Home?" Tommy said, the word sounding clunky and foreign, as though spoken by someone in an ESL class. He often wondered what had become of his old voice, a treasure lost beneath the windswept sands of time, buried in the absence of use. Now he was stuck with this spurious, clumsy replacement.

Dom searched Tommy's wistful eyes. They'd informed him maybe a week ago that his former apartment had of course been relinquished, his things boxed up and stored in their parents' attic. Dom had taken his brother's saltwater aquarium and a few boxes of his possessions, mostly books, the majority of which were authored by scientists and professors. Tommy had always been fascinated with marine biology, and Dom had often gone to the facility and read to his brother about whales and jellyfish, sharks and coral reefs, the latest discoveries and methodologies…hoping to spark something in his head, to jump-start the dead battery his mind had become.

It hadn't worked, yet still Dom had come with books, reading for many minutes until finally he tired out or lost himself to tearful despair. But after a while the tears had dried up and there'd been only hollowness – and thoughts of how long Tommy would want them to wait.

"You could use a little time away from this place," Dom said, rounding the table and placing a hand on his brother's shoulder. "We'll watch TV, stay up late – it'll be just like old times."

# GRIDLOCKED

Tommy brightened at the idea, a smile spreading across his lips. It wasn't *his* smile, though, distorted and strange, pulled up oddly at the edges. Other things were still way off, too. His head lolled occasionally, requiring of him an effort to straighten it and keep it from sagging forward or sideways. Sometimes he reverted to an inscrutable language, and it devastated Dom to see his brother like this.

Would he ever be the same again?

"Stay up late," Tommy laughed, taken happily back to childhood. "Yes, want stay up. Let's go. Ho…home. Let go home."

It didn't matter then that only half of his words came out right, the other batch burnt and malformed like cookies kept in the stove too long. It didn't matter that he wasn't exactly sure where home was for him now. It didn't matter – and he didn't dare ask – if he'd received clearance for this temporary discharge.

Tommy Sims was returning to the world.

# KEVIN FLANDERS

## Chapter 2

It was cold, dark, windy. Branches whispered and swayed overhead, blotting out the starlight.

Not for long.

Xeke Hamilton reached through the back window of his father's pickup truck and activated the Q (officially known as the vehicle queue system, colloquially known as the Q). Built into the center panel – a mandate for every vehicle – the screen glowed a soft blue.

"Let's roll, Q."

"Welcome, Xeke. Please name your destination," came the friendly southern accent over the speaker – a woman's voice as agreeably lilting as that of a hostess ready to serve a slice of key lime pie.

Speaking quickly, Xeke put the device's voice recognition software to the test, but still it managed to ascertain his desired destination. After a series of stern admonitions, his parents had permitted his voice and fingerprints to be entered into the system last year as "keys" for a sanctioned user (either was acceptable to get the Q started, and you could talk or tap your way through the manifest process).

Concisely, the Q read back the information, concluding with, "Is this manifest correct?"

"Hell, yeah, it's correct!" Xeke shouted, wanting to impress Amelia, still fearing sometimes that they wouldn't last. He wished he didn't feel the need to try so hard – *Just be yourself,* Mom had said – but what if he wasn't good enough? What if being himself sent their relationship careening off the rails?

"Manifest approved. Queue initiated. Level Three. No defects. Current traffic conditions…" Before the southern belle could provide an estimated time of arrival, Xeke snapped the back window shut and settled in the bed of the pickup truck beside his girlfriend, eager for another night ride.

"Ready, Amie?" he said, pulling a blanket over them, his breaths escaping in thick bursts.

"Eventually we'll get busted for this, you know." She was right, but it wouldn't happen tonight. Xeke's parents would be out until ten or so, the roads theirs to pursue.

"We're fine. No one can see us back here." Shivering, he took Amie's gloved hand in his. He couldn't wait for the summer, layers exchanged for skin.

Her smile shined amidst the shadows. "I love these rides, just us and the stars." She kissed him – icy, tingling majesty, the taste of strawberry lip balm lingering in his mouth. Suddenly the night wasn't so cold.

The truck eased into motion, not a soul inside the cab, its passengers lying abreast in the bed, out of sight, the alcohol tucked away in Xeke's coat pocket. Soon they would be out on Route 49, the stars dazzling above them.

"Maybe we'll *both* see a shooting star tonight," she said a while later, remembering their last ride, when Xeke had been the only one to claim a sighting.

"I can't believe you missed them. They were everywhere."

"You were drunk."

"No way. Two pops doesn't get me scrambled."

"Did you bring the Fireball this time?"

"You'll just have to wait and see."

When the truck pulled onto the next road and accelerated, the wind spread its chill over them, Amie's hair flying loose from her hood. In a few minutes she would put on her beanie cap, but for now she was content with her hair whipping about, the wind refreshing against her face, winter another minute closer.

Watching tree limbs and streetlights slide past, Amie felt like she was a bird, the truck no longer carrying her along but instead a set of wings enabling her to soar. The sensation heightened when she closed her eyes, and once again she was free of herself, free of the guys who'd used her and lied to her and made her feel worthless, free of the friends she felt compelled to please, free of her overly concerned, smothering parents, free of a stagnant town with nothing to offer her, free to be with Xeke.

Xeke was different. With Xeke, Amie was different. Herself. Free.

The truck picked up speed, the lights of the neighborhood falling away. Too bad they couldn't shake themselves loose of the godforsaken grid and start afresh, in a new place where they weren't just blips on a radar (or a red dot on the map of the lighted Q screen).

Amie hated the grid. She hated being controlled and monitored. All her life she'd been carefully guided due north by the shining moral compass of her well-intentioned parents, molded lovingly like clay, the daughter of a pastor and a Sunday School teacher, discipline and benevolence and selflessness her clingy siblings, following her everywhere. Worse, Amie had allowed herself to be malleable – had welcomed it, in fact – until that day last year she'd felt like she couldn't breathe, drowning in the too-still waters, wondering what it might be like to cast just one stone into the mirror lake her life had become. There had been a party that night, and an excess of alcohol. There had been a guy on the football team, not even the quarterback or an important player, some overinflated second stringer who, with a few shots of whiskey in Amie's system, had seemed legendary.

Still, he'd been significant enough to ripple the loathsome glass.

Amie couldn't remember much else from that night, only the pill the next morning and with it the realization that she'd finally disturbed the water. And the shame. The lake mirror, had she dared to gaze into it beneath an angry gray sky that morning, would have shown the fragmented reflection of a girl who hated herself. Months later, Amie's once placid lake churning with poison, she had drunkenly held a knife to her wrist, and she'd smiled upon applying thin pressure, wondering what true freedom would be like. She'd taken to the road that night, walking, walking, walking, not knowing where she was going, anywhere but home to her loving parents, who'd always shown her the right way, due north with integrity…

Now, at Xeke's side in the truck, the wind funneling down at her, the stars taking brighter form, Amie thanked God for showing her the path to happiness, certainly not due north but perhaps an oblique northeasterly course. She had abandoned Him for a time, but God had never left her, she'd realized. Amidst the deepest darkness He had extended a light to her – a light discovered not at church, where her father recited his sermons, but instead on the night road that had found Amie alone and despairing, walking aimlessly.

Xeke had somehow recognized her that night. He'd pulled over on E-mode, asked if she wanted a ride…but what had been waiting for her out there if Xeke hadn't come along? Whose headlights would have broken the lonely dark of the next hour?

The truck climbed to its max speed for the trip, an easy sixty without a driver, never any swerving or unexpected braking on the grid, vehicles falling into sequential formation like products on an

assembly line. The stars stretched across an enchanted ocean of mystery, an enigmatic tapestry interwoven with dreams past and present. Had she been by herself, they would have been just stars, meaningless, but whenever Xeke was at her side, they always reached her on a deeper level, evoking hopes and inspirations. Looking up at the stars tonight, achieving dreams really did seem possible.

"How many stars do you think are in the galaxy?" Xeke questioned above the wind. "A million? A billion?"

The truck slowed considerably, headlights rushing past in the same direction, obviously belonging to a Level One or Level Two vehicle. Amie turned to Xeke, his face cloaked in darkness beyond his hood. Yet again she wondered where she would have gone that night if he hadn't picked her up. Who would have found her?

"Billions," she said, indifferent to their continued deceleration, trying to focus solely on her boyfriend. The conversation reminded her of one they'd shared many years ago, staring up at the stars in her back yard, waiting for the Perseids to get off their lazy asses and justify staying up late to see them. They'd been neighbors for the early part of their lives, those summer campouts among Amie's fondest childhood memories.

"You ever wonder what's out there?" he said. "I mean, we can't be the only ones in the universe, right?"

"Definitely not. There's probably planets ten times more advanced than ours."

Xeke pulled her close. For a while they said nothing, Amie feeling suspended, weightless. They were perfect, these illegal rides beneath the stars, only him and her. They could be in the same position at home, on her bed, but the stars lifted the experience to surreal. It filled Amie with almost childlike wonder, as if the next moment would redefine all that had come before it.

Their kiss was tantalizingly short, broken when Xeke said, "We're stopped."

# GRIDLOCKED

It was true. The stars no longer rode along with them. The whirling, driving, buffeting wind no longer stropped its blade of ice against their skin. Half-dazed, craving more, Amie sat up and took in darkness to the south and virtual darkness to the north, a pair of lambent red eyes for tail lights waiting a quarter of a mile down the road.

Fear shivered through Amie's bones, deep and resonant.

"Something's wrong," she said.

"Nah, probably just a defect, maybe low tire pressure or something," Xeke assumed.

"So why is that car stopped, too?" Amie pointed to the northerly vehicle, which hadn't moved. Something about those red lights in the darkness, like the final embers in a midnight fireplace after everyone has gone to bed, made her stomach twist.

Xeke peered out beyond the cab. He hadn't noticed the other vehicle until she'd brought his attention to it. "You're right – that's really weird. Maybe there's a dog in the road or something. One time we were stopped on Route 20 for five minutes so the grid could redirect traffic around a bunch of turkeys."

Amie put a hand on Xeke's shoulder, glad he was with her. If she'd been on her own and the grid had come to a standstill at night, way out here on 49 in the darkness, she would have been frazzing out for sure.

Xeke reached through the back window to unlock the truck, climbed out of the bed, and slid into the operator's seat, surprised that the southern belle his parents had selected for the Q's voice wasn't rambling on about the reason for the stoppage. One of the many justifications for AVA's passage was the system's ultra-informative design, alerting operators to everything from mechanical problems to bad weather approaching. If you didn't have enough zip in the battery to reach your destination, you'd be redirected to a recharge station. If your motor faltered, the vehicle would pull itself safely into the breakdown lane and a technician would be automatically notified of your incident.

*AVA is one hundred percent dummy proof,* Dad had once said.

This time, however – for the first time in Xeke's experience – the Q was being a total dumbass. No matter what Xeke commanded, no matter how many times he reset the system, the screen remained an empty blue. The usual vocal prompt – *Welcome, Xeke. Please name your destination…* – was replaced by eerie silence.

Xeke slammed the door shut behind him. He hiked a foot up on the left rear tire, then hoisted himself back into the bed.

"What's going on?" Amie said.

He shrugged, glanced down the road, where the other car was still stopped. "I don't know. It's…dead."

# GRIDLOCKED

## Chapter 3

"Hell was that?" Paul Shannon exclaimed, stopping, the first thing he'd said in many minutes.

Paul and Steel had been soldiering through the darkness, determined to make up the lost hours overnight, the clunk, clunk, clunk, clunk of Paul's cane against the pavement having suddenly broken its metronomic rhythm.

Whenever a vehicle had approached these last several minutes, Steel had given his standard indication of, "Car!", and, arm in arm, they'd proceeded with caution. But that had been it for exchanges between them, until now.

"You hear something?" Steel said. Born Sherman Sylvester Sparks, he'd acquired his nickname in the cage fighting circuit and had stuck with it ever since.

Tilting his head to the sky, Paul said, "Gunfire to our right. Unequivocal. Sounded like a semi-auto, something heavy, sure wasn't no hunter. What road we on again?"

Steel lit a cigarette. "Route 49 North, somewhere between nowhere and oblivion. Phone's been out of service the last twenty minutes, at least."

"Paint me a picture." That was Paul's way of asking him to describe their surroundings.

Shining his flashlight down the road, then into the wilderness, Steel said, "Dark as hell out here – nothing but woods. Trees are as thin as toothpicks. I bet some of them have been here since Georgie Washington came through." A moment later: "Gives me the creeps walking at night. Everything's different in the dark, man."

"Any drones landing?" That meant: any vehicles approaching? Having served as Paul's guide for almost five years, Steel could decode even the most arcane of his many phrases.

"Nothing." Steel scratched his thick beard. "This road's dead."

Paul cleared his throat noisily. "Something ain't right. Well past amiss, buddy. Shouldn't be any shooting this late, and definitely not *that* kind of shooting. Send a SatCom alert to the police, would you?"

Steel pulled out the radio, but his report went almost a minute without response. At last a dispatcher took his information and said the troopers would check it out.

Paul started again, his pace quick. He was tall, approaching seven feet, his childhood dream to play for his hometown Chicago Bulls and mystify the crowd as Michael Jordan had. And he'd been on his way, too, a high school standout who'd pulled in his share of recruiters. He'd worked hard in spite of the fear that it would all be for nothing, that the curse of his genetics would strike. He even looked like Michael Jordan, with a sharp goatee and a pair of red-tinted shades that carried an enigmatic air. He spoke fast and with profound intelligence, his vocabulary sometimes seeming to Steel like another language. He'd been offered college scholarships by people who knew nothing of his curse.

But at age seventeen and seven months, Paul Shannon had been declared legally blind, the curse striking unusually rapidly over a three-month period, eating away at his vision until there was nothing left. Retinitis pigmentosa. The doctors had warned his parents after Paul's first episode of impaired nighttime vision at age seven that there was nothing they could do to cure the degenerative disease that had blinded his grandfather and skipped his father. If the curse came for Paul, there would be no stopping it…and so Paul, having recently watched an old western movie with his grandmother, had begun likening the disease to a faceless villain arriving by rattling stagecoach at dusk. The thought of what the disease did to people had scared him badly – *It took Grandpa's eyes. It might take my eyes, too* – and only faith and a nightlight had helped Paul get back to sleep after the scariest dreams.

But the curse had indeed come for him years later. His basketball career was over, his commitment to the University of Kentucky finished, his life in pieces. For a night he'd considered ending it, but his mother had held him and cried with him.

*There's always somebody worse off than you*, his mother had said, her words at first shut out by his devastation but gradually, a long while later, settling in.

The next morning Paul had woken with a mission – to walk every state in the nation seeking to share the stories of those less fortunate than himself. A calling, as he'd often described it, a quest to embrace his mother's words and be made grateful. Even if his vision was gone, his arms and legs still served him. He could still breathe and eat and experience joy and speak God's Word and fall in love – and he'd vowed to gain a new perspective through the catharsis of his journey.

"I don't like this," Steel said many minutes later. Something about dark, windy nights made his insides curl with unease, and the wind had been kicking up since sundown.

Paul kept talking about the gunfire – and with his exceptional hearing, it might have originated two towns away. The wind muddling everything into a whispery chorus, Steel knew he, himself, didn't stand much of a chance to detect additional gunshots at the current distance.

They stopped again. Paul listened closely, motionless, hands cupping his ears to break the wind. At last he said, "On we go," and they continued walking.

Steel kept his light on the road. Mostly. Each time he directed it into the woods, the imagined menaces therein became even more vivid, their faces taking twisted shape, peering out from behind trees.

"That a drone I hear on the landing route?" Paul said shortly after they resumed their trek, hearing the distantly approaching vehicle well before Steel saw its headlights round a bend.

"Your hearing's in top form tonight, buddy."

Paul chuckled. "Yes, sir. I can hear unborn babies' heartbeats before their mommas even know the little miracles exist, and that's no lie. Say, I ever tell you about the time my parents were petrified one Christmas Eve when they heard a soft shuffling on the front porch? My daddy was halfway across the room to grab his gun when I told 'em it was only Grammy, with her little susurrating steps. Woman's as light as a wraith, kind as your luckiest day. She'd come that night with grocery bags distended to the burst, gifts ready to spill out."

Paul's smile stretched deeply into the past, a contagious smile. They loved telling each other stories of family and friends, of good times and harrowing ordeals. Stories kept the miles rolling, kept the darkness at bay. Spend enough time hearing of a man's past, Steel had learned, and it often becomes intertwined with your own.

Steel had at first been reluctant to talk about his past, its lessons hard and painful, but Paul had never ceased his constant inquiries. He was most interested in Steel's career in the cage, five years that sometimes seemed like the ambiguous terrain of a dream – illogical, disconnected somehow – a world of blood and rage bookended by two major concussions. Above all else, there had been hate. Steel could remember his eyes twitching and hands shaking helplessly before the fights, the crowd a ghoulish composite of color and noise. Most of the time he'd been hopped up on speed and other drugs, but not even the best rushes had mitigated his hate.

Hate had gotten him through it.

# GRIDLOCKED

Steel had gone into the cage following his father's death. He'd eventually forced himself out of fighting to care for his mother, but he'd been too much of a mess to manage his own life by then. Addicted. Unemployed. There had been an arrest; rehab; living on the streets; hopping trains to somewhere new; somewhere new turning into the bright lights of Chicago; meeting Paul at the shelter, high on something that day – Heroin? Painkillers? Both? – the sightless serving the unseeing. Later, when the rain had ruled the night and kept them shuttered away, Paul had told Steel of his mission…

Paul jolted to a stop. "There it is again – even louder now! You hear it, man? You hear that? Hell's it coming from?"

Steel hadn't heard it.

A lash of wind ribboned across the road, careened into their faces, leaves once colorful scraping and swirling in its wake, crunching in cold death. Steel thought he saw someone at the edge of his flashlight's ambit, waiting for them in the middle of the road. Again the phantasm faces poked out from behind the trees.

Steel zipped his coat up to the chin. "Car's coming from behind."

They scooted further into the breakdown lane, Steel holding his friend's arm until the car passed.

Except it didn't pass. The headlights remained bright on their backs, Steel turning and squinting into the glare.

"Hell's that drone doing?"

"Good question." Steel felt as if an ice cube were slowly melting in his gut. Stopped fifty feet back, the vehicle appeared to be a sedan, though it was difficult to tell with its lights flooding.

"So damn bright I think I can see it!" Paul declared, removing his sunglasses. "Jesus, Steel, I can see it! Shapes, too! Wait, is somebody moving?"

Their voices arrived before their figures, Steel finally glimpsing movement at either side of the vehicle.

"You need to get off the road," one of them called. "It's not safe."

Shielding his eyes from the glare, Steel knew they were cops by the campaign hats. State troopers – finally they'd arrived. "What do you mean, not safe? What the hell is going on?"

The first trooper hurried toward them. "We're under attack."

"Get off the road now!" the second trooper repeated.

Turning back to the north, Paul saw only darkness, but, facing the lights again, both of the troopers' forms were visible.

Gradually, miraculously, the clarity enhanced to streaks and splotches of watery light.

"My Savior," Paul whispered, falling to his knees, tears in his eyes, oblivious to the troopers' orders.

# GRIDLOCKED

## Chapter 4

It was a brisk and sunny morning, the gentle wind refreshing against Tommy's face. He felt like he'd won the lottery each time he was freed from the facility, sunlight embracing him, the cold air reminding him he was alive.

This side of the coma, everything came to Tommy with heightened intensity. Colors seemed brighter. Sounds seemed sharper, louder. Strangely, the air smelled sweeter, like food at the fairgrounds. Though it was late fall, the wind had the renewing quality of springtime.

"Check out the new wheels," Dom said with a proud grin, pushing Tommy's wheelchair alongside a maroon Dodge Peregrine in the rehab facility parking lot. "Straight out of the factory. Got a great deal on it."

The car was small and angular – and ugly. Tommy was at first baffled when his brother helped him into the driver's seat, not a steering wheel extended before him but instead an empty space, the dashboard replaced by a widescreen. Then it all came hurtling back to him. Five years ago, just before his accident, they'd passed the Autonomous Vehicles Act of 2025 with stunningly little resistance. The memories were a bit hazy, but Tommy could recall some of the news reports. They'd called it AVA for short, an unprecedented law that required every manufacturer – from big rigs to motorcycles – to produce or retrofit all vehicles in accordance with groundbreaking autonomous innovations and traffic control systems.

For years they'd been improving vehicles capable of driving themselves using short- and long-range lidar sensors, microchips, cameras, and GIS accureaders, among other more recent inventions, but the technologies had been essentially useless without a revolutionary framework – a comprehensive system that could transform America's roads from chaos to order. What good were driverless automobiles, the primary argument had been, in a society still infected with dumb, impaired, distracted, and plain dangerous drivers? (Awesome – your vehicle can drive itself. Now sit back, relax, and wait for someone to blast your self-driving car off the map.)

"The grid," Tommy murmured when he saw the blue glow of another screen to his right. He hadn't been surprised by the domes rising from the roof and hood of the car. Driverless technologies had been around for decades, rapidly maturing; the grid, however, was still a new enterprise.

"Ha!" Dom exclaimed in celebration. "You remember!" He rounded the car and slid into the passenger seat, then pushed a button to activate the device that would connect them to the grid. What was it called? Remembering the name was like trying to catch a drifting leaf in the wind. Just when Tommy thought he had it lined up, the thing slipped through his grasp.

"Welcome, Dom. Please name your destination," came a man's voice from the speakers. Tommy remembered watching online demonstrations of how these things worked, and now he could see it live, his brother simply saying, "Home", and letting the technology go to bat.

In a moment the device confirmed his information. "Is this manifest correct?"

"Correct," Dom said, turning to Tommy. "Pretty sophisticated stuff, huh? You probably remember how skeptical I was of the grid at first, but the damn thing is flawless."

Tommy nodded, overwhelmed by the disparity of life on this side of the coma. The bridge spanning those five years between then and now – the middle, as he'd taken to identifying it – had brought him to a place he wasn't sure he wanted to encounter just yet. He felt like he'd obliviously stepped into a calculus class, ready to take on whatever challenges faced him, when he actually belonged a few grades back in algebra II.

Dom pointed to the device. "Check out what it says next. I've got the voice set to airplane pilot."

Seconds later, the grid's robot voice announced in an easy Midwestern accent, "Manifest approved. Queue initiated. Level Three. No defects. Current traffic conditions are manageable, no major delays out there. Should have you into Sturbridge within the hour." Dom was on his phone now, checking his messages as the robot carried on: "Current weather out in Sturbridge – 45 degrees, light winds out of the north. We thank you for your continued commitment to keeping our roads safe."

The interior lights forming a rim around the floor and ceiling flashed yellow, then took on a solid yellow band. "Caution, vehicle departing in ten seconds. Please keep doors closed for your safety."

Tommy felt a moment's panic when the interior rim went green and the car reversed, then eased forward toward the road. He glanced down at the pedals, but where there should have been an accelerator and brake was now just ample room to spread your legs. And where the hell was the e-brake?

Sensing Tommy's unease, Dom looked up from his phone and said, "Nothing to worry about, man. Check out the grid in action. Pretty soon I'm gonna buy those retractable window screens – it'll be like the fucking movies in this bad boy."

The car accelerated, made a right turn onto the road, and fell into place behind a van. Oncoming cars rushed by them. None of them crashed. There were no fires, no explosions, no blaring sirens, no screaming hordes, no bloody messes, no jaws of life, no reporters snapping photos.

They came to an intersection, slowed to a stop, yet there were no signal lights. No signs whatsoever. To their left, in the turn lane, a sedan was occupied by a pair of elderly ladies, one of them watching TV, the other eating a breakfast sandwich and reading her Kindle.

"No one's allowed to drive anymore, not even cops?" Tommy said.

Dom misheard the question and provided the answer to another. "There are hardly any accidents anymore, only when the Freedom Riders decide they want to raise Hell, fucking terrorists." He was silent for a moment, then said, "Still, even with those assholes and the wrecks they cause, it's a million times safer than before."

"Who are the Freedom Riders?"

Dom continued offering answers to questions that weren't asked. "You know what did it, don't you? All those Super Bowl commercials saying the grid would save lives. Combine that with scare tactics – a few reminders here or there of the San Francisco traffic signal hack – and we're talking instant mindfuck, Tommy." He shook his head. "When Mothers Against Drunk Driving and the state police unions expressed their support of Providence Devlin, it was all over. Congress just seemed to cave in at that point, and boom, it's on to the President and national law time, baby. Who would have thought it'd be that easy? People were predicting a half-century battle – now they're expecting Canada to come on board next year. Japan is making plans as well – heavy pressure from the automakers that lost a lot of business to American manufacturers."

"Providence Devlin," Tommy repeated, the name having struck a chord of recollection. Even with half a decade lost in the middle, Tommy could see Devlin's face – blue eyes, inviting smile, wavy blond hair, an air of mystery about him, perhaps originating from his glasses, an oddity for anyone under fifty to wear glasses these days.

They were entering the highway, Tommy taking notice of the driverless vehicle's unblemished performance. Never did it stray

# GRIDLOCKED

from the center of the unmarked lane (the lines had been paved over sometime between Then and Now). The ride was a smooth, efficient glide, almost as if they were flying.

The roads were smooth, too. No potholes, no debris, no litter – every road was as clean and freshly paved as the Mass Pike, a toll road that had always been kept in top shape.

"The man's a genius," Dom said of Devlin. Tommy watched as his brother pulled from his shirt pocket and maximized the latest version of the Apple iBook – the *Shifter*. He plugged it into a printer installed in the center console; then, with voice commands, he was printing multiple pages that sprang up from slits atop the console like slices of toast. "There was Einstein and Bill Gates, and now there's Providence Devlin." Dom stacked the papers, foldered them, printed a new batch, and produced a second folder from his satchel. "Difference between Devlin and the others is his ruthlessness. You remember the Boston Address? That must have been before your accident."

When Tommy shook his head, Dom said, "It was a speech for the ages, man. Mom was moved to tears when she heard this guy's story, how his kid brother was killed in a car accident and it inspired him to prevent other families from experiencing his pain. For me, the best part was when he went straight for his opponents' throats. The price of refused transcendence is paid not with money but lives – that was one of his best lines. And before every legislative session, he somehow convinced politicians to pass out pictures of kids who died in OUI and distracted driving accidents. He knew exactly how to manipulate people's emotions, and now he's a billionaire."

Dom leveled a hand over his heart. "As far as I'm concerned, I stand corrected, Tommy. I thought the grid would be an epic fail. I thought there'd be multi-car pileups everywhere. I thought hackers would send people over cliffs on day one, but the technology works. They say there's like twenty safeguards to make sure nothing goes wrong. It's layered like a damn wedding cake."

They reached Dom's house around noon, a raised ranch Tommy had never seen before. It was beige and black-shuttered, with a burgundy front door whose color, in comparison to the house at large, was less stately than incongruous.

There was a garden out front, and an enclosed swimming pool off to the side, each having been readied for winter. The porch flag was colorful and Thanksgiving-themed, turkeys in one corner, pilgrims on the left, a table of food at the center. In his head, Tommy tried to spell Thanksgiving but gave up after a few letters, the ability to maintain visualization of the sequence beyond his current capacity. It kept coming out as *Thks* or *Thangs*, and then he would lose his place and get frustrated.

"What do you think of the place?" Dom said, pushing Tommy's wheelchair into a cramped garage tucked beneath the house. "Cyri loved it at first sight. Me, it took a little while, but I came around."

"Very nice," Tommy complimented, sounding to himself like a man of Middle Eastern or Asian descent. It made him want to laugh and cry.

*Will it ever get any easier?*

Dom got him situated on the living room sofa, Tommy feeling hot with the shame of imposition. In high school, he and Dom had played football, hockey, and baseball – trivar athletes who'd ruled the school.

Now he was useless from the waist down.

"Cyri can't wait to meet you," Dom said.

# GRIDLOCKED

Tommy smiled thinly. A glint had come into Dom's eyes at the mention of Cyri, his fiancée, the mantelpiece and wall photos speaking kindly of their three years together. Upon first glimpsing those photos of Dom and Cyri together, Tommy had remembered that there'd been a new girlfriend in his own life at the time of the accident. They'd gone on a few dates, bowling at Bogey Lanes and dinner somewhere, maybe Applebees, maybe Olive Garden. He couldn't recall her name, though clearly she hadn't wanted to wait an indefinite period to see if the relationship would work out.

*The nerve of her*, Tommy thought, smiling at his humor. All had not been lost.

Later, Dom tried to get a little work done while the man recently hired as a home therapist attended to Tommy in private. It pained Dom to see his brother, who'd always been independent and robust, subjected to such miseries and redefined by everything he couldn't do. Sometimes, when Tommy's face twisted with a particularly oppressive anguish, Dom wondered if he wished he'd died in that accident.

"The lake," Dom said to his home office windows. "That's just what he needs. Can't wait to get down to Lake Lashaway and have a bonfire, just like old times."

## Chapter 5

Xeke tried the Q again. Nothing. Sharp stones piling up in his stomach, he climbed back into the bed of the truck with Amie.

Inwardly, he was beginning to panic. Outwardly, he was smooth and shrugging in his dismissal of trouble. He pushed his hood off, only to snap it back in place a moment later.

"You think it's the Freedom Riders?" Amie said. "Maybe they found a way to shut it down."

"No chance," Xeke said. "Those guys aren't smart enough to stop the grid. All they're good at is shooting people and getting splattered." Xeke checked his shifter, contemplating a call to his parents but also dreading the idea of an explanation. "It says no signal. What does that mean?"

She tossed up a hand. "That's what mine says, too. Maybe a meteorite hit, something crazy like that."

For the first time in their young lives they couldn't get reception, and without the Q they were stuck, no way to manually operate the truck. Since the passage of the AVA of 2025, vehicle operations had been conducted exclusively through the grid. People weren't even allowed to walk or ride their bikes on roads anymore, the cops in constant search of grid dodgers. To earn his driverless operation certification, Xeke had needed to learn that grid dodgers are defined as motorists who operate vehicles that do not conform to AVA 2025 standards. Such vehicles, the informational booklet had read, are not equipped with the latest technological upgrades and therefore cannot be guided by the sequencing system, the punishment for operation of said vehicles no less than six months in prison for a first offense.

Typically grid dodgers were easy to spot, the ones avoiding sequenced traffic by venturing into the breakdown lanes. The most dangerous of all grid dodgers – the Freedom Riders – zipped around on motorcycles and often weaved in and out of traffic.

"It's gotta be the Freedom Riders," Amie insisted. Even in the darkness, Xeke descried the shine of fear in her eyes. "Those psychos promised to take down the grid."

Xeke took her gloved hand. "It's not them. Those guys are a bunch of old dudes with fake limbs and PTSD. There's no way they could hack into the grid – the people who designed the security were hackers themselves, geniuses. Once they were done, I heard they hired a team of professors from MIT and Chinese exploit experts to try to crack it, and even they couldn't get in."

Amie sat back against the cab and glanced up at the stars. "Then what do you think happened?"

He kissed her cold cheek. "It's just a glitch with the satellite, probably. Don't worry, a vat will eventually come by and tell us what's going on. But while we're waiting, I'll make sure you don't get cold out here."

Amie let out an apprehensive laugh. The vat (vehicle assistance technician, hundreds of thousands of them employed by the government as part of the grid's launch) would of course report the situation to Xeke's father, the vehicle's owner. Then they would be in big trouble for taking the truck without permission, but this was a thought floating toward the edge of Amie's mind, a deeper, nameless fear having entrenched itself at the center.

Again Amie checked north and south, hoping for headlights. But aside from the vehicle stopped in the northern distance, there was nothing. "I don't like this," she said. "Something's wrong. I don't think this is just a glitch. Maybe we should go talk to whoever's in that car up there, see if they know what's happening."

Xeke eased in beside her and wrapped an arm around her shoulders, pulling her close. "No need for a frazfest, babe – I guarantee they're just resetting the system or something. It'll be up and running any minute. Meanwhile," – his lips were like ice cubes on her neck – "I'm sure we won't get bored."

A part of her wanted to indulge him. The memories of the others still clung to her – their lies and their deceit and, later, their mockery – thorns of regret digging into the woolen fabric of Amie's pride. Giving herself to Xeke would force some of the barbs to fall away, yet Xeke was the very reason she resisted such urges. She was a stronger person now because of him, the boy who'd always wanted the best for her, the boy who'd fallen miserably to obscurity while the others had taken their turns. Amie wished she could undo it…what she would give to extricate her name from the web that snared countless names, a web whose intricate gossamers twitched and silvered with shame, spun by boys exceeding with greed and self-importance. And once your name was snagged in that toxic web, it was there forever, no way to wrest it free or get back what you'd given.

*Boys are just users and abusers*, Dad had once said, *pleasure junkies looking for their next fix*.

Xeke wasn't like them. Xeke had told her he'd never hurt her.

"Nothing bad's gonna happen," Xeke said at last, realizing Amie wasn't up for it.

Instead she nestled into his shoulder, the wind raging again. To the south, the road was black, infinite, blending into the woods and the sky, ocean-like in its mystery. The stars were brilliant yet baleful. They glimmered with insights unknown to those trapped down here on the road, blocked in by the trees, harried by the cold wind. And something about those two red eyes to the north could make even the largest man feel small.

# GRIDLOCKED

When Xeke spoke again in a few minutes, his voice was panicked. "What's that?" he said, looking into the woods.

Amie felt something drop in her chest, then registered his laughter. She slapped him hard on the shoulder. "Plungelicker."

Their laughter shifted to kissing, a rising feeling in Amie's chest now, and this time she stopped Xeke from taking her further only because of the headlights breaking on the southern horizon, slightly inclined from their position.

When the lights fell level, they lanced brightly into their eyes, forcing them to look away.

"Q must be up again," Xeke said, hopping athletically down to the road. He'd never been overly fine in his looks, but he was wiry and strong – and after all these years Amie had finally begun to feel an attraction to his humor and kindness beyond the appeal of friendship. It had taken far too many falls, but she'd learned what was important. Plus, she'd spent a night with the finest boy in school, with eyes of an inconstant hue and a scar on his pretty cheek that could leave a girl with a frenny little craving ache, but inwardly he was an explicit horror, the blood from that stormy night last May still bright in her mind.

Amie's quickened pulse galloped even faster as the headlights approached. A tight foreboding lodged in her throat. "He's coming fast, Xeke! Maybe we should get off the road."

Xeke smacked the Q repeatedly. "Come on, you piece of shit." Amie was tapping the back glass. She'd shouted something a moment ago, Xeke too caught up in his assault of the Q to listen. When he gave up

again and snapped the door shut behind him, blue lights were flashing.

The state cop car stopped beside them, Xeke helping Amie climb down as the copper got out. The lights strobed into Xeke's skull, reminding him of the headache he'd taken home from last weekend's Shards for Breakfast concert.

Their backs to the truck, they exchanged a worried glance when the copper approached. He was tall, bald, rendered otherwise featureless by the adrenalized moment.

Xeke stepped forward. "Grid's down, officer. What's the deal?"

"You kids need to come with me." His voice was strangely stolid, the voice of a teacher nearing retirement who has realized he should have done something else with his decades.

"Wait," Amie said, returning to Xeke's side. "What's going on?"

"System's down for the night, miss." He was coming at them intently now, as if to take them by the arms like disobedient children and lead them to the car. "They're arranging rides home for everyone as we speak. We need to get you off the road, though. Every vehicle has to be towed and reset."

Xeke felt the chill of panic racing through him. Almost unconsciously, he was moving toward the cop car with Amie, dimly aware that this was a mistake, that they shouldn't get in. Amie was still questioning the copper, but their momentum seemingly couldn't be stopped, the guy's authority like an electric prod jabbing at them.

It wasn't until Xeke turned, his gaze following the perfect angle, Amie already ushered into the back seat, that he noticed the absence of the copper's belt, no gun jutting out from the usual spot, no handcuffs or radio, nothing.

# GRIDLOCKED

But the copper moved too quickly, back in the driver's seat before Xeke could shout a word of warning to Amie, who'd slid to the right side of the car.

There was a decision for Xeke then, but really there wasn't. He would not – could not – leave her.

## Chapter 6

"Paul, get down!" Steel shouted.

Already on his knees to thank God, Paul pushed himself flat against the pavement, his vision improving even with the asphalt glaring at him.

No sooner had he gone facedown than gunfire shattered the night. Paul, briefly deafened, looked up to find, at first, only a watery blur – and then his vision was flawless. He saw Steel shredding them down, every last attacker, though not in time to save the troopers.

The sounds were badly distorted, Paul's eardrums vanquished by a relentless ringing.

Time slowed.

The wind stilled.

The attackers didn't move, not even a gurgled cough of imminent death.

Paul thought he discerned the faintest of snowflakes drifting in the path of the headlights, glistening fiendishly. It wasn't until Paul gasped that he realized he hadn't been breathing, the sounds gradually coming back.

"Jesus, no! Come on, stay with me!" Steel shouted.

Shakily, Paul brought himself to his feet. Steel was thirty feet ahead in the road, attending to the fallen officers.

"They're gone," Paul whispered with sickly knowingness, stumbling to his friend's side, placing a hand on his shoulder, seeing his face for the first time, far different than he'd envisioned. It didn't matter. The only thing of weight was…

# GRIDLOCKED

The blood. It shimmered blackly against the pavement, puddles expanding around the fallen, seven in total, awash with the headlights. Stunned into a near mindless state – not only by the massacre but the miracle – Paul made a circle of the dead. He kept expecting a return to darkness, the blindfold slapped cruelly across his eyes again.

It didn't happen.

But was vision, in this moment, preferable to blindness? He'd dreamt of this miracle since he was seventeen years and seven months old, and here it was, arriving for him along with death.

Stars winked down at Paul. Had they always been this bright and unremittingly dire?

Steel was quiet and unmoving for a spell, though realization didn't take long to set in and slacken his knees. He'd seen death before, but never in such a violent portrait and never by his doing. He turned very slowly to Paul, their eyes meeting.

"Jesus," Steel murmured. "You can see. Jesus Christ, you can see!"

Steel holstered his Glock and embraced Paul, who felt as if a bear had wrapped its paws around him.

"What the fuck?" Steel finally said, stepping back, shaky, barely able to comprehend. "What the hell is going on, Paul? These guys try to kill us, and all of a sudden you can see? That's no damn coincidence!"

"The Great Tribulation," Paul whispered, not a statement or a question but a reaction. He looked searchingly again to the stars, which seemed even brighter, the wind cold upon his face. He didn't know if he was searching for an answer or praying for a savior, perhaps both. At one time he'd been convinced of the notion that, if ever his vision were to return, it would be at a beach, or in the middle of Times Square, maybe even at a chateau overlooking a sweeping, breathtaking expanse of God's precious earth.

But not here, never in a situation like this, where only the sheer violence could take your breath away.

Steel studied the dead men. He was slowly coming down from it, the shakes jittering out of him, replaced by jolts of urgent purpose. Paul receded to the edge of the road. Just ahead, there remained a slanted, rust-stained speed limit sign from the pre-grid days: **55**. Farther, Paul could even make out a sign for Route 49, his vision infallible.

A sudden presentiment came over Paul then, strengthened when Steel said, "Shit, these guys are wearing bulletproof vests. And they've got high-end gear and weapons."

Steel's pulse shot back up. He checked both directions of 49, glanced into the woods flanking the road, and ultimately leveled his gaze on Paul. "Whatever they were doing, it was tactical. Those shots you heard before – I don't think it was these guys, probably another team of shooters. This is large-scale, man, and we're right at the motherfucking center of it."

Paul's heart whaled away. "Tactical as they might have been, they certainly didn't include Steel Sparks in their preparations," he said, drawing a shrug and nothing more from a man whose face, until tonight, had taken another appearance in his mind's eye.

Paul hadn't envisioned a face quite as long and rugged, or hair as wild, or eyes as dark and raven-like. Steel's black beard, however, was pretty much how Paul had pictured it.

In a moment Steel spoke with remarkable calm into the fallen troopers' radios, his requests for help unanswered. His phone and SatCom were useless as well, the latter tossed into his backpack with exasperation, the former kept in his pocket.

# GRIDLOCKED

"This is way worse than I thought," Steel said, gathering weapons from their attackers. "These guys didn't just fly off the handle and grab their guns – this was planned for a long time. They even took out communications."

"Terrorism?"

"I don't know, but we have to get away from the road. We're sitting ducks out here."

For over half his life, Paul's cane had guided the way. Tonight, however, the stars as witnesses to triumph amidst tragedy, he threw down the cane and followed his friend toward the woods.

## Chapter 7

Tommy and Dominick were heading north, just past the entrance to Wells State Park on Route 49, when the car began to lose speed. At first it eluded their notice. Tommy was staring out the window, head pressed against the cool glass, brooding. Dominick, eyes glued to his shifter, was reading a website dedicated to sharing the stories of people who'd survived extended comas and went on to exceed all expectations.

Dom wanted to inspire Tommy, who'd been alarmingly quiet these past few hours.

Tommy wanted to fade into the night, wanted to be forgotten, no longer a burden. How many times had they gone up this road before, Tommy wondered, on their way to Lake Lashaway for family outings? But those days could never be had again or even imitated in adulthood, not with Tommy like this.

*They're all better off without me.*

"Greetings from the captain," chimed the annoying parody pilot's voice from the Q, a map of their progress displayed on the lighted screen, Route 49 in green and their position marked with a red dot. Tommy rolled his eyes. "Calm, clear night for travel out there," the Q continued. "Should have you to the lake in…"

Dom looked up from the shifter, wondering why the Q hadn't finished. In the upper right corner of the screen, the digital reading of MPH steadily dropped.

Then the entire screen blackened.

Tommy parted his head from the glass, their deceleration significant enough to draw his attention. "We're stopping," he mumbled, hating the sound of those two words. If his voice insisted on sounding this way, he preferred to hear himself as infrequently as possible.

# GRIDLOCKED

Dismayed, Dom tried to reset the Q. Nothing.

Meanwhile, Tommy pointed straight ahead, surprising himself with the speed and ease with which he did so. "That car's stopped, too," he said, the clearest his voice had sounded this side of the coma.

Dom gazed through the windshield. Maybe three hundred feet ahead, a pair of tail lights stared back at them.

"Something's wrong with the grid," Dom said. "I don't think this is just a precaution. Normally the system pulls your car into the breakdown lane when something's screwed up. It's called a default, but I've never been stopped in the middle of the road before. Maybe a grid dodger caused a wreck."

"A what?"

"Grid dodgers," Dom repeated, checking his shifter. No service, really? It had been ten years – before the launch of Satellite Awakening – since he'd gone without a signal. Impatient, he said, "I'll tell you later."

"No, tell me now." Tommy was growing agitated with the system and its absolute control. He wished there was a manual fallback so they could be on their way, but the grid wielded all the power.

Dom, sighing, pocketing his shifter, wondering at the improvement in his brother's speech, said, "Grid dodgers are people who, for whatever reason, refuse to get on board with the system. Some hate the idea of the government telling them what to do. Others don't want to give up cars that are too old to be updated with grid technology. Some are just assholes."

Tommy chuckled, an almost normal sound. "I can see why you'd want to dodge the grid. From what I've seen, it sucks."

Dom laughed in disbelief. "Holy shit, you're talking great, man. How—"

"I think I've turned a corner."

"Yeah, tell me about it. That speech therapist deserves a medal." He patted his brother's shoulder, momentarily forgetting the grid debacle. After a while, he said, "You probably remember how much I opposed the grid when they first came up with it, but the system really does save lives. The grid works because every vehicle is plugged into the same computerized system. You enter your destination, and the algorithms take over from there." Again Dom tried to reset the Q to no avail. "But if one vehicle is operating outside the system, it screws up the whole thing because the grid can't control its movements in relationship with other vehicles. To get grid dodgers off the road, they've set up scanners every few miles that read microchips in your car to tell if it's equipped with the proper technology. If you're driving anything that's not grid compliant, even a scooter, the scanners send out drones to track you till the cops get there. First offense is half a year in jail, second offense two years. Third offense – you're done for life."

Tommy remembered the news reports from the other side. With the billions of dollars the new system was expected to save from accident responses and investigations alone, cops were predicted to have significantly redefined roles – mostly to ensure that every vehicle conformed to the system.

A system that was currently failing.

"So what do we do?" Tommy said when it became obvious that the grid wouldn't fix itself.

"Looks like all we can do is wait for a cop or a vat to come. I can't believe the shifter's out – there must be something wrong with the satellite." Dom had checked his work cell phone as well, just to make sure, but it was also without service.

# GRIDLOCKED

Tommy sighed, though not simply from impatience. There was something uncannily familiar about those stationed tail lights ahead of them on a darkened road.

"What happens if no one comes?" Tommy asked.

Dom ignored the question, focused again on his brother's improved speech. "Your voice," he noted with a smile. "Dude, I can't get over it. Soon you'll be as good as new."

Tommy felt something soften in his chest at Dominick's words. There was an uplifted moment – genuine happiness – but soon it was shadowed by that other feeling, the one inspired by apprehension germinating in his heart. He'd felt it earlier, too, at the very first sight of his brother's house – and now it was even stronger.

After a while, following several failed attempts to get the Q working, they decided to share their bafflement with the operator of the other vehicle. The tail lights were still glowing up there, the operator probably just as confused and nervous as they were.

For the first time since the grid was initiated, Dom wanted control back. There'd been so many promises – no more accidents, no more OUI deaths, no more road rage – but opponents had always said there would come a day when the system failed.

As Dom helped Tommy into his wheelchair at the side of the car, Tommy's apprehension crept even closer to fear. But then, like the distant scent of chimney smoke driven off by a changing wind, it was gone, chased into submission.

"Ridiculous," Dom muttered, beginning to push his brother along. "Absolutely ridiculous. Even when the Freedom Riders have caused accidents, I've never seen the Q go totally black before."

Tommy's stomach was unsettled. The cold wind did nothing to refresh him. The sound of thin wheels caressing the pavement irritated him.

Up ahead, a white, ten-foot pole loomed beyond the right shoulder, green dots blinking from a dome. Dom pointed to it. "That's one of those scanners I was talking about."

Tommy's attention returned to the vehicle in the distance, which gradually came into better form, its shape emerging from the darkness. It was low, wide, muscular, "a Mustang," Dom identified a few moments later, the light projecting from his shifter a bright bluish beam, the device having been maximized in an instant to the size of a flashlight.

Drawing closer, the rumble of the Mustang's idling engine became exceedingly resonant, Tommy's bones thrumming with the currents of sound that coursed up through the wheelchair frame. They were close enough now to see that the driver's door had been left partly open. The headlights forged a ghostly path down Route 49, shadows shifting where they tapered, darkness beyond.

Above, stars limned the sky with indecipherable symbols, a vast map that could never be read. For a moment Tommy let his eyes skate across the open sky, wondering, reflecting on how Route 49 had never changed, not a single house or business added in thirty years to alter the wilderness road.

"Hello?" Dom called out, leaving Tommy's wheelchair behind the car so he could come alongside it.

Tommy looked behind him. The horizons remained dark, the woods on either side of them even darker, Tommy thinking then of a hallway through the night, the road like a portal to another place, the sounds of his accident coming sharply back to him, gone with the gathering wind.

# GRIDLOCKED

That had been the other side. And now he was here, on Route 49 with his brother.

Dom, meantime, poked his head into the Mustang. The Q was dark, Dom left with a tight, chilly, panicked consternation in his chest, a feeling typically induced by nightmares, the ones powerful enough to linger into waking hours.

"Goddamn screen's blank, too," he muttered, searching the glove compartment.

It was then Tommy noticed the license plate, an observation that rendered him slack-jawed, desperate to remember why those six letters – GRDLCK – were so familiar to him. The sight of the license plate immediately brought a strong sense of urgency, as well as a crisp fear for their safety.

But why was it familiar? Why was all of this so *familiar*?

Tommy strained his mind, but it was like grasping for a word just out of reach.

The wind lashed at his face.

He thought he heard a hollow sound down the road. Footsteps?

For a moment he wondered if he was actually awake, stranded on Route 49 with his brother near Wells State Park, or if he was still sleeping, still dreaming.

*Asleep. Dreaming.*

Then, jarringly, Tommy remembered where he'd seen **GRDLCK** – in the nightmares of the middle. The tail lights, too, he realized – and now he remembered what had happened in those nightmares, the monsters of the middle coming back to him (voices whispering from the woods; scraping shadows; rumbling; the green…)

"Headlights," Tommy managed with a choked, deathly whisper, his eyes expanding, bony fingers of dread curling around his shoulders.

Tommy looked past the Mustang, saw them off to the north.

The headlights were greener, sicklier, than they'd been in the middle, approaching fast, accompanied by the whir of a distant motor – and Tommy, somehow knowing what would happen next, reacted without thinking. He rose from his wheelchair, stood, ran alongside the Mustang, shouted for his brother to get out of there…for he was back in his nightmare now. He knew this place. He knew this night. He'd been here before, in the middle, and it was all racing back to him: whispers, tail lights, **GRDLCK**, green headlights.

"Jesus, Tommy, you're walking! You're–"

"Shut up and run!" Tommy grabbed his brother's arm, led him to the southbound side of the road, Dom at first resisting and then following Tommy up a hill toward the woods, both of them breathless.

The growl of the truck's engine strengthened, climbed even higher, crescendoed, Tommy looking back just as the clattering-shattering eruption came. Glass exploded. Metal shrieked. With the ease of a garbage hauler scooping up a dumpster, the Mustang was pinched and lifted by two massive hydraulic arms extending from the dump truck, claws at either end.

"Holy fucking shit!" Dom shouted, falling to his knees, hands on his head.

Green headlights menacing the road ahead, the truck had slowed considerably – the downshift's ferocity as vicious as a snarling Rottweiler – but only long enough to clear the Mustang from the road and toss it rudely into the breakdown lane. It came screeching down

with the crash of a piano thrown from a rooftop, sparks flecking away like the eyes of demons.

# GRIDLOCKED

Echoes clapped off the hills, thundered down the road.

"NOOO!!!" was all Dom could manage before his car was claimed next, the truck's arms flexible like those of an octopus, capable of both vertical and horizontal movement. Lashing out toward their victims, the claws were giant hooked talons of metal.

A similar, though smaller, dump truck passed in the opposite direction, green lights shining north. At the sight of this second truck, Dom felt as if he were sinking, the peace and safety of his existence that had always been guaranteed now shriveling to nothingness.

Even without realizing it right away, Dom was overcome with understanding. It initially circumvented thought, delving directly to his heart. The first truck had represented lunacy, psychosis – a lone shark out for damage.

But the second truck had represented planning, teamwork – a coordinated effort. Whoever was doing this had shut down the grid and rendered communications useless. Stripped of the abilities to drive and make calls, society was helpless, reverted back through the centuries. Well aware now of the colossal mistakes – *We gave up our freedom the day we let the grid take over. We set the table for this.* – Dom was momentarily numb with disbelief.

Then, Tommy's hand on his shoulder, the wind in his face, he was able to refocus. He turned to his brother. "You can walk," he murmured, the words barely forming. "But how?"

## Chapter 8

Xeke felt an insistent pressure in his chest. It was like he'd injured a rib that was now misaligned, every inhalation bringing discomfort. He was sitting to Amie's left in the back seat of the cop car, their hands, as if by magnetism, drawing together.

There was an urge to question the copper about his missing belt. Maybe the guy had been called to emergency duty after the grid went down and left his belt at home.

But a copper with no gun? *What?*

The thought made Xeke bite down hard on his lip. He squeezed Amie's hand. "Grid blows, huh?"

Amie's eyes shifted to the front seat. The officer was driving manually, his Q useless with the words **NO DEFECTS** blinking in white across an otherwise blue screen. All emergency vehicles were equipped with manual conversion capabilities, though they could only be used during Class 1 situations.

Tonight's events apparently qualified as Class 1.

"Where are you taking us, officer?" Amie didn't like the sound of her voice, small and shaky like that of a tremulous child. She felt foolish for being so afraid – there'd been a malfunction, that's all, nothing to have a frazfest about. There was no such thing as perfection, especially not for a brand new system; there were bound to be a few mishaps.

*And we're the guinea pigs*, she thought. *What's next to go wrong?*

"Everyone's being transported to emergency shelters for the night." The officer spoke in a flat, almost bored tone. "The Spencer shelter is just up ahead on the left. You'll be able to call your family from the landline once we get there."

# GRIDLOCKED

Xeke felt a rush of relief at that. They were almost to Route 9, the copper taking a familiar left turn off 49 before they reached the junction. Back when Xeke's mother drove him to elementary school, he used to take pictures of the car carrier trucks roaming up and down 49, each on its way to pick up or drop off vehicles at the automotive processing facility into which the copper was now taking them. The place had been shut down recently, rendered inefficient three years ago when trucks were banned from the nearby Massachusetts Turnpike following the completion of Midstate Subterranean Route (MSR), a two-level underground route that spanned the state, the higher level reserved for general traffic and the lower level for trucks and buses.

Lacking convenient access to MSR from Spencer, the owner of the processing facility had built a new complex along the recently constructed freight rail lines north of Worcester. That had spelled the end of the car carrier processions down Route 49, not that Xeke had cared once his interests graduated from trucks and trains to gaming.

The entryway to the facility was long and curving, a sliding barbed wire fence permitting their entry and closing behind them.

"So what do you think happened to the grid?" Xeke asked the copper, hazarding a question against his better judgment.

"Not sure," the guy mumbled. "They just told me to pick people up and bring them here."

They pulled in behind several cop cars – state, local, unmarked, even animal control – as well as ambulances and vans forming three lines ahead of a row of guard booths. They looked to Xeke like the border patrol checkpoints he often used to see on the news, before they put up the Invisible Wall. Illegal immigrants weren't a problem anymore, not with facial recognition scanners and drones.

On the other side of the entry road, oncoming, were several dump trucks rigged with devices Xeke had never seen before. They somewhat resembled log grapples, except the claws extended from the sides of the trucks and met in front of the cabs. The headlights were night vision green, many of the trucks carrying trailers loaded with equipment.

"What's with all the trucks?" Xeke said.

The copper sighed. "They need to clear the road for emergency personnel."

"Last I checked, they could do that with a tow truck." Xeke's uneasy chuckle was met by silence.

Leaning close, Amie whispered in his ear, "He's weird. I don't like this."

"Me neither," he muttered, then, in a louder voice: "We appreciate you taking us here, officer, but maybe you could just drop us off at a store or something. We can call from there."

They inched closer to the guardhouses, the officer remaining silent. Up ahead, Amie could see black-uniformed guards exchanging paperwork with drivers and then waving them through the booths, whereupon the vehicles were directed into a huge parking lot. With every release of the brake and subsequent movement, Amie felt the knot in her stomach twisting tighter.

"Hey, did you hear me?" Xeke rapped on the cage separating them from the front compartment. "This is taking forever, officer. Can you just drop us off somewhere in Spencer? Route 9's like two seconds from here."

"We're staying here," the copper said sharply.

# GRIDLOCKED

Xeke let out a huff of frustration…and fear. He didn't want Amie to panic, but this guy didn't act like a copper. Nothing made sense. If this had been a random malfunction, how had they found the time to arrange such an elaborate and secure facility?

No, something else was going on, he suspected. Something tilty. Something that had taken a lot of time to plan.

Amie took a deep breath, tried to relax. They were just a few cars back of the guardhouses now, the officer shuffling around paperwork up front. He was nodding rapidly as if to convince himself of something, and his repeated fidgeting and knuckle cracking suggested an inner turmoil brought on by a greater crisis.

"Please, sir, we don't want to go here," Amie pleaded, but the officer rubbed his eyes and kept his head down for a long while.

"Everything will be fine, just fine," the copper said after a prolonged silence. "We'll all just grab some Cokes once we get inside. Sound good?"

Xeke rattled the cage. "Bull! What the hell is going on? We have rights! You can't take us somewhere against our will!"

Xeke quieted when he heard Amie crying. He pulled her close, hating that he'd upset her, but his head was starting to scramble now. This was some real poodyloose shit right here, this spurdog copper thinking he could control them like this. They had to get out – had to get out now!

"We don't need a shelter," Xeke said in a far gentler voice. "Save the space for the old people, okay? Just let us go – we'll be fine."

But the copper was unreachable. Even when Xeke offered to pay for their release, silence prevailed from the driver's seat.

Amie's breaths seemed to catch in her chest. The officer pulled up to the guardhouse, a woman in the same black uniform as the other attendants accepting the officer's paperwork. In return, she handed him a clipboard and told him to complete the forms in the reception building.

"What's going on?" Amie shouted at the woman. "What is this place?"

They were back in motion, easing over a one-way spike strip and following the parade of cop cars through a series of gates. Once beyond a sizable windowless building to their right, they crept toward the parking lot, much larger than Amie had initially realized, seemingly big enough to accommodate ten football fields.

Xeke's and Amie's horrified gasps were simultaneous.

At first Xeke was speechless, capable only of watching as dozens of people were marched at gunpoint from the parking lot to adjacent warehouses. Some of the prisoners formed lines. Others were shepherded in pairs and trios. Those who resisted were tasered or beaten.

Amie's scream tore through her lungs, echoed in her head. She pounded at the windows and the cage, Xeke trying to kick out the glass.

"Don't make me have to restrain you," the copper warned.

"Fuck off!"

"You don't want to do this, kid."

"Fuck you!"

The car jerked to a stop.

# GRIDLOCKED

The doors flung open, uniformed guards on either side. One of them, a muscular black man, grabbed Xeke's legs and tore him out of the car, pain spiraling through his tailbone on contact with the pavement.

Amie, meanwhile, was dragged flailing and shrieking by the other guard. She couldn't see his face behind a ski mask, her fear blurring her surroundings to a vortex of lights and movement. Her head throbbed and her heart felt ready to burst.

"Amie! Amie! Let me go!" Xeke tried to tug free of the guy's grip, tried to search for Amie amidst the throngs of captives and captors, but he couldn't find her in the chaos.

Amie, having taken tae kwon do classes for three years, kicked the guard in the groin and sprinted away from the warehouses, her vision kaleidoscopic. She dodged one guard, then ducked and skirted to her right past another. But the officer who'd abducted them, along with two more guards, rushed her diagonally from the car and tackled her, one of them pulling her arms painfully behind her back and handcuffing her, another man slamming her head into the asphalt.

"Stop resisting!" the officer shouted, and the hand against her neck became a crushing weight.

"I can't breathe," she tried to say, mindless with fear, suddenly unable to take in air, but they wouldn't listen, wouldn't let her up.

"Stop resisting! Do it now! Stop resisting!"

There was a haze of pain and panic. Amie's desperation was mountainous, like that of someone trapped underwater, fighting to break the surface, thrashing away precious breaths, but it only made everything worse, sent her deeper, and she could practically feel death's skeletal hands clutching her ankles, pulling her down.

Steadily her vision faded, until there was only blackness islanded by a few twinkling stars.

The electric jolts daggered through every vein, every muscle, every bone, the pain astronomical, like nothing Xeke had ever felt or imagined. He would have voiced his resignation, but there was no air in his lungs with which to form words. He'd collapsed onto his stomach, arms and legs splayed out, clueless as to what had hit him.

Someone hauled him up, his sight cloudy. The picture wasn't clear again until after he'd been carried into the first warehouse and locked in a cell, kids about his age on either side of him. All around, the clanging and jarring of iron gates delivered migraine agony. There were whistles, screams, boots thudding against concrete.

"Get in there!" one man yelled.

"Hands inside the bars!" another commanded.

"Are you okay, dude?" one of the kids asked Xeke, taking his hand.

"Where am I?"

# GRIDLOCKED

## Chapter 9

Snaking their way through the woods, Paul and Steel were spared from darkness by the flashlights Steel always brought on their journeys, among other supplies tucked away in his backpack. They were well-prepared for the road, but nothing could have prepared them for this.

"Pretty damn lucky." Steel stopped, turned to Paul. "Your vision suddenly coming back right now of all times – don't seem like two things that huge could be random."

"A miracle…or perhaps a curse." Gripping the flashlight with both hands as if it were a pistol, Paul made a small circle, lighting up everything around him. The trees were tall and thin, mostly pines, the underbrush ample but not oppressively thick. The walk from Route 49 had been manageable thus far, but the idea of what was transpiring beyond these woods made Paul shudder.

Could this really be it, he wondered, the big one? His journey was far from finished, so many stories left to tell, yet the creator of all journeys and stories had set him down a new path, a twisting trail into darkness.

How far would it go? Where would it take them?

"How are you? Still good?" Steel asked for maybe the hundredth time since they'd left Route 49. He feared Paul's vision might be short-lived, a burst of sight sandwiched by blackness.

"Just fine. All systems go," Paul reported, no longer afraid to blink. Sleep, however, was another matter, the perfect opportunity for the curse to come riding in on its shadowy stagecoach and steal away his miracle. He wished he could stay awake forever, but his eyes would eventually force themselves shut and hopefully reopen to morning's light.

Steel tried to think. Before he was shot to death, the trooper had said it wasn't safe and that they were under attack. All lines of communication were down, and Steel's recently recovered weapons remained better sources of protection than the authorities. He'd left the rifles behind, grabbing up four pistols and stashing them as trusty backups to his Glock currently in hand.

Weapons notwithstanding, Steel felt a cold slither in his gut, the same sensation that had sometimes visited him before fights. Unable to use technology's maps, he relied on his father's compass to keep them heading north, a device he'd once considered removing from his backpack and adding to the shelves of Dad's memorabilia. Now it was the phone and other devices he thought about ditching. Whoever their attackers were, they likely possessed the capability of tracing electronic devices. Perhaps emergency responders were being targeted first (evidenced by what they'd seen on the road), and civilians would be next. They were probably aiming to cause as much damage as possible in the window of vulnerability before SWAT teams mobilized and put an end to it.

*Can't believe I killed them. How am I still alive?*

Based on his earlier review of a local map, Steel knew Route 49 intersected several east-west roads in Sturbridge and East Brookfield. If they could reach one of those roads, they could assess the situation from a residential perspective, Steel figured. At the very least, it would buy them a breather; maybe they could even find a resident to take them in until the attack was quelled.

"We should get rid of the phones," Steel said, whirling around after thinking he'd heard something over the wind.

"Good idea." Paul directed his light briefly to Steel, then swept it through the woods yet again. "The radio, too. We have to get off the grid."

"Literally."

# GRIDLOCKED

They kept moving, not looking back to second-guess their decision to abandon all things electronic, Steel leading the northern course. The ground rose and fell like waves, shadows darting with each pass of the flashlights. Paul was quickly exhausted, unaccustomed to the rigors of wilderness travel, slippery leaves and roots and rocks making for an uncertain walk.

"We should have stayed at the Brennaman place," Paul regretted. "I shouldn't have been so bent on making up time."

Snorting, Steel said, "Don't beat yourself up. How could you have possibly predicted *this*?" A brief silence between them accentuated the constant crunch-swoosh of leaves underfoot. In a moment Steel added, "The Brennamans might have been killed, for all we know. Your call to stay on the road could have saved our lives. Who knows how bad this thing is."

They were referring to the Brennaman family, of East Brookfield, one of several pre-selected host families for their trip. Paul had gathered quite a following over the years, especially after the release of his second book, *With Your Words I See*, and hundreds of families throughout the nation had responded to an online request for new hosts along subsequent routes. This had all begun as a quest to share stories from people across the country, and now Paul was on the bestsellers list. His publisher had even offered to provide a team to support them during their journeys, though he'd declined the extra help. These trips were both their tradition and their legacy – the miles had made them brothers, and there would never be a need for anyone else. Paul didn't even bring his wife and son along – everyone understood his reasons, no one asking questions anymore. This was his life's work, carefully culling stories from the nation's four corners and everywhere in between, his cane clunking mile after mile down the roads that delivered America's lifeblood.

But now that cane was gone.

Determined to make up time lost to a brief malaise, Paul had canceled their plans to stay at the Brennaman house that evening. They would walk all night, he'd said, then rest a few hours and refuel at an alternate host's house before hitting the road again toward New Hampshire. They'd been hoping to conclude their journey in Portland, Maine, but in a matter of minutes the goal of the trip had shifted to survival. Steel always carried the Glock out of an abundance of caution, and every last modicum of that abundance would seemingly be tested tonight.

"A light," Paul indicated, his eyes locked on a bluish glow in the distance, barely visible through the trees.

Steel huffed in surprise. "Guess I don't have to ask if you're still seeing okay."

"No further need to paint those pictures, friend."

Carefully, they navigated an obstacle course of fallen branches. The terrain was on the rise again, abruptly steepening, the light like an unreachable beacon for shipwrecked souls. Minutes passed, but the light seemed to maintain a precise distance, as though they were trying to chase down the horizon.

Paul was panting, his heart rapping heavily. "Is it me, or are we hardly gaining any ground?"

"I know, it's like we've gotten further away from the damn thing."

"Stop!" Paul urged. He'd been looking beyond the reach of their flashlights, toward that elusive bluish light, when he'd glimpsed someone weaving between the trees.

Steel readied his gun. "What? What is it?"

Paul directed his light to a hulking tree thirty feet ahead. "Movement. Someone's there."

# GRIDLOCKED

A cold gust ratcheted up, tossing leaves around. If there were footsteps out there, they'd be next to impossible to detect when the wind blustered.

"We're armed!" Steel warned, feeling exceedingly vulnerable with their lances of light barely scissoring the flesh of the night. After what the trooper had said back on 49, he knew there were more attackers out there, many more.

"We don't want to hurt you!" Paul added, guessing he'd seen a terrified resident, possibly even a kid. The figure, in its fleeting appearance, hadn't seemed very tall. "We can all work together. We can help you get to safety."

Silence.

Steel opened his pack and offered Paul one of the pistols he'd recovered. Earlier, following a quick tutorial, Paul had refused to accept a weapon. Never having fired a shot, he hadn't trusted himself to be of use if they were attacked again.

This time he made no objections. Panic constricting his throat, the gun helped steady his shaking hands.

Steel's follow-up tutorial didn't break a minute. "Don't think, just shoot," he advised. "You never know, maybe you'll hit a tree and the thing will ricochet into your target. Wouldn't be the weirdest thing that's happened tonight. Just try not to hit me."

Paul's chuckle was barely a sound at all. For a few moments he could hardly breathe, the air catching in his chest. Then they were

cautioning forward, flashlights making frequent arcs. Occasionally, at Steel's instruction, they clicked off their lights and waited, listened, perfectly still. When footsteps failed to arrive after a while, they were off again, closing down the space between them and the bluish glow.

Whoever he'd glimpsed, Paul realized, he or she wanted nothing to do with them – and somehow that provided not an ounce of encouragement. Perhaps the person had witnessed something even worse than what they'd endured.

And who could be trusted now? Who could people turn to for help if the cops were being murdered? For now, the enemy was faceless, infinite, as anonymous as the night woods, as enigmatic as that distant glow.

*We're under attack*, the trooper had said.

Now what? What picture would be painted for Paul when the sun angled back around? He could only pray the gift of sight had not been given with the stipulation that only suffering could be seen.

Ten minutes later, following additional stops – one of them marked by the calls of an owl – they finally arrived at the source of the bluish glow. But even though they'd reached the other side of the woods, they might as well have been at the center of the state forest, for a pall of desolation had spread mistily over them just now in the abstruse depths of the night, simultaneously seeping into their awareness like a scent…or an aura.

# GRIDLOCKED

## Chapter 10

Another dump truck rumbled southbound on Route 49, this latest green-headlighted rig featuring a massive yellow plow-like device. It reminded Tommy somewhat of the cowcatchers he'd seen in old western movies, everything in the truck's path rammed out of the way in a hail of sparks, including the remains of his wheelchair. Having already been blasted by the first truck, the shredded shell of the wheelchair rattled and dragged with the sound of a runaway shopping cart. A piece of debris – a wheel? – went hurtling ten feet up, landing in the breakdown lane with a pitiful clink.

Minutes later, a pair of street sweepers tidied up both lanes, the glass and other minor detritus of both vehicles and the wheelchair gathered up in an almost musical tinkling chorus. Robohaulers zoomed alongside the sweepers, tasked with collecting anything that had been missed, yellow flashing lights on their domes.

From the edge of the woods, Tommy and Dom watched all of this with cemented expressions of horror. Dom felt lightheaded, realization building to overwhelming heights.

He turned once more to his brother, took hold of his shoulders, unable to believe all of this was real. "What the hell happened down there, Tommy? One minute you're confined to a wheelchair, barely able to talk, and the next you're running up a hill with me."

Tommy shrugged. "Adrenaline?" he guessed, though he knew this response barely broke the surface of truth. Something epic was undoubtedly happening, well beyond the profundity of their combined experiences. This was the stuff of history books and movies, breaking news before it breaks…and here it was, unfolding for them on a darkened road, spectated by a million stars.

Tommy's gut roiled. He couldn't catch his breath. His legs felt a little rubbery but otherwise fine. He didn't know what more he could say – he didn't have the answers.

Dom stared at his brother, flabbergasted. "How did you know we were in danger? Why did you tell me to run?" When Tommy said nothing, he added, "This is insane, completely insane. Say something, man, you're scaring the shit out of me!"

Tommy thought briefly of how best to explain it, then realized he would sound crazy no matter how he conveyed what had happened. "Dreams," he finally said. "While I was in the coma, I was constantly dreaming. One of my dreams was of tonight." He clutched his brother's shoulder. "Dom, I saw all of those things – the tail lights of the car in front of us, the license plate, the green headlights, the trucks. It's like I've already lived through all this while I was…you know, gone. Who knows, maybe I got so scared that I shook myself free of the paralysis."

Forced into action by a sudden sensation, Tommy crossed into the shallows of the woods and unzipped his jeans, Dom cautioning him against "doing anything stupid." There was a moment's hesitation for Tommy, worsened by the fear that he wouldn't be able to access medical care if something went wrong.

Like before, though, Tommy relied on the guidance of instinct and, with only moderate pain compared to what he'd expected, he managed to relieve himself normally for the first time in five years. Initially the urine escaped in achy spurts, like water forced through a kinked hose, but soon it was a steady stream, Dom repeatedly asking if he was all right.

"You should take a few minutes to rest. This is too much exertion," Dom said with a disbelieving headshake once the chore was complete. "*I* can barely handle this. I feel like I'm gonna pass out, for Christ's sake."

# GRIDLOCKED

"No, we have to keep moving." With a look to the stars as he discarded medical equipment he assumed he wouldn't need anymore, Tommy couldn't resist thoughts that all of this was happening for a reason.

*Is there something I'm supposed to accomplish?*

Tommy wished he could slow the speeding train the night had become, everything funneling into an unstoppable twister and obliterating the columns upon which the grid had been built. Despite standing still, the world around him seemed to swirl, Route 49 like a theater stage in flux, new props and scenes occupying it every few minutes. What was next, he wondered, a reversion back to paralysis? A nuclear bomb falling? The ocean rushing over the land?

"So now what the hell do we do?" Hands clasped behind his head, feeling mildly vertiginous, Dom began to pace the treeline. "They hijacked the fucking grid, man. It's gotta be terrorists, right? But where did they get all of those trucks and equipment?"

"It's too large-scale for terrorism," Tommy said, searching Route 49 and seeing darkness in both directions. "Think about it – communications are sabotaged, the grid shuts down, and a few minutes later they're already clearing vehicles from the road. That sounds more like a government conspiracy than terrorism."

"Whatever's going on, we're screwed. The car's totaled, we can't call anyone – what are we supposed to do?"

Tommy wasn't nearly as rattled as his brother. Having received a series of miracles, his approach to this calamity came from a far different angle than Dominick. "For starters," he said calmly, "we've gotta stay off the road. Those truck drivers didn't care if people were inside the cars when they smashed them. They might even have orders to kill anyone who gets in their way. I think the best thing to do is just wait this out for a while."

"What do you mean, wait this out? We can't just stay up here all night. We have to flag down a cop or something. I need to get back to Cyri! And what about Mom and Dad? We have to see if they're all okay!"

"Do you see any cops down there?" With outstretched arms, Tommy regarded the empty road. "If the cops were coming, don't you think they would have responded by now?" Tommy went to his brother, took him by the shoulder. "The cops might very well be in on this thing, who knows."

"Why?" Dom shouted. "What would possess the government to turn on us?"

"I don't know – I haven't exactly been keeping up with current affairs."

Dom lowered his voice. "I'm really freaking out here, man." He resumed his pacing. "What if Cyri's hurt? Jesus Christ, we have to get back there!"

"So what's your plan, go back to the road? What if another truck comes?"

"I don't know, okay? My head's scrambled!" Dom stomped the grass, slapped the air around a little, the wind pushing back with a jab of its own. He willed his shifter to work, but it remained without a signal, almost four hundred dollars worth of near chemistry-transcending synthesized polymers in the damn thing…but without a connection it was useless.

"Let's just start walking," Tommy said. "We'll stay up here near the woods, see what happens on the road. Maybe we'll luck out and hitch a ride with a grid dodger later."

Dom couldn't believe what he was hearing. He'd never thought he would see a day when grid dodgers were coveted. The system had convinced him and millions more with false promises, and now people were paying the price.

"I guess you're right," Dom said resignedly.

Tommy started ahead, his brother left to wonder at the coincidence that the grid takeover and Tommy's miraculous recovery had been virtually simultaneous.

In the southern distance, green headlights were brightening. "God help us," Dom said.

## Chapter 11

"I'm scrambled," Xeke murmured. "Fucking harrowed. Plungelicker bastards kidnapped me and my girlfriend."

With help from the others, he managed to pull himself up, his head as dizzy as it had been following his first buzz, pain flaring up and down his body.

"What the hell is this place?" Xeke said, looking beyond their cell at a row of cages, each filled with no less than three inmates. All of the prisoners were male, but there were no other noticeable commonalities – some people were old, others only children; some wore suits and coats, others jeans and sweatshirts, even a few police uniforms; and the captors hadn't targeted people by race, either.

The taller of Xeke's two teenage cellmates extended his hand. His skin was coffee-colored, his hair black and tightly curled. "McCormick Martinez, not that names matter cuz we're all gonna die," he said, as defeated as a man overboard in a night sea. McCormick gestured to the other boy, a slightly overweight redhead on the verge of tears. "This is Kory."

Kory just stood there staring at Xeke, shoulders slumped, face shadowed in fear. His lower lip had been bloodied, his cheek welted. He exuded the complete abandonment of hope, an emptiness worse than despair.

Xeke introduced himself and quickly recapped the story of his arrival. The others shared similar horrors, McCormick on his way home from basketball practice and Kory heading to a restaurant with his mother for dinner. They'd both been picked up by state troopers and brought here within the last three hours.

"They dragged my mom away," Kory said, his first words to Xeke accompanied by tears and quivering lips.

# GRIDLOCKED

Xeke tapped him on the shoulder. "Don't worry, we'll get out of here and find your family."

"No we won't." McCormick spoke softly, plaintively, checking the aisle for guards and then letting his panic rise. "This is like fucking Auschwitz, man. I guarantee they did this for population control. They're gonna kill us all. They're gonna fucking gas us!"

"What are you talking about?" Xeke's legs felt leaden. His right cheek was puffing up and his jaw hurt when he spoke. He vaguely remembered someone punching him down and then the electric daggers, but his own condition was secondary, Amie's safety his main concern.

"Population control," McCormick repeated, his eyes awash with terror. "The water wars are getting worse, and it's only a matter of time before they happen here. The government is probably doing this across the country as a proactive approach. We'll be deported if we're lucky." He gestured to the cage to their right. "At least that's what I overheard from that old dude with the long hair. He said he's a professor. He said they're building a huge wall down south."

Xeke took a moment's appraisal of the man, whose unruly gray hair flowed over his shoulders. He spoke adamantly yet quietly to a thirtyish guy in his cell.

"Why separate guys and girls?" Xeke wondered aloud, panic creeping acidly up his throat. "If we're gonna be killed or sent down to Mexico, what's the need to split us up?"

McCormick's blank expression indicated he hadn't considered the question. "I don't know, maybe we're being sold into slavery. It's not like they told us anything when they shoved us in here."

Two warehouses to the west, imprisoned in a similar environment, Amie awoke with a soaring headache. She squinted against the light, her eyes burning.

*Where am I? What's happening?*

Until Amie heard soft whimpering, she didn't even notice the little girl sitting in the corner of her cell, knees pulled up to her chest, arms hugging her legs. Her face was tear-streaked and red. Her eyes were bright blue and enlarged like those of Disney characters. Her hair was hidden beneath a colorful beanie hat teeming with winter friends (penguins, snowmen, reindeer). She couldn't have been older than ten.

Amie, in spite of the pain brought by each step, crossed the cell and kneeled beside the girl.

"Don't cry, sweetie," Amie said when the tears commenced, wrapping her arm around the girl's shoulders and pulling her close.

As though a massive curtain had been drawn back, Amie became aware of the happenings in the immediate vicinity – girls and women of varying age confined to rows of cells. Some were shouting and railing against the iron bars. Some looked defeated. Many were crying.

Panic escalating, Amie squeezed the girl's tiny hand. "I'm Amie. What's your name?"

She glanced up at Amie with a haunted look, her eyes welling with fresh tears. Her lips parted as if to facilitate speech, but nothing came forth.

"Where's your mom and dad?" Amie pressed.

The girl lowered her chin to her knees. "I'm Jazzi," she said at last, in a voice as frail as talc. Her eyes remained on the floor.

# GRIDLOCKED

"Jazzi. I like that name. Is it short for something?"

"I'm not sure," the girl said, finally looking up at Amie again but only briefly. "It might not be short for anything. No one ever told me."

Amie waited a few moments, continuing to study their surroundings, then said, "So where are your parents, Jazzi? Did they take you away from them?"

"I don't know my parents, only my foster mom. I've lived with her forever. Well, it seems like forever."

"Who's your foster mom?"

"Arkansena," Jazzi said with a wistful smile. "She was born in Arkansas. That's how she got her name. Everyone calls her Sena."

"And where is Sena now? Do you know?" When Jazzi's silence persisted, Amie recounted her own story, the girl blinking as though she might cry again when she heard about what had happened to Xeke.

"I know you're scared." Amie spoke even more softly now, touching the girl's icy cheeks. "I'm scared, too. I don't know what's happening, but we need to stay together. No matter what happens, we stay together, okay?"

Jazzi removed her hat, revealing not a wisp of hair beneath, her blue eyes magnified. "You don't want to stay with me. I'm sick," she said in a fading voice. "Sena was taking me home from my treatment. She would have been safe if she hadn't gone with me."

Tears springing, Amie embraced the girl once more, words a momentarily impossible feat. Locked in each other's arms, they absorbed the horrors of the prison – every scream and clang amplified – but then there were other sounds.

Distant gunfire.

Rumbling.

Vibrations.

Uniformed guards sprinted down the aisle, guns in hand. With the bulging eyes of a terrified fawn, Jazzi watched the guards run past. Many of them were women, some barely a few years older than Amie.

Who were they? Why were they doing this?

A thunderous explosion. Xeke dropped to his knees, shielded his head from the singeing heat with his arms. He was in the middle of a long line of prisoners, the railroad yard before them, hundreds of autorack cars linked in the sidings, waiting to be loaded.

Upon Xeke's shaking hands the blood was still warm.

Cell by cell, the guards had ordered them out at gunpoint, then herded them to the back of the warehouse, where they'd been stripped of their possessions. Even Xeke's necklace and Swatch (short for **SMARTWATCH**), the one Amie gave him for his last birthday, had been stolen during the session the guards referred to as a prisoner inspection.

But not everyone had stood still and submissive like Xeke while their things were torn away. A handful of prisoners had rushed the guards and were shot, falling to the concrete floor with sickening *thwunks* and *schlats*, the shock rendering Xeke momentarily paralyzed, until finally a guard had shoved him into motion.

# GRIDLOCKED

The inspection had culminated with monitored visits to the throom – a huge, centrally located setup of urinals and toilets. There hadn't been much pissing in the throom, mostly vomiting. Later, overhead doors at the back of the warehouse had lifted to expose a railroad yard half a mile wide, with multiple sidings branching off the main line and running east-west.

During the downhill walk to the yard, a group of prisoners immediately in front of Xeke had tried to flee. Two of them had been shot, three more tackled and forced back into the line. One of the prisoners shot and killed had been McCormick, Xeke running to his fallen cellmate's side, trying to stem the relentless blood rushing from his neck, the wound a hideously deep and shredded chasm that Xeke had instantly known would prove fatal, yet still he'd tried to stop death's march, slow it, even just a little. The clap of gunfire limiting his hearing to a dull ring, he'd recoiled at the sight of the reaper's shadow creeping into McCormick's eyes, tall and swaying. It had lingered there briefly, the expanding shadow, Xeke was positive of it. Staring into McCormick's chestnut eyes, hands syruped in blood, he'd been hyper-aware and yet straddling the border between what the mind can take and what snaps it, and then there'd been nothing for him to glimpse in those lifeless eyes, vacant and unseeing as the guards hauled Xeke up and away, back into line.

Now there was even greater chaos. Xeke turned in the direction of the explosion, which had induced a temporary deafness, the heat still pulsing at his face. The midsection of the warehouse they'd just left was destroyed, the impact zone curling with fire, ruined prison cells visible within.

Lights flashed from the surrounding woods. Gunfire clattered with the rapid repetition of automatic weaponry. There was a moment of surreal, time-defying stillness before sound engendered result – then, with whizzing pelts, the rounds expelled from the woods tore into several guards, riddling them, dropping them, destroying them.

His world reduced to a slow-motion phantasmagoria from Hell, Xeke saw blood misting from the nearest guard's head. He somehow heard the solitary sound of another guard gurgling as his life poured out through his lips. The eyes of a third guard locked solely upon Xeke as the big man fell, death intercepting his soul before he hit the pavement.

Many of the prisoners, Xeke among them, dove instinctively to their stomachs as the gunfire raged and rockets whined into the rail yard. Then, during an eventual lull in the storm, the prisoners stood, ran. Some rounded the warehouses, heading back toward the entrance. Others crossed the tracks, hopping over couplers linking the cars. Rows of light towers glared down at them. In one of the sidings, three locomotives were burning.

For an extended moment encapsulating other moments – a slowly creeping photograph of sorts – Xeke was motionless, thoughtless, almost sightless from what he'd endured. He was shaking uncontrollably. He didn't know what to do or where to go, watching with horrified transfixion as wounded guards and prisoners warred, the inmates quickly taking the advantage, mashing their enemies' heads in until they looked like ruined watermelons.

Suddenly Xeke was on his feet again, driven by a single image in his head, a single word on his tongue as the warehouses burned and the battle surged around him – Amie.

# GRIDLOCKED

## Chapter 12

Paul gazed up at the light that had guided them here, its blue-tinged glow painted along the shallows of the woods, a foreboding portrait having been limned for two hapless viewers, subtly changed with each brushstroke of wind.

And now what?

Paul, though gifted with a miracle, felt as if he were still sightless. He could not see beyond the woods, beyond the night, beyond his fear. He couldn't formulate a strategy. At least in blindness there had been societal predictability and safety...but now, with sight, the world was an overwhelming peril.

And it seemed like years had passed since his last call to his wife and son.

The bluish light drizzled down from a lamp affixed to an otherwise darkened outbuilding – a large garage with three bays and two sedans parked out front, hoods lifted. Farther ahead, the cones of their flashlights bobbed and swooped against the windows of a two-story house. They were approaching the house from the back, sneakers thudding over a slightly downsloping driveway that split into a Y about where they'd met it, then branched in opposing directions through the woods. To the right of the house, a detached shed and a host of junker cars were nestled in darkness.

"What's the plan?" Paul said. They'd turned onto a back sidewalk flanked by bare plants ready for winter.

Pistol and flashlight pointed ahead, Steel led the way to the back deck. "I want to get a look at the other side. Then we'll watch the road for a while like we talked about, see what happens. Right now we trust no one." Steel glanced back at his friend. "You still good?"

"Good as gold, man." Paul held up his weapon. "You remain about as insufficiently backed up as possible."

Steel permitted himself a chuckle. "Maybe you should go on ahead of me, just in case you start shooting at shadows."

Paul was shivery from the cold and fear, the wind acquiring a sharper bite with the deepening hour. He guessed it was probably around nine now; if that was true, it'd be eight back home in Chicago, where his family would soon be worrying.

"Sounds like a good idea to me," Paul said. "Let's just pray I don't kill someone's cat. Last thing we need at a time like this is bad luck."

Rounding the house, they fanned their lights across the cover of a rectangular in-ground pool at the base of a steeper hill. Aglow with colorful solar lights, a staircase cut through a garden to an empty pool deck still repining over summer's departure. On the opposite side of the front lawn, the driveway meandered precipitously down to the road, surely a beast in the wintertime.

"Let's get to the road." Steel tried to maintain his resolve, but he couldn't ignore the dread heightening in his heart. A part of him wanted to check the house right away. If it was empty, they could grab a quick meal and rest, then move again at sunrise, at which time the authorities would hopefully have the remaining renegades in custody or body bags.

But for now it would be the life of a vagrant for them, a life Steel had adapted to during his days of instability, when the clanks and clatters of railroad cars had lulled him to sleep and he'd awoken at dawn in a new state. Nothing had been guaranteed during that abject chapter – not even his next meal – and now he was back to it, ready for a brief return, but not Paul. His heart hurt for Paul, that pistol as foreign to him as China, far too many miles between him and his family. Paul was a man of higher purpose, a man of calling and inspiration, Steel just a guide, a worker with no family. Yet even though Paul's vision

# GRIDLOCKED

had been restored, Steel knew he would have to guide him now more than before. Paul had once helped save his life, and Steel, looking briefly to the stars, vowed to keep returning the favor. He would see Paul through this as he'd done for years, just another road, he told himself, a new destination awaiting their arrival and with it a new story.

They sidled carefully down to the edge of the road and kept their flashlights dark for a time. From this low angle, the house seemed like a fortress up on the hill, a massive shadow extending from the woods, backlit by the spectral blue glow.

For several minutes they waited, hidden behind an ancient tree, watching the empty road. There wasn't another house in sight, woods in every direction. Though the road wasn't likely heavily traveled at this hour, even on a normal night, the sustained absence of vehicles sent chimes of alarm ringing through Paul's bones, the relentless wind seemingly their only company.

According to Steel's watch, ten, fifteen, thirty minutes passed without a single vehicle, until finally the raw wind sent them back up to the house just shy of ten o'clock. Though they'd worn cold-weather apparel in anticipation of November in New England, the wind nonetheless found its way through to their skin. Paul had even pulled the hood of his coat tight around his face, but still his cheeks and nose felt half-numb.

Steel rang the doorbell three times and allowed lengthy intervals in between, ready with a quick explanation for their weapons. When silence prevailed, his hand fell instinctively upon the handle. Unlocked, the door opened to darkness.

The foyer was cold, bare, uninviting, the stairwell before them rising up into a black abyss.

"Follow me," Steel whispered, his flashlight sweeping into an empty room to their left.

Paul found a light switch, flipped it. The room was large and stripped of furnishings, nothing on the walls, either. "No one lives here," he said, relieved.

Steel frowned. "So why didn't they kill the electricity? And why are there vehicles outside?" He shook his head, lowered his voice. "Something's off. I don't like this."

The next room was also empty, the chandelier hanging at its center likely indicative of a dining space. Yet the adjoining kitchen hadn't been fully cleared out; the cabinets boasted cereal and crackers and bags of candy. And the refrigerator, stocked with soda, bottled water, and a bowl of fruit, among other offerings, seemed to suggest at least one current inhabitant of the place.

"Anyone here?" Steel shouted, checking a side room and a closet before returning to the kitchen. Silence. "You've got nothing to be afraid of…at least not from us. But out there it's real bad. *Terrorism*. We saw cops killed right in front of us, and we're just looking for a place to hole up for the night."

Silence.

Steel sniffed the grapes and blueberries inside the bowl in the refrigerator which had been covered with plastic wrap, then popped a handful into his mouth. "Not fresh, but not too old," he noted, extending the bowl to Paul. "Want some?"

"Heavens no!" Paul backed away, as if in atavistic revulsion to the fruit. "Should we leave, you think?"

Steel shook his head. "Not before we refuel and load up. We've got ourselves a long day ahead."

# GRIDLOCKED

After hastily treating themselves to some of the foods left behind, then stuffing nonperishables and bottled water into their backpacks, they embarked on a thorough review of the house, searching for a landline but finding no tools for communication. In many rooms, especially those on the second floor, boxes had been left half-packed, mostly filled with clothes. The beds and most of the other furniture were gone. In what had evidently been a child's room, a few articles of clothing remained in the drawers of a bureau, many of them shorts and summer clothes. Even stranger, the master bedroom closet looked as if it had been ransacked, a few old suits left in their bags at the end of the rack and dusty footwear forgotten on shelves.

"Looks like someone didn't have time to pack up all of their stuff," Steel observed, examining the things forsaken.

Paul, meanwhile, had removed a photograph from the master bedroom wall. At first he noticed nothing of its subjects, swept up by the simple notion that he was looking at photographs again, yet another of life's treasures he'd assumed lost to the cruelty of The Curse.

"This is real," he murmured, bringing a hand to his forehead. "Dear Lord, it's really real."

It wasn't until Steel, on his way from the walk-in closet, said, "Whatcha got there?", that Paul studied the occupants of the photograph: a family, the parents on either end, three colorfully dressed little ones in the middle.

Paul handed the photo to Steel. "A beautiful family, indeed. I pray for their safety."

Scratching his beard, Steel regarded the silver-framed photograph. "I'd save your prayers for now, buddy. It's almost like these people knew something was about to go down. They were planning to move, but things got on them in a hurry and they had to blow town before they could even finish packing."

Paul, at first, couldn't find the words to respond. "Nonsense. Foolishness," he finally spurted, taken aback by the idea that this family had learned of…whatever was going on out there and thus expedited their moving plans. "How could anyone have predicted such a calamity?"

Steel whisked a stolen package of peanut butter crackers from his pocket and tore open the wrapper. Snapping a cracker into his mouth and crunching it to bits, he said, "Think about it. Why would anyone leave all of these things behind – photographs, clothes, shoes? Why are boxes half-packed? And why the hell did they leave their cars out there?" He pried another photograph from the wall. "Plus, why is there still food in the kitchen? Maybe they're planning to come back for the rest of this shit later, after the dust settles."

A chill curled between Paul's shoulder blades, fading before it could spread. There had been a spark of suspicion just then, a thought that maybe Steel was right.

*No, it can't be. It just can't be.*

Paul thought of his wife and son, prayed they were safe. He thought of his religious teachings. He thought of what his parents and Father Guillen had said long ago. He thought of the upsetting accounts he'd heard along his journeys in recent years, fear and uncertainty ruling minds young and old. There were many problems, building and building and building, and now there was chaos.

Steel, in that same span of seconds, as he progressed on the package of crackers, licking his fingers after every one, thought of where he might find a drink. He thought flashingly of the troopers who'd been murdered, their wives and children left behind. He thought of his latest girlfriend, who'd been too kind and wise for a man like him. She hadn't understood his penchant for the road or his friendship with Paul. She'd wanted to change him, so much talk of college and bettering himself – and it had all been too much, the moon and the stars asked of a man who, at his apex, could not hope to reach the clouds.

If only this house had offered a few drinks. Then the troopers' blood might not burn so brightly in Steel's head.

*They spent their final moments trying to protect.*

*Don't think of it. Just keep moving.*

But the horrors were surging back at Steel, worsened by the soughing, wicked night wind that traced along the eaves and pressed at the windows. The world had changed out there beneath the stars, and Steel worried he wasn't strong enough to protect Paul until normalcy returned.

Exploring another bedroom that had belonged to a child, the little girl in the photo, they found stuffed animals piled up on the indented carpet where the bed had been and others tucked away in the closet, something sickly sentimental about such toys left behind. Steel, bored with these finds, took a bathroom break, but Paul continued his exploration of the closet. Lifting a threadbare pony with a missing eye, he felt suddenly as if he were sinking. Maze had once loved a stuffed bear named Hero, its fur about the same texture as this little pony, though Paul had only been able to guess at what it looked like based on Maddie's descriptions.

Squeezing the pony, Paul looked to the ceiling and whispered, "I love you guys. Stay strong. I'll be home as soon as I can."

An apprehensive sigh escaped Paul. He would gladly live in the dark for the remainder of his days if it meant he could get home safely to his family, a wife and a son whose faces he'd never seen.

But there were no guarantees, nothing to take for granted anymore, their lives suddenly churned with chaos and chopped by a cold wind.

Paul shifted his attention back to the closet. It hadn't been cleared out as thoroughly as the others, its shelves still cluttered with appurtenances of pink and purple. There were shoeboxes crammed with drawings and markers and crayons; a shifter-compatible dollhouse that could play any song of a child's choosing; and a magic kit replete with cards and strings and dice. At the bottom of the pile was a pink mirror about the size of a makeup compact, Paul grabbing it up eagerly and then tossing it away, as if the thing were as hot as a baking tray in the stove.

Gathering the mirror again, he lifted it slowly to eye level, bracing himself for major changes but not expecting a total stranger staring back at him.

Paul's breath caught in his chest. His face was fixed in a broad grimace. He brought both hands to his cheeks and pressed lightly. He'd last seen himself as a seventeen-year-old kid, but the adult countenance in the mirror bore no resemblance to the face of memory, the eyes dark and foreign, the chin an inch too long and covered in thick stubble, the ears too big. For a moment the weight of the dark years and everything Paul had missed hit him with untrammeled force. Looking at himself now was like a recently released inmate coming home after twenty years and seeing a drastically changed neighborhood, the infant next door now wearing a university hoodie, the woods at the end of the street cleared out and replaced by a subdivision, the sweet old lady two doors down who used to give you extra Halloween candy now residing across town, haven't you heard, at St. Anne's Cemetery.

"Find anything we can use?" Steel said, returning from the bathroom, his hair and beard damp.

# GRIDLOCKED

Paul held up the little book that had come with the magic kit. "Not unless you want to learn some magic."

Steel crossed the room and checked some of the boxes stacked in the corner. Going through these people's things, he felt as if he were a crime scene investigator searching for that one item that would bring sense to the confusion. But what if no such item existed? What if they were wasting their time here?

There was a flexing discomfort at the pit of Steel's stomach as he went through the boxes, brought on by urgency. He kept glancing back at the hallway, thinking he'd heard footsteps. Outside, the wind railed against the windows. Distantly, or perhaps only at the edges of his mind, there were faint cracks of gunfire breaking above the wind.

But they had to keep looking, Steel told himself. Maybe they really were close to stumbling across something that could explain what had caused these people to leave in such a hurry.

Paul, searching an abandoned toy chest, found a few construction paper drawings of religious inspiration. Bolstering the drawings were images – crosses, churches, angels – that had been roughly cut from computer printouts, edges and corners snipped off here and there. All around these images were the colorful swirls of sky and water rendered by a young hand, words interspersed, some of them alarming.

**THE END**, one drawing was titled in youth's penmanship, with scribbles of fire drawn recklessly around a throng of stick figures.

**JESUS SAVES!** another drawing proclaimed, a massive crucifix tilted against a gray-black scratch of sky. Upon a thin path leading to the crucifix, serpents lashed at shackled prisoners consigned to damnation, these details understandable for Paul because they had been printed, not drawn. Otherwise, had the job been left entirely to the kid, the serpents might have appeared as windblown worms whirling past a family of sticks.

Yet another drawing featured swarms of insects, no printouts this time, just hundreds of dots to convey the message without mistake. A fourth drawing ran red with a river's blood, empty rowboats floating down the middle, a rippled spiral hinting of recent submersion off to the right. In a fifth rendering – this one augmented by printouts as well – the damned were but hamsters in a spiked wheel, their chests exed out in angry, brazen red, the artist caring little about straying from the lines.

***They will all die***, came the small-handed scrawls. Beneath it: ***Sinners suffer and die.***

The drawings and messages scraped through Paul's head like sand gritted between teeth. Following the madness on Route 49, it seemed beyond coincidence that he should find such things in a child's room.

"Steel," he called, gathering the drawings.

"Religious fanatics," Steel said, handing the drawings back to Paul. "Parents probably forced the kid to draw this shit. Churches have been obsessing on this End of Days stuff lately, right?"

Paul shrugged. "I wouldn't say, *obsessing*, though the tenors of many congregations have grown noticeably…darker in recent years. With the water wars out west and down south, some have certainly sought the hand of prophecy."

Steel huffed. "In other words, they're obsessed that the world's gonna end."

Paul returned the drawings to the toy chest. "A growing number of people," he conceded, taking a final glimpse at the **JESUS SAVES** strangeness before closing the chest's lid. "I sure hope they're wrong."

# GRIDLOCKED

They went hurriedly through the rest of the house, finding the attic and basement mostly full. There were still awards and plaques on display in a basement trophy room; beyond it was an almost fully furnished office (but still nothing for communications). The attic, meanwhile, was a maze of boxes and old appliances. Some of the boxes held Christmas ornaments, others photo albums – surely not the kinds of things that would be willingly left behind.

Finally, Steel discovered an attic box full of bank and credit card statements. "Looks like the Sterlings had it made," he said, riffling the documents.

Paul, sifting through a larger box, had come across another stack of useful papers. "Richard Sterling, Sr., President of Sterling and Sons Builders," he read, the transfer of ownership document before him having faded to yellow. "So I take it he's the grandfather, and Richard Sterling, Jr., inherited the company. Simply put, these people are loaded."

"Maybe they aren't finished moving, after all," Steel suggested. "They must've known the shit was about to hit, I'm telling you. I just get that feeling."

"Nah, there's gotta be another explanation." Paul shook his head, unwilling to settle for the conspiracy theory. "Can't tell you what in God's name that explanation is, but there has to be another answer."

Eventually their investigation yielded to a few hours of fitful sleep in shifts. When Paul woke, immediately thanking God for his continued vision, he availed himself of a hot shower and then stuffed a few last-minute items into his backpack, among them the one-eyed pony he'd found. He couldn't explain what had prompted him to return for the pitiful little creature, but something in his heart had latched onto it and wouldn't let go. Though just a toy, it was a vestige of the world he'd always known, and now, the ground trembling beneath them, the order of society shaken, Paul clung to every last shred of normalcy.

*It'll all be over soon*, Paul thought as they stepped outside into the predawn dark, the eastern sky lightening beyond the treetops, fear and excitement clashing in his heart at the idea of seeing his first sunrise since he was seventeen years and seven months old.

## Chapter 13

Tommy and Dominick walked a little over a mile, ducking into the woods whenever headlights emerged in the distance, until finally Tommy came to an abrupt stop and kneeled.

He was staring off to the south, his eyes following the road, yet he took in very little of the night on this side of the bridge. Without even a precipitating thought, he'd been wrenched back to the darkness of the middle, drawn as if by magnetism to that road of his dreams where **GRDLCK** had first appeared on a license plate and green headlights had poured violence into the senseless black.

Now he was there again in his mind, taken bit by bit to the depths of that place existing infinitely between then and now. Looking closer, he noticed an arched door – dungeonlike dark beyond it – and he could sense himself sliding inexorably toward that open door, through it, and now he was on the other side…

But he heard his brother's voice calling his name, strangely distant, and suddenly he was returning.

Dom went a little farther before realizing his brother no longer walked alongside him. The wind, in its duplicity, had fabricated the crunch-sweep of footsteps to his left.

Dom looked back, saw his brother kneeling on the grass, head lowered to his chest. He was shaking, mumbling. When Dom called out to him, he said nothing.

"Tommy! Tommy, are you okay?" Fearing that his brother's ability to walk had indeed been a miracle of adrenaline, Dom grabbed his shoulder.

"Tommy, can you hear me?" His eyes lifted lazily, fluttered, then shot open, wide and confused.

A little dizzy, Tommy wobbled to his feet. In a moment he regained his orientation, the night returning to him. There was Dominick, stabilizing him. There was the road at the hill's base, barely distinguishable in such a thick swaddle of black. And there were the stars, friend or foe? Tommy had seen them but seconds ago, bright and disturbing, not just stars but something more – spectators.

"We have to get to the road," Tommy rasped, his voice at first unfamiliar. Soon, like the rest of him, it was fully restored. "The truck. We can't miss that truck."

"What truck?" Dom suddenly realized what was happening. Again. "Jesus, Tommy, did you remember something else from the dream?"

Tommy nodded, led his brother down the hill to 49, just as green headlights swept around a distant curve.

"This is a mistake. It's the same kind of truck as the others." Dom started back up the hill, but Tommy shouted for him to stay.

"Trust me!" Tommy pleaded. "This is our only chance. I just saw what happens if we miss it."

Dom, torn with combating thoughts, managed a few more steps of reason up the hill, then realized he could never leave his brother. Guided by God or madness, Tommy had already saved them once, and even if this was suicide, even if gunfire would shred them to nothingness, Dom hurried back to his brother at the bottom of the hill.

The whir of the truck grew louder, the headlights brighter. Dom's chest knotted. Tommy's throat clenched. For a few moments neither of them breathed as they stood in the breakdown lane like destitute vagabonds waiting for a downpour to add to their misery.

The truck rumbled closer, slowed.

# GRIDLOCKED

Dom could see the contraption jutting out from the front of the truck, its claws ready to snap them up…and anything else daring to remain on 49. The headlights brightened to impossible strength, predatory eyes widening at the sight of two victims soon to be claimed.

Dom sensed himself stepping back, but his brother seized his arm. "Trust me," he repeated, his eyes squinting but without fear.

Tommy wondered fleetingly if he'd been tricked, but then the warmth and calm of the vision took over. It wouldn't lead him astray, he somehow knew. If he held firm to its wisdom and stayed unfalteringly within the path carved out for him, then they would survive – this all coming to him with a second's instinct.

The truck downshifted, angled to the right, a turn signal preceding its shift into the breakdown lane. Dom gasped in astonishment when the blinker came; they'd become obsolete in the new system.

"He's not on the grid," Dom murmured. "Jesus, Tommy, he's stopping for us. You saved our asses again!"

The dump truck groaned to a stop. It was a tri-axle heavy hauler, equipped tonight not for hauling but destruction. The driver's door flung open, a tall guy with a leather jacket and a Red Sox hat hopping down to the road. He crossed quickly in front of the truck, a pistol in hand but facing downward, his boots bringing hollow thuds.

"Get in. Hurry," he said.

"Wait, who are you?" Dom demanded. "What the hell is going on?"

The man, already striding back toward the driver's door, said, "Do you want to live or not?"

The brothers exchanged glances, then stepped up to the passenger door.

## Chapter 14

The gunfire quickly ascended from pops to cracks to thunderbolts. Screams and chaos rose to such a height that time stilled, Amie and Jazzi hugging each other as war ravaged the building.

Amie held the girl tight, tried to remember the stars, infinite stars winking down from the blackness, the wind jagging icily at her, Xeke's gloved hand in hers – and at last there was a strange moment of improvement, a hole in the storm, the gunfire diminishing.

Amie pulled free of their embrace and glanced behind her, where the aisle was red with death. The bodies were like those in one of Amie's recent theater productions, heaped luridly. But those had only been actors, death imagined, faked.

This was real. The eyes were vacant. Blood flowed and pooled. Wounds gaped and glared, forcing Amie to retch, Jazzi screaming upon exposure to the horrors.

The thunder faded incrementally, the storm slowly pulling away. There were remnant cracks at each corner of the building, vibrations pulsing through the iron bars. Amie clutched her head with both hands, feeling an odd detachment from herself, as though she were floating. Her vision wasn't quite right, either, a little blurred and swimmy.

Not comprehending what she was doing, Amie took Jazzi's hand and led her out of the cell, realizing once they were in the slippery aisle, dodging victims of the massacre, that they were the only prisoners to have escaped. She'd opened the gate without issue and walked out, not even acknowledging that it was unlocked.

Prisoners screamed at them, begged them. "How did they get out? Find the keys! Get us out of here! Hurry!"

"Just keep going. Don't look down," Amie said, her hand never separating from Jazzi's.

"Save us! You can't leave us here! They'll kill us!" girls and women pleaded, slamming the bars and rattling the gates.

Though terror impelled her forward, Amie stopped, forced herself to look down. The majority of the victims were guards clad in black cop-like uniforms, yet there were no badges or pins or logos of any sort, nothing to identify them. A few of the victims were men with black leather jackets and bandanas and plenty of pins/patches – the Freedom Riders. Their guns were strewn about like the remains of an armory after a tornado.

With shaking hands Amie searched a few of the guards for keys, her fingers slick with blood.

"There's no keys!" she shouted at no one in particular. "I can't find any keys!"

Outside, the gunfire opened up another downpour.

"Please, you have to save us!" a prisoner begged. "Don't let my daughter die in here! You're our only chance!"

The captives beseeched her to keep looking, a chorus that soon drowned out individual pleas, but Amie was suffocated by urgency, utterly out of time. They had to keep going. If they stopped again, they'd be killed, she sensed. More guards would come and shoot them – they'd shoot until no one was left.

"Come on, Jazzi," she urged, and the little girl nodded, running with Amie to the end of the aisle.

Xeke was sprinting east, ignoring the pain, when, three hundred feet to the north, an explosion of sound and brilliant light momentarily stripped him of his faculties, the world reduced to a blinding sphere of orange. He could feel the intensity of the heat upon his face, could smell gasoline. When his eyes and ears took control again, he saw the row of guardhouses ablaze. Distantly, the purr of motors came surfing in on the wind.

Headlights appeared to the north, rushing toward him from the entry road, breaking across a slight rise like waves. Motorcycles. Dozens of them.

Fear arrived first, followed closely by relief. The Freedom Riders, he realized, throwing his hands up as the riders cruised past into the parking lot. "Help! My girlfriend – they took her!"

But the riders ignored him. They couldn't hear him, their engines blasting. Most of them veered right and came alongside the warehouses, the others following an access road leading down to the rail yard.

Another surge of escaping prisoners, meanwhile, headed north toward the burning guardhouses, freedom half a mile beyond.

Xeke was directionless. He made a little circle, flinched at a new swell of gunfire between the nearest warehouses.

Amie. Where was she? Locked up? Taken away by train? Injured? Killed?

"You looking for a bullet to the head, kid?"

Xeke stumbled. The deep voice had boomed from behind him, its owner standing with his arms crossed and his chest pushed out. He wore a black leather jacket and a fedora of the same color, a pistol gleaming in his right hand. There were myriad patches displayed on his jacket, and his belt buckle boasted a rhinestone cross. It wasn't until the man glanced north, toward the ruined guardhouses, that

Xeke noticed his motorcycle idling twenty feet away – a Harley with an oversized black-tinted windshield.

"Well, don't just stand there. Ride or die, kid," the man said, motioning to the bike. His gray beard was neatly trimmed, his eyes smoky with intensity. There was a strange calmness to him, an aura inconsistent with the abounding pandemonium. Xeke wondered if he was one of them, the people who'd taken them here.

"My girlfriend. She's still here. I can't leave." Xeke's words were rapid and conjoined, barely intelligible even to him.

Yet somehow the man understood him. "Don't you worry about her. Our group won't leave no one behind. Our first liberation team probably already got her out of this godforsaken place."

They both turned in the direction of a flare-up, a handful of guards put down by Freedom Riders with assault rifles. A massive hulk of a guard rushed at them from the nearest warehouse, running clumsily but not for long, a flurry of shots claiming him. The Freedom Riders, with leather jackets and heavy weaponry, moved swiftly, tactically, and why wouldn't they? These people had fought in the wars. They knew how to kill. For a time they'd known nothing but violence and death, and now they were mostly drunks and grid dodgers, often referred to as the Wasted Warriors. But on this night Xeke would have been wasted if not for their arrival.

Apparently confident with the ensuing calm, the man holstered his weapon. "Look, kid, the next team is gonna firebomb the shit out of this place in about" – he checked his watch – "half an hour or so, give or take a few minutes. You don't want to be here when that happens."

"But my girl–"

He held up a hand, then pointed to a fresh legion of headlights in the distance. "You see those buses coming? Those are to take people out of here, but not everyone will fit. We'll have to do quite a few pillion jobs to get you all to our camp in Sturbridge. But you have my word, no one gets left behind."

Again Xeke worried that he couldn't trust the guy, but why would these people have killed the guards if they meant to hurt the prisoners?

"Okay, I'll go with you," Xeke agreed, realizing amidst his desperation that, even if they searched the entire facility, it would be next to impossible to identify one girl among hundreds of people. The guy was probably right anyhow – hopefully Amie had already been rescued.

Yet still Xeke searched the sprawling site of mayhem, his eyes sweeping down to the rail yard, where Freedom Riders were ushering people off the autorack cars. Their faces all twisted into one, as if Xeke were sitting behind the dugout at Fenway Park and trying to pick out a single face from the seats wrapped around Pesky's Pole.

The man led Xeke to the Harley and tossed him a helmet. "One rule," he said before hopping onto the bike. "Don't let go."

Amie raced trippingly down the aisles with Jazzi, made a series of lefts and rights, her head hammering, the taste of blood in her throat. With each turn she expected a guard in their faces. With each forward burst she dreaded footsteps closing in from behind.

Finally they reached a steel door, pushed it open, and found themselves in a large room mottled with bodies and streaked with blood. The dead were stacked over chairs, strewn across desks, splayed out on the floor – all of them guards.

"There!" Amie pointed to an exit sign above a corridor in the far right corner, but halfway there she stopped, a thought springing to mind, ambivalence taking hold.

# GRIDLOCKED

Was there time? Could she pull it off? And what about Jazzi?

"Come on!" the girl urged, but Amie called her back and explained her idea.

"It might be our only chance," Amie said, wrenched by the fear in Jazzi's eyes. She had to free the girl of this nightmare, every second spent here a second too long, but the alternative – rushing out unprotected – was suddenly unthinkable.

Amie squeezed Jazzi's hands. "I need you to be really brave, okay? I can't do this without you."

With a resolute nod Jazzi approached the nearest guard, whose head was haloed in a pool of crimson. "We can do this, Amie." The girl spoke with a quiet confidence, her eyes a little brighter now. "Sena said you can do anything if you have faith and don't give up."

Faith. There had been a time when Amie's faith was broken, her days long and bleak – but then Xeke had redirected the course of her path.

Where was he now? Amie envisioned the worst, impossible to think positively with death entombing them.

"Ready?" Amie said, biting back the tears.

"Ready," Jazzi confirmed.

## Chapter 15

Paul and Steel were in the woods again, walking parallel to the road, the house they'd just lightly ransacked now half a mile back. Another house crouched in the distance, a sheepish little two-story job crowded by trees. The porch light was on, its dim glow spilling out; otherwise the place would have been nearly invisible.

Through the trees, the sky had adopted a scarcely lighter blue, birds rousing with their earliest tunes, the wind having finally subsided. It was cold, winter cold. Thanksgiving was less than a week away, Paul to see his meal for the first time in two decades…if there was a Thanksgiving meal to be had this year.

*Of course there'll be a meal. This will all be long finished by then, another tragedy in the archives.*

Yet Paul had grown increasingly fearful that the damage was widespread and irrevocable, that the world he'd known was gone with last night's sunset, a new world dawning. And what picture would the morning paint? When they were finally free of this wooded East Brookfield neighborhood, what devastation would they encounter? Maddie and Maze were surely stricken with fear by now – he had to find a way to reach them.

They edged closer to the road, Steel leading the way. He hadn't heard a siren – not even the distant sound of traffic – in several hours. It was as if life had been paused, everyone but them frozen in place.

Steel pointed to the house. "How about we see who's home?"

Paul nodded. "Maybe we'll find a landline this time."

On Steel's call, they hurried across the road into the empty driveway. The house, with its dark windows and severely pitched roof, was stern, uninviting, somehow watchful. It filled Paul with even more apprehensive thoughts, but without hesitation Steel went up to the front door and rang the bell. After another try, he went for the door. Locked.

"I'm really starting to dislike this damn neighborhood," Steel grumbled, his face pale.

They came alongside the house, following a path that led behind it. The back deck was illuminated as well, Paul nearly bumping into a grill he'd somehow overlooked. There was a glass table back here, an umbrella looming over it, the perfect place for cookouts in the summer. These details brought Paul briefly back to his Chicago home with Maddie and Maze, where the fire pit provided countless memories – ghost stories and marshmallows and huge gatherings of friends and family on the Fourth of July. Paul had seen none of these experiences, yet he nevertheless knew the place infallibly from the portrait his family's descriptions had painted. He could see home in his mind, could feel moments of the past fill him with warmth on a cold predawn morning.

But Paul no longer needed to rely on his imagination to create a setting, the real thing sprawled out darkly before him. He watched with trepidation and a tightened chest as Steel pushed the back door open and stepped inside, his flashlight peeling through the house.

"Anyone home?" Steel called. "We don't mean you any harm, just looking for a phone so my friend can call his family and let them know he's all right."

Again they switched on lights, searched the first floor, Steel poking his head out the breezeway door and discovering a garage devoid of vehicles. At least the garage and house were fully furnished, Paul experiencing a moment's relief that the owners hadn't moved out half-packed as well. That would have brought a fury of suspicions better left unsaid, neither of them possessing enough energy to sort through fear's thorny thicket for an explanation.

Back in the living room, after they failed to locate a landline, Steel clicked on the TV, desperate to learn what was happening out there. But no matter which channel he entered, the message at the center of the screen remained: **NO SIGNAL**.

"Dammit!" He tossed the remote onto the sofa. "Can't catch a break."

They continued through the house, its walls cluttered with dozens of pictures of children at varying stages of youth, as well as family photos with a white-haired couple often at the middle of the group. There were newspapers outspread on the dinner table, pairs of reading glasses scattered about, and not a shifter in sight. The computer in the study was troglodytic (Steel hadn't seen a screen that large in years), and the internet browser unsurprisingly did not come up.

Clearly an elderly couple resided here, but where were they now? Certainly not out for a walk of the dog at this hour.

"Can't believe they don't have a landline." Steel scratched his beard. "Old people and landlines are like PB and fucking J."

Though strikingly antiquated to Steel, the house was quaint and nostalgia-inducing to Paul, who'd been confined to darkness during the technology boom of the last fifteen years. He hadn't seen a Robopup. He hadn't witnessed clothes and shoes printed from a Comex. He hadn't seen what eighty miles per hour looks like with no one behind the wheel, or a pizza delivery drone struck down by hellion teenagers on Damage Night, or a two-hour maglev ride from Chitown to New York on Transrapid's Liberty Limited. And he was very thankful he hadn't gotten a glimpse of Leapland, which you could visit simply by popping in specialized contact lenses and then popping a corresponding pill that served as activator of the encoded data in the lenses. Those drugs were capable of taking you to outer space or the front lines of battle or a trembling high-wire stretched between skyscrapers, among countless other "destinations" – drug addiction turned into virtual reality (and one of the many reasons for the passage of AVA). The technology had been sold into the wrong hands by a rogue engineer contracted to work on revolutionary biosensory gaming conversions. And the rest was history, a multi-billion dollar drug network.

Paul felt a little dizzy at the thought of such things. When he'd last been able to see, there were still mail carriers, vehicle excise taxes, deliverymen, contact lenses capable only of improving your vision in one dimension, dogs that went to the vet when they broke down, not the factory for new parts. You ordered shoes and clothes online – and sometimes you even bought them at the store. You drove your car to work and school – and sometimes you crashed it. Twelve- and ten-year-olds texted, not six-year-olds.

A sound. They both heard it on the second floor. At the base of the stairs, Paul flicked on the staircase light.

No one up there, at least not in view.

Another sound – a thump. In unison they glanced up the stairs, which, after the landing, turned left to reach a second floor hallway mostly out of sight.

For the first time Steel was consciously aware of the house's smell, like old textbooks and forgotten basements. An almost liquid cold seeped through the walls.

"Is anyone up there?" Steel eyed his pistol up to the second floor. He could see a partially open door up there, as well as a wooden crucifix on the wall to the right of the doorframe. The cold sickened through him, bringing a mild barb of nausea.

"What do we do? Should we leave?" Paul whispered. He couldn't keep the gun still, nor could he quell the drumbeat insistences of his heart. He wished he could find an inner quiet, everything suddenly too loud and motional within himself, like a carousel circling with great speed.

"Be ready to shoot on my say-so." Steel crept up to the landing, waving for Paul to follow. He could see into the first room now, a candle flickering in there, a fruity scent wafting out.

Paul thought he heard slight rustling in the room, but Steel didn't seem to notice it.

*Relax – it's in your head.*

The next sound was not in his head. An unmistakable thud.

Their pace quickened up the remaining steps, Paul feeling as if he were drowning on dry land, his lungs unable to process the air. He coughed, choked a little, lagged behind.

Steel, already striding around a corner where the second floor hallway made a right turn outside another bedroom, lurched violently backward, away from the gore, the horror, the evil.

Paul, soon behind him, could not keep his snacks down.

Neither of them looked for a moment. Then, needing to confirm it was really there, Steel, like a recently awakened man allowing his squinting eyes to adjust, took in the gruesomeness in small doses that were no less intolerable.

The woman's head had been severed and reattached, then rended vertically into a bloody zipper line that split all the way down to the neck, everything rezipped with black thread. Blood-soaked bits of brain and skull and once cotton-white hair stained the gray carpet, chunked like the remnants of a smashed pumpkin. The head had been positioned upright again upon the stump neck after the atrocities were complete, the lips and eyes held open with clamps, the corpse then

# GRIDLOCKED

suspended from the attic hatch, dangling by the drawstring twisted around the neck.

Stumbling back, falling into the darkened second bedroom, Paul pulled himself up and beheld the next installment of insanity.

The husband.

He was hanging from the ceiling fan, his severed head affixed somehow to his paper-white hands. In the terrible half-dark, with only the light from the hallway sliding in, the corpse was like a headless scarecrow with bursting straw at the neck, unreal, impossible to be real, Paul wishing he was blind again, this new world a cruelty beyond comprehension.

Paul heard a scraping squeak. It sounded like a taut rope pulled through a winch, or a metal door jerked open.

Steel heard it, too, his jaw dropping when he saw the mutilated husband.

The shrill sound might have issued from the overstressed ceiling fan canopy, or maybe it came from up above, in the attic–

They ran, not looking back, stopping only when they were in the woods again.

Panting, every inhalation a slow burn, Paul wondered if they'd died on that road last night and gone to Hell.

# KEVIN FLANDERS

## Part II: Through the Woods

### Chapter 1

Death moves swiftly, silently. Into the next house, up the stairs, hooded, ready, a shadow, a flash gliding forth.

Flicking with the serpent's tongue. Gleaming with the marauder's eyes. Itching with the need, the calling.

Fingers flexing. Muscles coiled, hand of the huntsman eager for more blood.

It hasn't always been this way. Death, at one time, in another life, allowed his victims to go unclaimed. Grandparents. Siblings. Teachers. No longer. Crouching that moonlit winter night in his previous incarnation, the shadow of his hood upon the road, there was a connection achieved, a brilliant instant of realization, an acknowledgement of the calling. The demons whispered gleefully from the woods. Emerged. The nonsense of the day having sloughed away, night, in its infinite mystery and wisdom, sang verses of coronation.

Death found a vagrant that night and took his head as a souvenir. Bored the next night, Death visited the hole he'd dug by the side of the road and disinterred his prize, reuniting head and hands in incipient ritual.

Now Death stands among the envoys, armed with a new night, a new name, a new purpose, a new victim, the window having opened and let him back into this world. It won't stay open long, they tell him, that jagged portal of ancient black, but Death refuses to rush, not yet, not until he has stayed a little longer and gotten to know his victims better.

Death, not with a knife or a gun but his scythe, arcs a hooked shadow across the bedroom wall. He does not appear this way on the other

# GRIDLOCKED

side of the portal, only in this realm to facilitate the ageless promulgation of fear – for who is the conqueror with no one to fear him?

Lying before Death in the bed, another man sleeps soundly.

Death leaves the house without hurry, his scythe painted red, the man's blood sweet upon his tongue.

Pulling his hood tight around his face, savoring the mask it forms, Death glides obliquely down the road, gladdened that the window is open wide after remaining shut for so long.

Soon Death will end even more of them, just as he ended the pastor in his previous life. The man's head, perfectly smooth, made a fine tribute. Grandmother's display, however, wasn't nearly as neat.

Death gazes up to the next house, knowing he must return to his duties, yet he is drawn to this house by the scent. Their rage and agony smell like iron and firewood.

It is time for more sobbing. And fresh blood.

## Chapter 2

The man behind the wheel of the dump truck, a single bullet hole in its windshield, had introduced himself as Rocco Alidante. He went by Rock. About six-five and two-fifty, he could go by whatever he damn well pleased.

They drove in silence, the hydraulic claws looming hungrily out front, ready to snap up more vehicles. They were headed south toward Sturbridge center, where the military, state and local police, and members of the Freedom Riders had allegedly teamed up to establish a base at the high school on Route 148 and, across the street, at the junior high school. They'd fortified Route 148 from the Brookfield Town Common to Route 20 in Sturbridge.

"They're making progress," Rock said, breaking a long silence. "We're gonna win this war."

War? Tommy still couldn't stretch his mind around it. War was for other places, barbaric places. Since terminating its engagement in the latest Middle East campaign, the U.S. had spent a decade strengthening its borders and revolutionizing its transportation methods and infrastructure. This was a time for peace and transformation.

But war had struck, the enemy still faceless. Rock thought it might be a Chinese-funded initiative, billions invested into striking down the grid and communications systems on a single night.

"Think about it," Rock said a while later, getting back to his earlier indictment on the Chinese government. "You take out the grid, take out communications, kill everyone you can, cause chaos. The stock market crashes. People panic. You combine that with the problems we've already got with the water wars, and *bang*," – he snapped his fingers – "the government starts to collapse. This country has been a weak muscle for a long time, and this is the overstrain that was bound to happen. Someone saw the weakness and took advantage."

# GRIDLOCKED

"They might have been planning this for years – maybe all the way back to the start of the grid," Dom suggested. "But wouldn't attacking us also hurt their own economy?"

Tommy couldn't find any words. He imagined the White House and Pentagon on fire, as Rock had claimed. Before picking off the previous driver of the dump truck with a single shot through the windshield, then shoving him out of the rig, Rock had barely escaped death during a raid of a bar on Lake Lashaway. He'd been talking to himself about the lousy week and drinking whiskey, thankfully not too deep in the well to be useless when the shots were fired. Later, making his slow way south toward home, he'd heard from a badly wounded cop that D.C., New York, L.A., Chicago, Boston, and others had already been overrun.

The cop had collapsed shortly after informing Rock of the base on Route 148 and telling him to keep off the roads. With a round lodged in his stomach and another in his chest, he'd died a few minutes later, no time to bury him properly, the side of Route 49 to serve as his gravesite.

Now they were at the southern end of 49, crossing an overpass above the Mass. Pike, six lanes of highway below flooded in a river of headlights and tail lights, dozens of motorists having abandoned their vehicles.

When Route 49 spilled them out at the junction with Route 20, they proceeded west toward the center of Sturbridge. The road was verging on apocalyptic with vehicles piled up on the shoulders, all four lanes completely clear. Headlights persisted out from a few mangled vehicles, cutting their final paths into the night, and even the buses and big rigs had been downed like card houses and shunted aside, many of them overturned on the grassy flanks of Route 20. Passengers of the nearest bus limped among the wreckage, trying to extricate survivors. A panicked golden retriever in a red bandana zagged across the road and ducked into the darkness, Rock braking to give it space. Two women cowered behind a van, their faces bloody. An old guy waved a rifle around in search of the next attacker. In the distance, an SUV and an ambulance were on fire. Overhead, a formation of planes rocketed west, then another a minute later.

The totality of the madness was just starting to take effect for Tommy, seeping slowly through the numbness. It was much like the 2020 Massacre, the violence so extreme and unprecedented that it had initially left him stunned and disbelieving. Though Tommy had only been an infant on September 11, 2001, he imagined his parents had endured a similar speechless horror on that day, their apartment just a few miles from the World Trade Center.

Tommy tried to force back fears for their parents, their extended family, their friends. Rock had promised to drop them off on Route 148 (somewhat near Dom's house), but he'd refused to take side streets. Doing so was simply too risky, he'd maintained, and Tommy could see that now. The truck was a major asset. Manually operable, not even a Q on board, it wasn't a prisoner to the grid as most other vehicles were. In fact, it had seemingly been designed specifically for the comprehensive attack that would headline this night in the annals of history (people were referring to the perpetrators as Gridhacks, Rock said, the event itself the Gridlock).

The truck was outfitted with a specialized set of controls for the claws: a pair of levers mounted to platforms on either side of the driver's seat. Rock hadn't tried to use them yet, and he didn't plan to, his only focus getting to that base on 148.

Dom was seated in a tiny middle seat Rock had cleared for him by pushing forward the retractable tray that held the GPS and GIS accureader monitors. Tommy, in the passenger seat, remembered with a dazzle of discomfort in his gut the license plate he'd glimpsed in the middle, then in the real world.

**GRDLCK.**

# GRIDLOCKED

He kept wondering what it all meant and why he'd been entrusted with these psychic gifts of premonition. It couldn't all be coincidence, and it certainly couldn't be a gift previously unbeknown to Tommy. Long before his coma, he'd failed to guess the color of the cards Dom held up during their drunken attempts at sibling telepathy between poker games, never mind the suit. And one time when they were teenagers, higher than a transatlantic flight, they'd put their heads together and tried to transfer thoughts to each other.

It hadn't worked.

So how the hell was he calling the future now? And how had his body miraculously recovered?

Tommy knew something well beyond a manmade war was happening. Greater powers were involved, though he and Dom hadn't told Rock about his…ability. Whatever it was, it scared him as much as it astonished him. It made him sweat and shake. He felt an enormous weight, as if he'd been chosen for an extraordinary purpose.

But God had picked the wrong guy. He should have targeted someone who could fight or shoot or build missiles or perform surgeries or keep the vactrain tunnel technologies advancing so that Americans might one day reach Australia in ten minutes.

*But what am I supposed to do? Before the coma I graded science tests.*

Dom stared out at plaza parking lots. Droves of abandoned vehicles waited patiently for their owners to return, the entry roads crammed with cars as well, just a typical Friday night before the grid had shut down.

A chill edged through Dom at the sight of three middle school-aged boys walking along the side of the road. A few hundred feet west, an old lady was crossing the road in a wheelchair, her eyes bulging with terror as the truck approached. Rock had repeatedly said the truck had no more room for passengers, not unless Dom and Tommy wanted to exchange seats with someone else. The Sims brothers were the first people Rock had seen after hijacking the truck, and that was the only reason he'd picked them up. If two other guys had been a quarter of a mile north of them, Dom and Tommy would still be on Route 49.

"Wish I didn't panic after shooting the bastard," Rock regretted, lifting the Red Sox cap to rub his forehead. "I just threw his ass out of the truck, didn't even think to check his pockets. I could have figured out who these people are, maybe even grab a radio off him so we could hear what's going on. But I panicked, thought more hacks would be on me."

"Don't be too hard on yourself," Tommy said. "You must've been in shock."

"Nah, I've killed before." Rock looked over at them, an awkward silence coming between them. "Don't ask," he finally said. "Anyhow, after I ditched the guy and drove off, I knew right away I'd screwed up. I pulled over when I saw it was clear for a while, checked the glove box and beneath the seats. Nothing, totally clean. The driver probably didn't have much on him, either, I guess. These guys aren't sloppy – I'll give 'em that."

They passed a large group headed west. Assuming the truck was driven by the enemy, a few men hurled roadside rocks and chunks of asphalt at the windows, managing not a single crack or pock in the glass.

"It's bulletproof, or so they thought," Rock said. "But I've got the latest and greatest ammo, boys." He grinned crazily, did a little drum roll on the steering wheel. "Even the thickest glass can't handle the caliber and propulsion I'm packing with these new kevshredders."

# GRIDLOCKED

Before climbing into the truck, Dom had noticed that the tires were protected by sheets of glass dropping to within inches of the road. When not in use, the hydraulic arms from which the claws extended were also tucked into cylindrical sheaths of glass. Apparently these trucks had been mass-produced for war right here in America, then deployed once the grid was disabled. But why destroy billions of dollars worth of vehicles and heap them in piles like worn out sofas? What was coming next? Why did the roads need to be opened up?

A few more miles down Route 20, just past the entrance road to the former Old Sturbridge Village – which had recently been sold to the owner of several New England driving parks – they spotted a boy on the sidewalk in the distance. He walked alone. Judging by his size, Tommy guessed he was younger than ten.

"Stop the truck," Tommy urged.

"There's no room," Rock said with irritation. He'd already shut down multiple requests to bring aboard passengers.

But this time Tommy was adamant. "Stop the fucking truck!" he shouted. "The kid can sit in my lap."

Rock bit his lip, shook his head, then swung the truck into the right lane. They slowed to a stop fifty feet behind the boy, who turned and squinted up at the truck. Tommy was shocked he didn't run.

It wasn't until the kid started toward them that Tommy noticed the blood dripping down his face.

## Chapter 3

Xeke sat alone at a cafeteria table inside Tantasqua High School, menaced by fears for his family and Amie and his dog, Zombie, who he'd left a few hours ago with a "later, Zombo" and a bone.

Fear had harried Xeke relentlessly, like waves intent on caving in a sand castle. Now he was raw and sick, barely in possession of enough energy to hold a bag of ice against his swollen cheek. He watched the door, praying to see a loved one, *anyone* he knew. But they were strangers, all of them. Old people; little kids; babies; people in wheelchairs; a guy on oxygen; wounded cops and military; frantic parents, grandparents, friends. Some people had brought their pets; others carried bags and backpacks. Every face was glazed with terrified disbelief.

Xeke considered leaving. He was of no use to these people. He needed to get home, needed to know if his family was okay, even if it meant walking all night. What if his parents were waiting for him there, holed up in the basement, refusing to leave until he arrived? Worse, what if they'd gone out looking for him?

Xeke was about to stand when Virgil Kalas, the Freedom Rider who'd rescued him, returned to the table, a kit of food in hand. He tore it open and set down a small bottle of water, an apple, and a package of peanuts, among other snacks.

"You should eat, kid."

"Nah, my stomach feels septic and my jaw kills. I need to get out of here."

Virgil took the seat opposite Xeke and handed him an Advil packet. He looked weary, depleted, much older than he was. He smelled like cigarettes. "And go where?" he said. "Walk back to your house? Back to the main roads? You'll get yourself shot quicker than a pog in the heat, buddy."

# GRIDLOCKED

Xeke swallowed two pills. "But I have to know if my family's all right."

Virgil removed the fedora and scratched his shaved scalp. "Come on, kid, don't be a little dumbass on me now. I know how bad the urge is. I know how scared you are, but we all need to compartmentalize here." He reached across the table, clutched Xeke's arm. "I have no idea where my wife and kids are. No idea where my parents are. My youngest son's in college in Ithaca, New York. Who knows how bad it is up there, maybe nothing at all, maybe Hell itself." He shrugged. "This is it – war. We survive now, that's our only focus. They want us to panic and run. They want us to be desperate, but the tide is turning." He tapped a radio attached to his shoulder like the ones coppers used. "We're getting good reports. Bases just like this one are being set up all over the place – Westover, Monson Developmental Center, Smith and Wesson, Barnes, Bradley, Worcester Centrum, just to name a few. Munitions are in strong supply. We've got enough food and water, at least here, and we're bringing in everyone we need – doctors, communications people, soldiers, engineers." He allowed himself a flickering smile. "They caught us with a nasty cheap shot, but we'll beat them down, kid, don't you worry about that. We just have to keep fighting. Then everyone gets to go home to their families…well, almost everyone."

Gulping sorely, Xeke twisted open the water bottle and took a tiny sip. "What am I supposed to do, though, just wait here for it to end?"

Virgil's eyebrows lifted. "Hell, no. This is war, kid. You think there's time to feel sorry for ourselves? Everyone's got a job to do. Consider yourself enlisted."

"What's my job?"

Virgil stood. "You can shoot, right?"

Xeke cringed. The way Virgil had said it, a strange knowingness to his tone, it was as if he'd glimpsed into Xeke's past.

"Yeah, I guess," Xeke said, afraid of where this might be going.

Virgil's grin was unnerving. "I think you'll do all right with an assault rifle, maybe even man the fence for us," and he winked at Xeke before receding into the fray.

*Jesus, he knows! Who is this guy?*

Overwrought, Xeke lifted a cold hand to his face, Virgil's words bringing him reluctantly back to that night almost a year ago. It had been a frigid night, school already canceled the next day. JV hockey practice had been boring as always with dumb drills, but afterward, in the locker room, the things they'd said…

Dalton Rose had started it. He'd dashed acid over Amie's name, and their insults had knifed at Xeke's heart, rendering him momentarily breathless, as if he'd been punched, kicked, stabbed. Only a longtime friend of Amie's at the time, not yet her boyfriend, Xeke had nonetheless wanted to defend her, but stunned silence had prevailed from his corner of the room.

*Are they just making up bullshit? Did they really–?*

Xeke hadn't found sleep that night, wishing through the twisted, turbulent hours that he could reach back and grasp those moments not long ago, when Amie's name hadn't been desecrated by their words, when she hadn't ignored Xeke on certain occasions, when weakness hadn't stopped him from standing up to others on her behalf. But those days could never be reclaimed. They could never return to their childhood sanctuaries and search the stars of yesteryear, could never undo the irrevocable truth that assailed Xeke with darts of realization – frigid, visceral, sickening, paralyzing.

# GRIDLOCKED

Unable, through speech or action or even thought, to vindicate the girl he would always love, Xeke had torn himself free of sweaty, heavy sheets later that night and, shakily, fetched his father's assault rifle from the gun cabinet, then headed out to the driveway. Dad had been teaching him to shoot an array of weapons since eighth grade, and out there in the freezing dark – the snowy, wind-burnt lawn sparkling in the glow of Christmas lights – the rifle had empowered Xeke as he stood in the driveway. It had made him feel strong, like maybe he could defend Amie now.

He'd held the weapon up, pointed at the watchful hint of moon, envisioning their faces, hearing their words, trembling, hating them, abhorring those who'd hurt Amie, those who'd laughed at Amie, and if only they'd been there that frigid night in the driveway, facing his muzzle, smug and sneering, if only they'd called her those things then, in the lonely dark, he knew he could have done it, could have pulled the trigger, could have made them powerless, could have shut them up forever.

Xeke had ultimately retreated from hatred's ledge and sought guidance that night…and meaning. He'd fallen to his knees and prayed, but it had all seemed so empty out there on his own, so useless. He'd shouted at God, asked Him why Amie had changed. Why was he invisible to her now at times? What had happened to her between those starry summer nights of childhood and now, when the parties and the pretenses ruled? This wasn't her.

And what about him? He'd once shoved down two kids who tried to take Amie's phone during recess in elementary school, but now he was weak, manacled by an all-encompassing need to impress, to fit in, to be one of them, to forever remain in concurrence with the teenage whirlpool, to not resist or even hint at subversion. Conformity had a price, he'd discovered, realizing it in steady increments, among them the day the cheerleaders' bus had driven past and one of Xeke's friends had shouted, "Make way for the pussy bus!" Xeke and the others had said nothing, the whirlpool such a beast to resist, and if you did you were explicitly alone…but if you didn't resist, you lost yourself a piece at a time. Later, Xeke had remained quiet when a teammate insulted Jannie Jablonski, a girl confined to her wheelchair, calling her a defect and making her cry. Later still, Xeke had reported nothing when another kid on his JV team confessed to stealing money from a girl's backpack in the science lab, because what if they learned he was a snitch?

There had been other (even worse) moments of acquiescence. Shameful, really, a blazing urge in Xeke's heart each time to stand up and confront – but the manacles of conformity had held him stiffly in place and suppressed his words. What few words remained the whirlpool had drowned.

And now Amie. They had insulted Amie. They had to pay.

But with morning's light things had been dulled and different, Xeke accepting it once more and heading off to school, where he would play the game for another day. His rage had shriveled away, replaced by resigned acceptance.

Amie and Jazzi carefully left the building, pushing open the final glass door and gasping at the dozens of motorcycles blasting into the facility and the conflagration off to the left, the row of guardhouses burning furiously. There had been a roaring boom while they were still inside, Amie hurriedly changing into the bloody uniform, Jazzi repeating the story they'd concocted so she wouldn't forget it. The walls had shaken, ceiling panels crashing down around them.

Amie and Jazzi turned left and followed a walkway around back, where they found a small parking lot filled with vehicles. The majority of them were sedans, with a handful of SUVs mixed in.

Amie held the key ring she'd found in the guard's pocket, a single key and pad attached. She pushed the unlock button repeatedly, but none of the vehicles responded with an interior light switching on.

# GRIDLOCKED

"She has to have a car around somewhere." Amie was jogging, Jazzi at her side.

"Maybe her car's in the front," Jazzi panted, remembering the front lot they'd seen upon leaving the building, its vehicles smashed, tires slashed. Some of them had been burnt up.

"I hope not. Those cars were totaled."

They flinched at a rise of gunfire down in the main parking lot near the warehouses, a battle raging between their captors and the Freedom Riders.

"Let's just run to the woods!" Jazzi urged. "We don't need a car."

Amie tried the unlock button once more, half-expecting a light to flip on. But there was nothing, another burst of gunfire spurring them on.

Amie pocketed the key. "You're right. The woods – let's go."

They came around the building again – and nearly bumped into a guard.

Amie felt something plummet in her chest. She was about to pull the pistol she'd recovered, when the guard asked, "Are you all right, Captain?"

It took Amie a moment to realize her disguise had worked. The guard actually believed she was one of them.

Theatrical skills taking over, skills she'd honed almost her entire life, Amie assumed the part.

"Yeah, fine," she blurted. "What's going on? Who's attacking us?"

The guy motioned for them to follow him around back. In the parking lot, he stopped suddenly and clutched his right shoulder, his hand coming away red.

"You're shot," Amie murmured.

"Can't believe I wasn't killed. Two guys were shooting at me from close range, so I just played dead." He nodded at Jazzi, then looked back at Amie. "Why do you have a deportee?"

*A deportee?* "I caught her trying to escape." Amie leveled her stare on him, taking in every feature with the heightened clarity of terror – from his thin brown goatee to the mole on his right cheek – and now there was a hot hatred bubbling up and twisting her face into a scowl.

Her hand brushed against the gun in the belt holster.

The guard let out a pitiful chuckle. He was young, probably not even thirty, his face blanched with fear and pain. "You don't have to worry about deportees no more," he said. "Gig's up. Fucking Freedom Riders blew us away. We're decimated." He shook his head, pulled a shifter from his pocket, his face softening in defeat. "I can't get anyone from dispatch in Sturbridge." For a moment it looked like he might cry. "Guess it's back to work soon, no brave new world. This was supposed to be a cakewalk, not a goddamn war."

The guard pulled his own key ring from a pocket and started toward an SUV. The light came on inside. "You coming?" he said, looking over his shoulder at Amie. "Why don't you just shoot the stupid kid and come with me? Freedom Riders'll be back here soon – we stay any longer and we're dead."

Amie was afraid he'd seen her recoil from the inhumanity of his words. "Stay here," she whispered to Jazzi, and the sound of her voice in that moment was as she'd never heard it before, papery and eerily purposeful.

# GRIDLOCKED

Tremors vaulting coldly through her, Amie jogged to the SUV and settled into the passenger seat while the guard, with a series of groans and swears, tried to start the vehicle.

Amie's hand was on the pistol. With exceeding caution, she pulled it free and concealed it to her right. She was strangely calm, as if none of this were really happening, her surroundings nothing more than the fabrications of a nightmare – or the scene of another play, a tragedy as dark as any.

The guard wasn't looking at her, too preoccupied with his pain and failure. Unable to find any strength in his wounded right arm, he was reaching across the steering wheel with his left hand and trying ineffectually to insert the key in the ignition.

He didn't see Amie lift the gun.

He didn't see her point it, steadying the weapon with both hands.

He didn't see the change in her eyes.

The world went quiet, Amie's head thrumming. For a second she was adrift in a sea of infinite depth, fear at its surface, the rest beyond the limits of words, beyond the capabilities of imagination.

Her thoughts crashed together, joined now by a thin ringing. She wondered if she could do it. She'd gone shooting with Xeke and his father a few times, and though she'd been a terrible shot, her current target did not demand tremendous accuracy.

Still the guard was oblivious.

*I can't! I can't do it!*

Her hands shook violently. She worried she might drop the gun. Then he would kill her. And then he'd kill Jazzi.

Amie leaned to her right, wanting to run, suddenly aware that the guard was looking at her. It was over, run or die. She reached for the door handle, ready to flee.

Instead she shifted left and pulled the trigger.

# GRIDLOCKED

## Chapter 4

Birds departed noisily from the tree looming above them, sending Paul and Steel into a moment's frenzy.

Paul, peering through the trees at an electric blue sky peeled with layers of black, was almost certain it was just a notch darker than it had been before, when they'd left the house of horrors.

Steel made a little circle, tried to expunge the last ten minutes from his mind. He couldn't get a handle on his thoughts, much less form a plan. "What was that? What the hell *was* that?" he kept saying. He spoke not to Paul, not even to himself, his reactions escaping as words.

A little lightheaded, Paul shrank down against the thick tree. "We need to go," he murmured, but *go where?* Where exactly would they go after seeing an old couple mutilated in their home?

The police station? The police were dead.

Home to their families? No, they sure as hell weren't going home.

Paul thought back to the drawings in the penultimate house: THE END; JESUS SAVES; THEY WILL ALL DIE; SINNERS SUFFER AND DIE.

Again Paul looked skyward. He thought of his wife and son. He wondered if they were safe…and the sky, how was it possible? Even in the last few seconds the sky had tinged a darker blue, he was sure of it.

"What would You have us do?" Paul shouted, searching the visible patches of sky. "Paint me a picture, Lord, I beg of You."

Beyond an ebbing whisper of wind, there was no response.

"Is it getting darker?" Steel said a moment later. He'd noticed it, too. Arms crossed, he looked disbelievingly at Paul, as if he'd just witnessed a flash of brilliant light and the slow descent of an alien starship.

Steel had once been caught in a riptide off a Long Island Sound beach. The helpless panic had exceeded, his only thought that he would die, and then, after seconds that for a ten-year-old boy had seemed like hours, the lifeguard had snatched him away from death.

Steel felt the same all-consuming panic tonight, but this time death's grip was even tighter. Remembering those terrifying moments in the Atlantic, he shook his head and thought, *You might get me this time, but not before I empty these guns.*

An hour later, at the edge of a stream, their slow wilderness trek got a needed rest, Paul's thoughts having stumbled upon one of the last people he'd interviewed. A resident of Sturbridge, the sixty-nine-year-old widow, Brenda Leitner, had moved from place to place after Hurricane Josiane leveled Galveston. She'd forged an indiscriminate northeasterly path through Arkansas, Kentucky, Pennsylvania, and Connecticut before settling in Massachusetts, charmed by Sturbridge's endless antique shops and a little coffee house where she'd found the patrons to be unusually agreeable.

A leaf in the wind, Mrs. Leitner had called herself, claiming she might take to the road again on a whim. But then she'd amended her analogy. No, not a leaf in the wind, she'd said, because although undetermined, her next location would not be chosen entirely at random. Seaside towns were out – too great a risk of dangerous weather, not to mention the ocean eventually ruling the streets. Additionally, she'd nixed the idea of returning to the south or heading west, for these were the battle zones of the expanding water wars; in fact, money saved from the grid and pumped back into the national economy was the only reason, according to some experts, why parts of the southwest hadn't declined to anarchy.

# GRIDLOCKED

Indeed, Paul's interview with Mrs. Leitner had accentuated the nation's negatives. She'd even been down on the grid, describing it as a clandestine arrangement with the Chinese government.

"The technology is too advanced," she'd said. "We don't come up with that kind of technology here. It was probably given to us by the Chinese, but I bet they'll use it to control us. You watch – one day they'll take over. Everything."

Paul, tossing stones into the stream, wondered who was really behind this attack. He resisted urges to assume that a greater entity was responsible as he'd done earlier, for the sky was lighter again (the further they got from that last house, the more clearly they were thinking). Back there, they'd obviously been subjected to an illusion of shock – the light had only *seemed* like it was shriveling away.

No, this was not the Great Tribulation or another chapter of eschatology, Paul kept telling himself. This was the work of extreme human evil, the likes of which Americans had rarely seen on their own soil. Like a virulent sickness, it would be severe yet curable – and together Paul and Steel would eventually get through it.

But far more important than their own survival, Paul prayed for the safety of his wife and son. He hadn't heard their voices since yesterday evening, much too long when chaos abounded and he didn't know how far it stretched.

All the way to Chicago? Paul didn't think the sickness had spread that fiercely, but without a way to contact his family he would be forced to continue grappling with his fear–

And was he losing his mind a single grain at a time, or was the sky darkening again through the trees, just a little?

## Chapter 5

Rock lurched the truck into gear and they were off, rumbling back onto Route 20.

"It's okay, you're safe now, buddy. It's gonna be all right," Tommy comforted.

The boy was sitting in Tommy's lap in the passenger seat, still wide-eyed and word-deprived. He was even younger than Tommy had initially estimated, maybe as young as six. Etched shallowly into his forehead was a large bloody X stretching nearly from hairline to eyebrows. He trembled like a beaten puppy, and it made Tommy sick with rage to see him hurt and scared.

Dom had stripped off two layers to reach his undershirt, which Tommy again applied to the kid's forehead. After wetting the shirt with water from a bottle Rock had found earlier in the truck, Tommy had wiped and dabbed much of the crusted blood away, enough for the X to take shape on the kid's forehead, his blond bangs matted red.

"Who did this to you?" Dom repeated.

The boy only blinked and shook. Tears fell silently down his face.

"Kid's traumatized," Rock said, then, glancing over at the boy, added, "We'll get you to a safe place, okay, pal?"

"He'll find me," the boy whispered, a ragged, ghostly sound, Dom barely able to hear it a foot away in the middle seat.

"Who?" Tommy said.

More tears spilled.

"Who will find you?" Dom touched the boy's shoulder, but he recoiled with a violent jerk.

# GRIDLOCKED

"Just let him be," Rock advised.

They were on a straightaway cutting through the western edge of Sturbridge, darkened shops and destroyed vehicles on either side of them, the old Blackington Building looming not far ahead like a phantom's tower. The stranded motorists out this way, upon seeing the truck's green headlights, sprinted into the recesses of the night.

The truck hummed down Route 20, indifferent to the suffering all around, its claws hungry for their next victim. At last, as they turned right onto Brookfield Road (Route 148), the boy said in a small, wounded voice, "I'm Gene."

There was a brief silence, no one knowing what to say, followed by the three of them announcing their names. Additional questions ensued, and, wiping his tears away, Gene told them that his grandmother had been shot.

"I think she's dead."

The tears exploded, Tommy hugging the boy halfway to Tantasqua High School, until Gene eventually regained himself and, following a series of sniffles, reiterated that, "He'll find me. He said he'll find me anywhere."

"Who will find you?" Tommy pressed.

"The man."

"What did he look like?"

"His face was blood. He had a hood. He said exes are for things that will die."

For a few seconds, only the truck's voice was heard.

"What did he look like, besides the blood and hood?" Rock said.

Very slowly, the boy looked over at him. "I don't know, but he can fly."

# GRIDLOCKED

## Chapter 6

Death stares down upon the darkened church, its doors opening to a group of survivors. Soon they will all meet Death.

Landing, returning to a vacant building that serves the Huntsmen, Death collects his latest list.

"Finished already?" the dispatcher says, raising his eyebrows, fool of a man who believes he controls. "All of them?"

Death presses a bloody palm against the glass partition, below which rests a slot for the exchange of lists. Death smiles. Imagines shattering the glass, reaching across the counter, throttling the man's scrawny neck. He can feel the bones snapping, a sound somewhat similar to twigs underfoot, though considerably thicker, more sinewy and substantial. He can hear the man's screams – tending toward the strident end of the spectrum – not musical like the screams of a larger man.

But Death mustn't kill, not this man, for this is one of the chosen men, and the job must be done right. Each of the chosen men/women must be carefully crafted. New thoughts must be properly had, for the window will close and they all must stand together as leaders of the army. Their hands cannot be held forever.

The man's eyes fall to his device. "Sure you don't want a shifter? It'd make things a lot easier for you."

Death lets his fingers smear down the glass. "I told you, boy – none of that. Just drink now, yes, yes, that's it."

Sipping from his can of Coke, the man reviews the database. "And no trackers, either, I see. You know, I could get in big trouble for giving you this list without a tracker." His eyes lift briefly to meet Death's stare, then return to the device.

"What about your hamsweeper?" the little man calls as Death walks away. "He needs to check in, too. Where are his recovered materials?"

"Your Coke," Death murmurs, looking partway back at the man. "Just drink."

# GRIDLOCKED

## Chapter 7

Amie was explicitly scrambled, rendered immobile by the shock of sight and sound. Time itself was postponed. Even her thoughts ceased to exist, only the colors of horror before her. An overarching, mildly painful force crushed her from all sides.

It wasn't until Jazzi opened the passenger door and shook her that Amie reacted.

"You killed him," the girl said with strange calmness. "Amie, you did it, you killed him!"

Amie nodded, mindless, and looked wonderingly down at the pistol, which felt considerably heavier than it had a few seconds ago. She stumbled out of the SUV and came around to the driver's side. Had she stared for too long at what she'd done, she might have come unhinged, the smell of death diving down to her viscera.

If not for Jazzi, Amie might have stood there for hours, frozen, or perhaps run off with her heart and soul heading in opposite directions. But Jazzi was right there beside her, tugging at the guard's legs, and soon Amie joined her, their combined strength more than enough to tear the dead man from his seat.

The crack-squish of lifeless flesh and bones against the pavement sent them both leaping away. Like water from a soaked dog's shake, a spray of blood had splashed against their ankles. Neither of them noticed the rapid decline in distant gunfire.

"Come on! We have to go!" Jazzi urged, rounding the vehicle and hopping in through the passenger side.

Amie climbed back into the SUV and clenched the wheel. She felt heavy and sick, her arms and legs like logs. For a moment she couldn't remember how to drive. She hadn't done it since August at her grandparents' house in Monson, where Grandpa Joe kept a few manually operational cars hidden out back beneath the willow tree at the edge of a rolling field. Even though the government had offered trades for brand new, grid-compatible vehicles, including exchanges for junkers, Gramps had refused to give up his cars. Additionally, he'd refused to apply for permits to enable him to keep his pre-grid automotive property (a $500 fee per vehicle…under the condition that such vehicles were operated exclusively on private land or transported via trailer to driving parks for recreational use).

Good old Gramps. Amie, in a flash of septic thoughts, wondered if her grandfather and the rest of her family were dead.

"Faster! Hurry!" Jazzi exhorted as Amie tore out of the parking lot and sped past the burning guardhouses in a narrow access lane that had been reserved for the guards.

Swinging right onto the entry road, Amie nearly lost control around the final curve leading them to Route 49. A pack of motorcycles and fire engines and buses passed them in the opposite direction, all of them turning in from Route 49 North, many of the Freedom Riders hollering and waving weapons around as if declaring victory.

"Not that fast!" Jazzi squealed when they ratcheted up to sixty on 49 South, Amie remembering him then, Dalton Rose, and their night together in May.

*Let's blaze the grid, Ames!*

Heading south, the road was dark. Amie couldn't catch her breath. Her throat burned. Her head throbbed. A Godsend, Jazzi discovered a bottle of water beneath the passenger seat. Half full and cold, the two of them took turns with it until there was nothing left.

"I think that's my boyfriend's truck," Amie said a short time later, slowing the SUV nearly to a stop. "Well, it's actually his dad's truck…*was* his dad's truck."

# GRIDLOCKED

Amie pointed to their left, where the truck sat mangled in the breakdown lane, two more crushed vehicles within fifty feet of it, their roofs caved in and windshields shattered.

Tears pooled in Amie's eyes, the road going blurry. "We love to ride in the back of the truck and look at the stars. That's what we were doing when…you know."

"I'm sure he got out," Jazzi said with tender certainty. "You'll find him, just like I'll find Sena."

Amie fought an urge to return to the truck. It was useless now, yet still she was reluctant to leave it behind, for it served as a confirmation that she was leaving Xeke back there in the burning devastation, perhaps still imprisoned as the flames licked forth.

*The Riders will find him. They'll get him out.*

Amie held on tightly to those thoughts. Clutched them along with the wheel.

"Why did they crash all the cars?" Jazzi said after a while.

They'd just passed another wrecked vehicle in the breakdown lane, this one a small box truck that had been overturned and cleared from the road, as if it were nothing more than a toy kicked angrily from a parent's path following a stubbed toe. Amie felt something sickly rise up through her chest each time she saw a ruined vehicle – the freedoms and safety she'd always known had been obliterated.

And for what?

Whoever was responsible had tried to round everyone up and…what? Ship them somewhere in those rail cars? Kill everyone else? Searching for a motive was like trying to solve a math word problem that went in circles, but she knew they weren't dealing with a fringe terrorist cell or a small group. These people even had uniforms!

"They want to control us," Amie said, wishing she could just blink and be home. Her parents would know what to do – they always knew the right thing to do. "By taking away communications and shutting down the grid, we're helpless. We're so dependent on those two things that society will fall apart without them, at least temporarily."

"And I'll die, I think," Jazzi said. "I need my treatments for the next five months, maybe longer."

Seized by hurt for her new friend, Amie reached for Jazzi's hand and squeezed. "You're not gonna die." She glanced across at the girl, who was staring blankly ahead. "We'll find a way through this, and tomorrow everything will start getting back to normal. Remember what Sena said – you can do anything if you don't give up."

Amie couldn't believe she'd remembered the woman's name, much less what she'd said. She hoped her name really was Sena, though Jazzi offered no correction. She was like a frail little doll, her colorful beanie cap pulled down low, its snowmen and other winter friends smiling.

It shredded Amie to imagine what the girl was fearing – the crisis compounded by her sickness.

"We'll get through this," Amie repeated, words that brought no assurances with the road black and empty ahead, a road that seemingly led to nowhere, haunted by all that had been lost.

A few miles farther, having passed dozens of ruined vehicles – many of them afire – Amie made a right turn off Route 49. She prayed she would find her parents waiting for her at home, but with every revolution of the tires her dread heightened, until each indrawn breath brought an ache in her side.

# GRIDLOCKED

What if her parents had gone to Xeke's house to look for her? If they'd been on the road…

There were more vehicles up ahead, cars and vans and SUVs overturned on people's lawns. Some of them had been pushed into parked cars and slammed right up to the bases of garages, others tossed against trees. People were huddled together in their driveways, still trying their useless phones and shifters, perhaps waiting for coppers who weren't coming.

The residents turned to the road as Amie drove by, watching and wondering. A few people sprinted into their homes.

Amie didn't see the man with the shotgun, not until the windshield split into spiderweb cracks and Jazzi's screams answered the roar of gunfire. A creeping shadow beside a tree, the shooter was aiming at them from a lawn ahead to their right.

Another shot.

Somehow he missed, Amie hammering the accelerator, both hands clutching the wheel. "Get down, Jazzi!"

In the distance, people scattered back to their houses, away from the onrushing SUV.

Amie wheeled around a tight curve, nearly losing the road, the SUV edging up onto the curb and clipping a mailbox, then joggling back down to the road. To their left, a cane-bearing old woman hobbled up her front walkway, glancing back with transcendent terror, as though she'd seen the costumed beasts of Halloween made real.

Jazzi returned to her seat (she'd somehow squeezed herself into the floor space) and looked out the window. Amie, expecting tears, was surprised when the girl said, "I think we need a sign telling people not to shoot us."

Amie managed a thin chuckle. "I should have realized we'd be a target. The grid's dead and these people see us coming down their street – of course they want to kill us. Maybe we should just ditch this thing and walk the rest of the way."

"No." Jazzi's response was emphatic. "We have to get to your parents' house quick. Then I have to get to Sena."

Over the last little stretch back on Route 49, Amie had built up Jazzi's hopes by describing how her father was an amateur survivalist. He hadn't constructed a military-grade subterranean bunker or purchased a truckload of canned foods and bottled water. He hadn't acquired an assortment of weapons or fortified the house with fences, but he and Grandpa Joe were both experts in ham radio. They'd even put together a fairly complex setup in Dad's basement (which they referred to as "the station").

Relying on a covert flagpole antenna to access radio frequencies, Dad and Grandpa operated tri-band transceivers that could pick up specialized channels; their equipment could even receive transmissions from across the country. And since Dad's brother was with the Worcester County Sheriff's Department, he'd been able to acquire several devices from the mobile command vehicle after the latest system upgrade two years ago.

If anyone was prepared for something like this, Amie had said, it was her father.

A minivan was burning at the corner of Elm Street and Valley Drive. A quarter of a mile farther they arrived at Glenwood Drive, Amie shivering when her street opened up before them.

She accelerated around familiar curves, her fear like a never-ending hill. It kept rising and steepening, but the neighborhood looked like it always did at night. The same vehicles were parked in the driveways, none of them mangled. Nothing was on fire. The power was on. If the

# GRIDLOCKED

night had gone as planned, this was the scene Amie would have expected at its conclusion.

But Amie and Xeke hadn't made it to Friendly's for ice cream. And the night was far from over.

Almost home. One final curve, just a few more seconds – but when they rounded that last curve, the crest of Amie's fear arrived like a roller coaster's first drop.

Amie crushed down on the brake. "Jesus!" she gasped.

Jazzi let out a little yelp of surprise.

There was a man standing twenty feet ahead, in the middle of the road, dressed in a black hooded robe. He was staring at Amie's house, arms rigid at his sides. He did not turn in their direction.

He just kept on staring at the house.

"What's he doing?" Jazzi's voice was small and fearful. "Is that your house?"

Amie could only nod, too afraid for words. But he was only a man – how could he bring such inexplicable fear, especially after everything they'd endured? Was it the way he was standing, stiff and unmoving? Was it a pulsing, radioactive vibe he exuded? Amie didn't know, but she could hardly withstand the fear, drowning in the idea of a life without her family.

Amie blasted the horn, the man pivoting slowly to face them, his face little more than a shadow beyond the hood, even with the headlights scrutinizing him.

Amie felt something strange skate through her, a watery sensation fraught with a spurious combination of cool and warm. It was like her insides had been frozen, and now the thawmelt drips were creeping through. Moreover, a septic ache originated in her stomach and surged outward in waves.

The man started toward them.

Amie let off the brake, honked again, yet still he came at them, his arm lifting from his side to reveal a massive blade.

"Hit him!" Jazzi urged, though Amie was already accelerating, bracing for the collision, headlights swallowing the man and then…

Nothing. Not a sound beyond the screeching of brakes.

Amie had closed her eyes at the last second, but she was positive the man hadn't leapt away. He'd just stood there, impact unavoidable.

"What the…what happened?" Amie murmured.

"He jumped."

"What?"

"I think he jumped the car." Jazzi looked in the side mirror. "He's behind us."

Amie, with a lurching stomach, checked the rearview mirror.

A short distance back of the SUV, the man stood facing them within the orange ambit of a streetlight, wide-stanced and motionless. Waiting.

When Amie looked back again before entering the driveway, he was gone.

# GRIDLOCKED

## Chapter 8

Virgil had given Xeke an assault rifle and told him to help man the fences. He hadn't given him instructions on how to use the thing, not that Xeke needed instructions.

Undoubtedly, Virgil knew about him somehow, a perplexity that made Xeke bite his lip as he stood guard at the fence. The Freedom Riders and the people they'd rescued had managed to surround most of the school grounds with sections of fencing, some taller than others, some barbed, some black and speared with ornamental wrought iron.

"If someone threatening comes at you from the woods, don't think – just shoot," Virgil had said. "Our people will only be coming from the road."

Xeke stood about one hundred feet from the next kid on patrol. They were near the back entry road behind the high school, facing the woods. An occasional motorcycle or van swung around, following the road all the way to the end to drop off people or supplies at a makeshift outpost they'd apparently set up at the intersection with Webber Road. Convinced that the enemy would strike from the north or west, Virgil had been emphatic about guarding against attacks from Brookfield and Brimfield, dispatching dozens of men to the Webber Road camp.

Xeke felt a boost in confidence whenever the vehicles came around. Still, what would he do if people actually came from the woods? Shoot them? He wondered if he'd be quick enough, accurate enough. He'd become a decent shot during practice, but now, with fear driving at him and the wind relentless against his face, the weapon felt heavy and foreign.

Mostly, Xeke wanted to set the gun down and run. He needed to find Amie and his parents. He needed to know if the rest of his family was okay. But...

*I'm stuck here. If I leave, I'll get killed for sure. Without the Freedom Riders, I wouldn't have gotten out of Spencer.*

Xeke kept wondering if his family was somewhere in the Tantasqua camp, an urge dominating him every few minutes to search the school. But Virgil had entrusted him with a task. He'd said this place was only as strong as those who defended it.

He'd spoken to Xeke not as a child but a–

The motorcycle blasted up behind him, its rider waving Xeke and the other kid over.

"Head on back to the school," the rider hollered. He was a big guy with an unruly red beard. Wearing only a leather vest up top, his bulging arms exhibited a gallery of tattoos. "We're rotating people out every half hour. See Tracy in the library – she'll give you new jobs."

Back in the school, Xeke was in no hurry to receive his next job from Tracy or anyone else. Having handed the gun off to one of the "weapons guys" in the lobby, he did not proceed as directed up the stairs to the library, instead passing through the cafeteria and then the gymnasium in search of family and friends.

The gymnasium had been turned into a makeshift hospital resembling a wartime scene. Camping cots and gurneys were arranged in rows, Xeke at first unable to differentiate between doctors and helpers because everyone wore plain clothes. The medical equipment, like everything else, had been brought in and hastily set up. There were crash carts and IV poles and monitors, new supplies being rushed in, medical people explaining to volunteers where things were needed and then hurrying to the next person, dozens of Freedom Riders serving as substitute doctors for people with non-life threatening injuries. Some wrapped bandages. Others applied pressure to wounds. Many delivered medications. And there was Virgil in the back row, hugging a little girl.

Xeke moved away from the back, not wanting Virgil to see him, his legs seeming to drag him to an area of greater commotion. Here, at the right side of the gym, doctors and nurses scrambled and shouted, navigating by the sounds of agony, weaving through the rows of the critically wounded and pushing past people who stood in their way. Xeke wanted to get a better look at the patients, praying he wouldn't recognize a face, but one of the Riders stopped him.

"Get to your next assignment, kid," the hulking black man ordered. "If you ain't hurtin, you workin."

"But my family–"

The man held up a hand. "This ain't about you and me." He pointed to the nearest bed, where three people were attending to an old woman who screamed through gritted teeth, blood surging from a stomach wound. "This is about survival. Chain's only as strong as the next link." He crossed his arms and looked severely down at Xeke. "You gonna be the weak link?"

Xeke turned away from him and scanned the room, the gore and chaos reducing his vision to a spinning haze. Here, a man was missing his right arm, his eyes bulging and deranged. There, a child's face was covered in blood. Across the room, Virgil was staring at Xeke through the crowd, and then, just seconds later, a few people passing and shifting between them, they stood face to face.

Virgil frowned, put a hand on Xeke's shoulder. "Remember what I told you, kid? This is war." He let a moment pass, allowed Xeke to absorb the madness yet again. "You know what they say about war."

Lightheaded, Xeke dropped to a knee. "I can't do this."

Virgil took his hand and pulled him up. "If you say you can't, you can't. God gave you the gifts, kid. Up to you to use 'em."

Nodding dumbly, Xeke started toward the double doors that had been propped open. "Good on you, son," Virgil called. "To the library you go."

Again the scene was distorted, as if Xeke were seeing through the eyes of an insect. He kept bumping into people en route to the staircase; a few steps up, he nearly fell.

"This isn't happening. It can't be happening."

Xeke delayed a while outside the library, pacing and tugging at his hair, wishing he could forget everything he'd seen. For a moment he convinced himself that he really was dreaming – a moment shattered by shouting on the first floor.

Looking down from the balcony, Xeke saw a stretcher being hauled into the school, another one right behind it. The victims looked like they'd taken showers in blood.

"Make room! Multiple gunshot wounds!" yelled a Rider carrying the first stretcher.

"It's real," Xeke murmured. "It's realer than real." In his head a single word tolled with a foreboding clang: War.

The library, maintaining expectations amidst pandemonium, was quiet and orderly. At the tables people were collaborating, books and maps and printouts scattered about. One heavily armed man was vigorously circling and underlining points on a map for two of the Riders, Xeke left to wonder at what sort of plan Virgil and his crew had in mind. They clearly weren't content to control the Sturbridge-

# GRIDLOCKED

Brookfield line and wait for the authorities to put down a faceless enemy.

They were going on the offense, it seemed.

Two lines of about twenty people extended from the circulation desk at the center of the room, people of all ages waiting for their next assignments, even a few kids as young as eleven or twelve. No one asked questions.

Xeke, watching them depart with their orders, felt a trace of his earlier doubt take residence. What if Virgil and the Freedom Riders were in on it? What if this was all just a ploy to get people out of the way and divert their attention?

When it was Xeke's turn at the desk, he shifted uneasily, neither receding nor stepping forth.

The woman behind the desk, thirtyish and narrow-faced, looked up at him from a laptop. Her glasses hung primly over her nose. "Your next assignment is the prisoner area," she said with stolid detachment, as interested in Xeke as the delivery robots at hotels. "Go down the stairs and take the left wing past the gymnasium. Look for signs for the pool locker rooms. Someone will direct you from there."

Halfway down the stairs Xeke stopped, the relief that spread through him perhaps exceeding what the situation deserved. His next-door neighbor, Mr. Korach, was bumbling around the lobby, going ineffectually from person to person in search of answers, his lips quivering in panicked confusion.

"Mr. Korach!" Xeke called.

The white-haired Korach looked up and squinted as if facing the sun. Per usual, a collared shirt poked out from his sweater, though tonight he wasn't merely wearing a sweater but also an argyle vest and one of those Godawful scratchy old people jackets. He was a pretty zesty old guy, Mr. Korach, although he always pissed off Xeke's dad by lawnmowing early in the morning and grinding over every jutted rock, which made a terry sound like a drunken skate sharpener trying his luck on dull blades.

It wasn't until Xeke was within twenty feet of Mr. Korach that the dude actually spotted him, a glimmer of recognition in his eyes. "Xeke! Thank God for a familiar face!"

Korach's words mirrored Xeke's thoughts. "Have you seen my parents?"

Korach shook his head. "So sorry, but I haven't a clue where they are, Xeke. I was out shopping tonight. Had the bags in the car and everything, but it wouldn't start. Kept saying something about defects." Korach's eyes receded with the haunt of memory, taking him back to that moment. He looked bewildered, scrambled, his stomach probably as twisted and septic as Xeke's.

"I looked out at the road," Korach continued, shaking his head, "and that's when I knew it was bad, real bad, Xeke. All of the cars just stopped, both sides of the road, people getting out and yelling and cursing, a total debacle." He managed an exhalation of reeking breath. "Maybe five minutes later the trucks came – goddamn bastards tore up the whole street, cleared out every car."

"How many trucks?"

"Oh, I don't know, at least ten." Korach confirmed that no one was watching them, then leaned in close. "This is a government conspiracy, kid, you mark my words. My vision ain't what it once was, but I swear those trucks had special equipment – gadgets up to the wazoo, hooks and claws and God knows what. They were snatching up cars like it was nothing."

In a moment Korach said, "So what about you? How the hell did you end up here?"

Xeke was about to recount the horrors when a familiar grip found his shoulder. "Talk is overrated," Virgil said. "Too much talk'll get you killed."

Xeke huffed. "He's my neighbor. I'm trying to figure out if my family's okay."

Virgil extended his hand to Korach. "Howdy, neighbor. My sincerest thanks for your service to this nation."

Korach could only blink. Xeke, remembering what Virgil had said about the assault rifle, shrank back a few steps.

"Who are you?" Korach finally said.

Virgil shrugged. "Just a fellow defender of freedom, that's all." He turned to Xeke. "Talk will do us no good. We've all been put to sleep by authority, and now it's time to wake the fuck up."

## Chapter 9

The wind lost its voice after a while, night having reluctantly yielded to day. Birds were chirping, squirrels and chipmunks cavorting from tree to tree. It was ostensibly a day like any other, the woods free of the surrounding violence, oblivious to the chaos.

Paul and Steel walked in miserable, scarred silence. The gruesomeness of moments past and the uncertainty of the immediate future combated in a toxic tug of war, impossible to stay in the present when each second jerked them either way.

With every step, Paul liked to think he was a little closer to his family and not a notch or two in the wrong direction. Beyond the trees, the clouds were breaking apart like springtime snowbanks, windows of brilliant blue revealed – and Paul knew his wife and son were thinking of him in that quietly strained moment, fearing for him as he feared for them, desperate to bridge the time and space separating them.

Far too many states between them.

"I don't like this," Steel growled, pulling out the map again and checking his compass. "We should have reached 49 by now."

They stopped to survey what was essentially the same scene as the one presented to them last hour: trees as thin and condensed as teeth on a comb, the ground gently rising and falling all around them. Presently they were starting into one of the rises.

Steel showed the map to Paul. "We're right about here," he said, pointing to a spot just east of Route 49. "Or at least we should be. We've been keeping northwest for an hour – we should have run into the damn road by now. Can't believe how far off course we got."

# GRIDLOCKED

"It's probably on the other side of this hill," Paul guessed, but his attention was stolen by something far closer. "What in the blue blazes is that?"

Shining in the soft morning light that coruscated between the trees, protruding from the hilly earth, the sword at first seemed unreachable, moving as they moved, gaining two feet for every foot they managed. But soon Paul was upon it, pushing through a copse of young pines and climbing halfway up the hill.

The hilt dazzled with resplendent gold. Surely no one would have forgotten such a piece out here – but why would they have brought it out to the middle of the woods in the first place?

"It's sensational," Paul noted, expecting an Excalibur-like scene as he gripped the hilt. Instead, with a gentle effort he removed the thing from the damp earth as easily as a candle from a birthday cake.

A closer inspection revealed diamonds encrusting the hilt. The blade was a perfect mirror, not a nick on it.

"Shit," Steel said when Paul handed it to him. Curious, he fished through his backpack and produced a sheet of scrap paper. "Feels sharp. Let's see exactly how sharp we're talking."

The sword rended the paper with near soundless ease, Steel amazed not only by the sharpness and extravagance of the thing but also its surprisingly light weight.

Steel scanned the hill, thinking he'd heard something up there – maybe footsteps – and then returned to his examination of the sword. A single word was engraved in cursive into the bottom of the hilt.

"*Abandon*," he murmured, showing it to Paul.

"What in God's name does that mean?"

A light breeze stirred up, whispering weakly through the trees. Thicker clouds scudded overhead, tinged dark with their contents. A fresh scent of rain capered into the forest, and Paul was convinced he heard a child's voice from the top of the hill: "Colder."

Paul pitched the sword back into the ground and turned to Steel. "You hear that?"

Steel rubbed his beard. "Hear what?"

"Sounded like a kid – a girl. She said, *colder*." He pointed up the hill. "Sounded like it came from up there."

"Colder?" Steel shrugged. "I didn't hear nothing but the wind just now, but I thought I heard footsteps a few minutes ago. Probably just an animal, but your hearing's ten times better than mine, man. If you say you heard a girl, I don't doubt it."

Paul blew into his hands, more so out of habit than a desire to warm himself. He recalled one of the many stories he'd translated from spoken word to written word – a story about an old woman who'd survived nearly a week lost in the wilderness. Turned out she'd finished her harrowing ordeal in roughly the same place where she'd initially gone astray in the West Virginian Appalachians.

"You can get turned around in the woods," Paul said absently. "Easy to go in circles."

Steel scowled at the sky. "Not with Dad's compass, you don't."

Paul didn't like the frantic gleam in his friend's eyes. Steel kept swiveling his head, looking as if he'd heard something again.

"Come on," Paul said, putting a hand on Steel's shoulder. "Road can't be far."

# GRIDLOCKED

Leaving the sword behind, they continued up the hill. The clouds drifted apart again, the forest suffused with light once more; arriving along with it was optimism in Paul's heart that the worst had passed.

Steel, meanwhile, was tormented by his memories. He could vividly see the old woman's eyes – he would always see those lifeless, blood-sodden eyes held open by clamps, he feared. He would see them in wake and in sleep, and on every day for the rest of his life. He forced himself to think of something else (the sword was the first thing that came to him), but what had it been doing out there in the woods, with its odd engraved word?

*Abandon.*

Paul offered another prayer, made the sign of the cross. They were almost to the top of the hill now, even sunnier up here with the trees more widely spaced.

Steel began to jog, wanting to get it out of the way and confirm whether the road was on the other side. He nearly tripped on the wet leaves, but with a final leap over a rocky patch he was at the crest, looking down, the atrocities they'd seen still so fresh in his mind that, when he took in the carnage, he at first ascribed it to a hallucination.

It couldn't possibly be real.

But Paul gasped behind him. "Lord, Jesus, no! Take my eyes! Take them back!"

Neither of them advanced any farther, the extent of the slaughter bringing them down.

Then they heard the scream. Saw the girl.

# KEVIN FLANDERS

## Chapter 10

Death must not give in to his urges when the children's eyes meet his.

He once attempted to claim a child, but the lightning pulsed strange and violet when he descended that night, a profound roar coming from above, turbulence shaking Death about. He didn't know then of the great plans for the children.

He knows now.

Rather than killing, Death must establish fear. It is a higher command. The creation of fear must be had in every neighborhood, not merely with words but action, terror always purest in their eyes when his blade approaches, their tears flowing forth along with crimson.

Death has yet to render a perfect X, right-angled and symmetrical upon their flesh. He wonders what the perfect X might look like. One day, perhaps, he'll find out. Perhaps he'll create an X that not only imbues fear but transcends it, an X that climbs mountains, an X that flies.

Death often imagined flying in his previous existence, fantasizing about what it might be like to inhale at such a rate that he could inflate himself and lift gently away, then test a set of wings that must surely be awaiting discovery. His aspirations of flight were always confined to the chambers of the unreal, but then one moonlit night he really was drifting above the houses, watching the chimney smoke wisp away, searching for the next victim among the twinkling lights.

Similar to flying, if Death envisions that perfect X frequently enough, he knows the conversion from thought to reality will be inevitable.

Such notions please Death as he carefully sews another head back together, his supply of thread limitless, spooling blackly from his fingertips. This task, though not nearly as joyful as killing, will soon triumph. Within each corpse Death has embedded the seeds, and before long his army will rise.

Lights.

Death looks first upon his next target residence, then pockets his task in a cloak of infinite darkness, in comparison to which midnight could be mistaken for twilight.

An approaching vehicle. Is that a child Death scents in the passenger seat?

Intrigued, Death grins. He is still facing the house. "And who might you be?" he whispers, his words like stropped blades.

## Chapter 11

Gene's eyes, wide and tormented, told of the terrors he'd endured. His gaze dropped, the others remaining silent. Up ahead in the breakdown lane, a school bus was overturned, football equipment scattered about.

"He can *fly*?" Tommy finally said.

The boy nodded, refusing to look up.

"What do you mean?" Dom asked. "Did you see him fly?"

Another nod. "He said X means I'm dead." His voice was frantic, shivery. "He said he'll come back for me. He'll find me – he'll find everyone. He said they put exes on trees, houses, anything that will die."

Tommy clutched the boy's hand. "You're safe now. No one will hurt you again."

A quarter of a mile farther, Dom told Rock to pull over at the next street, Northridge Drive, the street sign slanted nearly flat after a sedan had been pushed into it. In the roadside gulley beyond Northridge Drive, a dozen other vehicles were piled into a makeshift junkyard.

"You sure about this?" Rock said. "It's only a few more miles to the shelter. You really wanna go off on your own?"

"Don't go," Gene implored, his eyes springing with fresh tears. He'd adjusted himself so that he was facing Tommy, the X carved into his forehead impossible to grasp. That someone could hurt a child in such a way left Tommy spent of words – and somehow he felt responsible, like he should have foreseen what would happen to the boy and found a way to prevent it.

# GRIDLOCKED

*I've been useless for five years. I have to do more.*

Tommy knew something profound was happening within himself, but the chaos was cycling all around, too fast, too heavy, not allowing him to harness what he'd been given. He felt as if they'd been cast adrift, the waves battering endlessly down on them.

"We'll meet you at the camp. We need to find our family, but it's too dangerous out there for you," Tommy told Gene. "You'll be safe with Rock. He'll take good care of you, I promise."

"No, don't go. Please don't go." Tears slid down his cheeks.

Tommy climbed out of the truck first and, with Dom's help, he brought Gene down as well. "Here, you take this," Tommy said, unclasping his necklace and handing it to Gene. "This cross will keep you safe. If you feel scared or alone, just give it a squeeze, okay?"

The boy's tears stopped. Briefly studying and then pocketing the necklace, which Tommy's mother had returned to him a few days earlier, Gene offered a hopeless smile. "Don't die."

"We'll be just fine," Dom said with impatience, starting toward Northridge Drive. They still had a long walk ahead of them.

"He's right. It's all gonna work out, buddy." Tommy kneeled and hugged Gene. He wished he could add something more assuring, but Rock was waving urgently for him to get Gene back on board.

Tommy lifted him up to the seat. "Buckle up," was all he could manage.

Another round of tears welled in Gene's eyes as Tommy snapped the door shut – and the true weight of their calamity crushed down on him in that moment, with the boy's face pressed against the window, his haunted eyes staring down at him, the X on his forehead like a sigil from Satan.

The truck jerked into motion. With both hands Gene palmed the glass.

Even as Tommy ran to join his brother, he watched the truck continue north on Brookfield Road, green lights fading sickly into the night.

The street was strangely quiet, ghostly. Around the first curve, a pickup truck remained where it had come to a stop when the grid shut down – in the eastbound lane. The fleet of dump trucks apparently hadn't cleared out residential streets yet, so maybe there was still time to reach Dom's fiancée…if she was home.

"Cyri," Dom kept murmuring, his fear that they'd be too late like glass in his gut. He'd sprinted for a time, but Tommy hadn't been able to keep up.

Refusing to leave his brother behind, Dom had brought it down to a jog, the clomping of their sneakers far too loud when the road was otherwise quiet.

Tommy felt the fatigue at first as a burn in his sides, then as a repeated stab in his chest. He tried to keep his panting down, afraid someone would come from the woods or one of the houses. He kept thinking he heard footsteps creeping up from behind them, but the most alarming result of each backward glance was a pain in his neck.

Finally, after a few miles that alternated between jog-walks, the house came into distant view, a few lights on upstairs. Tommy sucked in the brisk, wind-bitten air, but it brought no relief. Like a circuit, pain flashed through his legs, jabbed at his back and chest, and finally returned to his ankles for another round.

Dom, a frequent runner, felt only the strain of fear. He had to get to the house, had to be with Cyri – but what if he was too late?

# GRIDLOCKED

Tommy willed himself up the final hill, fighting through the agony of exhaustion. Then, as if time had been stopped and spliced, they were in the house, calling for Cyri even though her car was gone from the garage.

"Fuck!" Dom shouted. "She must have gone out looking for us."

Tommy put a hand on his brother's shoulder, Dom's expression like that of a widower at a funeral. Tommy hated that look. Again he wished the words would come, words capable of inspiration, words powerful enough to impel Dom through the storm.

"She probably went to the shelter Rock was talking about," Tommy said after a while, settling for vague optimism.

Dom let out a tortured sound that made Tommy shudder, though it wasn't the sole contributor to the chill that suddenly seized him. He'd seen something new in that moment.

Tommy tried to hold on to it, the details there but only for an instant. Still, he'd seen enough.

"We have to go!"

## Chapter 12

Xeke remembered the stars. Remembered the night rides with Amie. Their troubles had all fallen away out there on the road, no past or pretense, nothing lost or squandered, no one between them, only the stars as they had always been, the nights no different than those of their childhood.

Xeke stuffed his hands into his coat pockets…and discovered that the young guard hadn't been thorough in his pat-down back at the facility. Two nips of Fireball remained in his right pocket; he and Amie should have gulped them down on the trip home, warmth infused on a cold night. Ice cream and then whiskey, only a young stomach capable of handling the combination, and was it ever frenny.

But there hadn't been a trip home.

Xeke uncapped one of the bottles and allowed himself a sniff, but he couldn't bring himself to drink, not without Amie.

"Where are you?" he said, closing his tear-stung eyes as he leaned against the wall.

The corridor was chlorine scented. A flurry of sounds rushed out from the pool locker rooms opposite Xeke – laughter, shouting, muffled wails, rattled lockers. Virgil had brought him down here a few minutes ago, refusing to answer Xeke's questions about how he knew him. Maybe he was one of Dad's neighborhood friends, he'd thought, which would explain his knowledge of Xeke's experience with assault rifles and also Mr. Korach's military service.

Yet Xeke couldn't escape an intuition that Virgil played a far more prominent role than distant acquaintance. Without even saying a word, Virgil commanded the respect of everyone he encountered and somehow made them feel like the result would turn out all right.

# GRIDLOCKED

"You ready?"

Xeke flinched. He hadn't even heard Virgil coming.

"Time to stand guard, kid." Virgil nodded at the first door. **BOYS LOCKER ROOM**, it read. "Rules are pretty simple for this assignment. If a guy gets out, shoot him."

With that, Virgil led him into the locker room, where Xeke was issued a Glock 22 by a raggedy guy with a long gray beard. He wore a Grateful Dead T-shirt bearing a skull, his eyes shadowed beneath the worn brim of a Red Sox cap. A toothpick poked out from his badly cracked lips, and when the man handed over the gun he made a deep grunt that might have been contemptuous or simply indifferent.

Beyond the weapons lockers and their dustlord sentry, the room had been made into a makeshift prison. Temporary fences spanned rows of lockers; penned within them were the prisoners, dozens of them crammed into the little spaces. Guards armed with Glocks monitored every row, watching nervously as a few of the prisoners pushed and kicked at the fencing. Xeke recognized the prisoners' black uniforms – the same ones worn by the guards at the facility.

Virgil snapped his fingers in front of Xeke's face. "From what we've gathered so far, this was a massive national operation." He nodded as his eyes passed over the prisoners, the spray of showers echoing in the distance. "It's pretty obvious a great deal of planning went into this. They've already killed thousands, and they've transported thousands more. They shut down the grid, took down communications, took over the railway system – all within a few hours."

"The trains," Xeke remembered. "They were forcing people onto the trains. The cars were full."

Virgil raised his eyebrows. "And where has history seen *that* before?"

"I...wait, what?"

"History!" Virgil exclaimed, throwing his arms out. "Do they not teach history anymore?"

"What are you talking about?"

"Never mind, kid. Never–"

There was an eruption from the showers, where yet another prisoner holding area had apparently been set up.

Shouts rose above a strained gargling sound. Virgil hurried toward the commotion, Xeke and a few others right behind him.

"Move the fences!" Virgil ordered a guard posted outside the showers, and then they were inside the giant square, shackled prisoners parting to let them through, Xeke slipping on the tiles.

At the far wall, three armed guards had a prisoner pinned down on his back, allowing a teenager to direct water from the showerhead into the victim's mouth.

"Open up wide, or I'll break another finger," one of the attackers warned.

"You're gonna talk," said another. "Talk or drown."

"Enough! What is this?" Virgil demanded, and the four of them moved clumsily away like ants scattering beneath a boot's descending shadow, leaving the victim to his soaked, coughing misery, little spurts of water choked back up.

Xeke smiled at the guy's suffering. It was another black-uniformed bastard, his nose bloody and left eye swollen. But after everything these terrorists had done, after all the people they'd killed, a few facial injuries were nothing, the red swirls running down the drain barely even scratching the surface of retribution.

Xeke gripped the Glock, aware for the first time since entering the locker room of its presence. With a frisson he looked down at the gun, checked the magazine – as fully loaded as a Saturday night in a country song.

An urge burned through him along with a memory, Xeke taken briefly back to that scrambled night in his driveway, when it had been just him, the assault rifle, and his hatred.

"Where did he go?" Amie said.

Jazzi looked through the back window, the passenger window, and finally the front windshield. Her voice was soft, paper thin, almost a whisper. "I don't know. Keep going. We have to get inside."

With a screeching acceleration Amie jolted the SUV into the driveway, each look in the rearview mirror met first by the menacing renderings of imagination, then the relief of reality.

No sign of the man.

"The gun. Where's the gun?" Jazzi said.

"What gun?"

"The gun you shot the guy with!" Jazzi's expression was twisted with dismay and desperation.

Amie fumbled for the light switch, found it, searched the floor and the space between her seat and the door. Nothing, no gun. "I…I don't know, I must have dropped it. Come on, let's get inside. Dad has plenty of guns."

They ran for the house, not even sparing a second to close the SUV doors behind them. The terror that rallied in Amie's heart made it difficult to breathe, every shadow on the lawn manipulated by the night's trauma. The man would attack them. He would spring from the bushes and slash at them with his blade, she just knew it.

*Where did he go? What does he want?*

They reached the front door, their sprint feeling like it had covered the length of a football field, Amie immensely grateful for the recently installed voice recognition locks.

Inside.

Safe.

Amie checked the rectangular windows flanking the door. It came screaming through the slits right then, a cold, harrying wind, its breath upon Amie's face.

But the wind, for now, was their only pursuer.

*Is he gone? No, he's out there. Somewhere.*

"Mom? Dad?"

Footsteps on the basement stairs, thumping quickly.

Amie brought a hand to her heart when she heard her grandmother's voice.

"What did I tell you?" Virgil said, getting in each of the attacking guards' faces. His voice was calm yet somehow worse than the most scathing shout. It was a creeping sort of calm, one that got beneath your skin and burrowed deep.

# GRIDLOCKED

None of them could maintain eye contact with Virgil. It looked like the kid would cry.

The victim, meanwhile, had rolled onto his side, still hacking and spitting, his eyes red and turgid. The other prisoners cowered in the opposite corner, a mass of chained wrists and trepidatious stares.

Xeke gradually came down from that hate-poisoned place, the gun dropping once more to his side, its muzzle facing the floor. He grabbed one of the Fireball nips in his pocket, and this time, almost mindlessly, he downed the whiskey. Later, he would wonder if the alcohol had brought him to a new headspace, one in which his urge was not to kick the captive in the gut…or shoot him in the head.

Virgil switched off the shower faucet, rubbed his beard, and crossed his arms. The predominant silence alone was enough to crack the first guard, a heavyset guy who'd said: *Talk or drown*. This time, however, his voice was desperate and defensive. "Come on, man, give us a break. We were just looking for information." His eyes fell abruptly to the floor. "It's the only way to get it out of these assholes."

Virgil looked to the other two guards, then the kid, waiting for another response. When silence prevailed, he drew to within inches of the first man's face. "What were your orders?" he said in an almost bored tone.

The man took a few steps backward, Virgil matching each one until he had the guy against the wall. "Screw orders!" the guy finally blurted, defiant now that he'd been cornered. "Who are you to tell me what to do?"

Virgil stepped aside. "You're free to leave. Go ahead, try your luck out there, but don't bother calling 911 when there's trouble."

The man seethed in silence, gnawing on his lower lip.

Virgil started into a pace, his eyes flashing from one person to the next. "Let's get one thing dead straight." He pointed at them, his voice remaining level. "In my camp, we go by my rules." He stopped, loomed for a moment in the first man's face. "If I were in your camp, you could do whatever in God's name you please, sir, but this is *my* camp."

Virgil looked back at Xeke, whose fingers curled around the other bottle of Fireball. Tracks of sweat broke out on his face. The victim, through all of this, had crawled to his cohorts' corner, where he sat sopped and crumpled up like a black-clad puppet left out in the rain, his nose still running bloodily.

Virgil let out a long exhalation. "Torture doesn't work, boys," he said in his library-quiet shredder voice. "I learned that a long time ago in Afghanistan. Torture will make people tell you what you want to hear." He tapped his temple. "Closer the brain senses it's getting to death, the more creative it gets."

Virgil stopped before the kid this time. He waited a moment, and when the kid refused to look up, Virgil took him by the chin and lifted his head. "Be careful who you listen to in this place. You follow a bunch of dummies too close, and you'll be just another car in the pileup."

Virgil arrived next in the prisoners' corner. He tossed the wounded party a handkerchief, then directed the first scolded guard to get them all back to the cells. "And somebody find him some new clothes," Virgil said, nodding for Xeke to follow him. "These people will receive proper justice once things settle down. Until then, they are to be treated humanely in our custody."

"Where will we find new clothes?" the first man called, suddenly obsequious.

Virgil shrugged, stopping at the threshold of the showers but not looking back. He took off his fedora, made a quick examination of its interior. "You'll think of something, boys. It may take a while, but you'll think of something."

Amie's grandmother, Grammy Gigi – somehow short for Julia – came lightly up the basement stairs, followed by Amie's mother, Carmen Valenzuela, whose pistol poked out of her belt.

With spouting tears and a sudden weightless sensation, Amie lunged into their arms, then turned to face her new companion. "This is Jazzi. We escaped together, but…"

Xeke's name poured out with the next rush of tears, along with a diced up account of how they'd been separated and a description of the man who'd been watching the house.

"Where's Dad and Grandpa?"

Their faces darkened with fear, deep lines skating across Grammy's forehead.

"They went looking for you and the rest of the family," Grammy said, putting both hands on Amie's cheeks. "Thank Heaven your grandfather kept a few old cars around. He brought me here in the truck, then picked up your father." She checked the wall clock, eyes severe. "They've been gone a few hours now."

Mom's face was tear-streaked. "We tried to reach you, but there's no cell signal. The landlines are dead, too – there's this weird static, and no calls are going through." She started toward the basement, motioned for them to join her. "I don't know what we'd do without the radios. We've been keeping in contact with Dad and Grandpa that way, and also talking with people across the country. This attack – it's everywhere. Some people think it's terrorists. Some think anarchists. It might even be war, the Russians maybe, or the Chinese."

They proceeded into the basement shelter, Mom locking the double-cylinder deadbolt behind them. The "station" was reinforced with bulletproof panels and glass, the ham radio equipment set up on a long table against the far wall. In one corner stood Dad's gun cabinet; the other cabinets housed food, water, and medical supplies. It was a far shot from a doomsday bunker by current standards, but Amie nonetheless felt like she was in a fortress.

Mom scooped up the transceiver. "Freddy, can you hear me? Amie's home! She just got here!"

A moment later Dad's voice scraped over the radio. "Thank God. Is she okay? Where was she?"

"We'll tell you everything when you get home. How are you guys? Find anyone?"

"Not yet. It's Hell out here." A crackly pause, then: "It's really bad – lawless. They're shooting people and lighting things on fire. We just left Uncle Johnny's house – we couldn't find him or the family. People shot at us on the way out, took a few rounds off the frame but no major damage."

Mom brought a hand to her mouth. "Jesus, just come home! Please, Freddy, we need you here!" She was crying, Amie helpless to provide comfort beyond a hand on her mother's arm.

"Don't trust any cops, Dad – don't trust anyone," Amie added, and then it was Grammy who spoke into the transceiver: "Is Joe all right?"

"He's good to go. We're heading toward Route 49, away from the bad areas, which is pretty much anywhere with people."

Amie warned them to stay away from Spencer, then told them about the man they'd encountered outside the house.

# GRIDLOCKED

"He better hope he's long gone by the time we get there," Dad said.

Grandpa Joe spoke for a while, but Amie's focus shifted to Jazzi. She was staring emptily at the transceiver, her face exceedingly pale.

"Do you feel okay? Are you hungry, thirsty?" Amie asked, aware once more that, no matter how desperate her own situation became, it could never reach the depths Jazzi knew.

The girl let out a deep sigh. "That man we saw," she said, turning to Amie. "Do you think he's still out there?"

## Chapter 13

"Stop, please, we won't hurt you!"

Paul's voice was broken, agonized, a voice like shards of glass clinking together.

Down the hill, in the flat wilderness of ruin, the little girl ran, stumbling over corpses and forging a sanguine trail. If Paul were a child and he'd seen what the girl had seen, then spotted two men at the top of the hill, he surely would have run, too.

They started down the incline, Paul's prayers for strength not enough to stop the suffocation. He could go no farther, brought again to his knees and crushed by the sweeping death. The eyes. The faces. The tragedy of stories unfinished, some barely even begun.

Clouds marched in overhead. The wind cycled up a notch, wafting the stench around.

Steel, realizing Paul had stopped, came back to his friend. "There could be survivors," he said, taking Paul's arm. "Come on, we have to see if we can help."

"Look at them!" Paul screamed, squeezing his eyes shut. His voice fell to a trembling whisper. "Do you see any survivors?"

Not sure for a moment if he was awake or what was real, Steel scanned the expanse of death. No one moved. Not a sound came from the mass grave, not a lifted finger.

Steel was wrenched back to his drug-addicted fighting days – everything going briefly blurry, dizzy, distorted – and he thought he might pass out. He was breathing but somehow taking in no air, seeing but no longer with clarity.

He turned from it. "You're right," he said, but when he looked down at Paul, for a millisecond or less, his friend was replaced by something else, a face that wasn't quite a face, floating and without shape, a phantasm with eyes as empty and glassy as those of a doll.

"Warmer," Steel heard a child whisper from afar, followed by a titter echoing through the woods. The clouds parted, sunlight shafting down.

Steel grabbed Paul's shoulder, crouched beside him. "I heard it!"

"Heard what?"

"The kid! The one you heard earlier. It wasn't the girl we just saw…someone else."

Steel glanced back down the hill, where something was moving among the corpses, mistily amorphous but not entirely faceless, flashing with disjointed scuttles between the trees.

"These woods," Steel murmured. "They're fucking possessed."

## Chapter 14

Though his vision had already shown him a glimpse of what would happen, Tommy nonetheless jumped when the flaming bottle crashed through the living room window.

In his panicked warning, Tommy had described the projectile to his brother as a Molotov cocktail. The fire had come to him in the middle and again now, the curtains going up first, flames clawing up to the ceiling, the sofa instantly afire as if previously doused with gasoline. In the vision, it had all been black and white and sparkling gray, the fire entrapping them within seconds, Dom's house to serve as their incinerator.

This time, unlike Tommy's first vision back on Route 49, Dom had asked no questions and made no objections, enabling them to escape the room before the second bottle came through – the one that would have struck Dom in the head.

"Christ, you're a fucking psychic!" Dom hollered as they ran through the garage.

Outside, on the front lawn, their eyes were first drawn to the row of orange. Every house on the street was burning, the collective roar like a waterfall, the heat pulsing out in waves.

"Stay down!" Tommy saw the vans approaching before his brother. They were traveling abreast, violet headlights corrupting the night.

Slowing nearly to a stop outside Dom's next-door neighbor's house, the nearest van's side door slid open. Using a swiveling cannon-like device, a masked man in heavy tactical gear fired bottles in rapid succession – *THWOONK! THWOONK! THWOONK!* They ignited on contact, shredding the house and garage with fire.

# GRIDLOCKED

The other van, meanwhile, obliterated the homes and vehicles across the street, a little sedan catching orange like dry brush in an April wind.

The vans jerked forward in violet waves.

"Run!" Tommy's shouts rang in his head, but it was like they were running in slow motion. The faster Tommy wanted to move, the slower he seemed to go.

Behind them, rocketing whines sounded like incoming mortars, spiraling flames born in their wake. The earth shook, the heat singeing the nape of Tommy's neck.

He didn't look back.

They angled left, into the woods behind the row of houses. Back here, the violet glows were like sweeping searchlights, vans moving down the street in pairs.

"They torched my fucking house!" Dom clasped his hands behind his head. "Tommy, my house, it's...*gone!*"

Dom wobbled in a shaky circle. Was the ground quaking, he wondered, or were his legs failing him?

In a surreal flash, Dom remembered touring the house with Cyri. There'd been a storm that day, and they'd later shared a sundae after dinner at Applebees. They'd talked a lot about the future that night, another round of storms creeping in, but those had been the times when the future was seemingly theirs to dictate. It hadn't belonged to someone else. No one had possessed the power to take it from them. They'd been the authors of their own calendars...weekend hiking trips and weeknights at the movies, a trip to Boston when they both had time, making love up and back in the blackened depths of the MSR.

But now what? Like a setting moon, their freedoms had disappeared with inexorable speed, the chains of a new life snapped down on them with each new color of the enemy's headlights, the cats reduced to mice. And where were the cops, the Armed Forces, the fucking FBI? Dom couldn't fathom the irony – the only person doing a solitary effective thing was his brother, who, until a few hours ago, had been confined to a wheelchair.

Dom searched the smoke-veiled sky, wondering, fearing.

"They're doing this in rounds," Tommy said, watching as the last of the violet lights drifted off, leaving the neighborhood to the custody of orange. "First, the trucks came and cleared out the roads. Then the vans came and lit everything on fire. They've got this so carefully planned that they even had time to break everything down to the color of the headlights."

"So what do we do?" Dom threw his hands up. "You're the one with the visions. How do I find Cyri?"

Tommy knew his brother was unraveling – and what else could be expected with his fiancée missing and his house ravaged by fire? Yet Tommy managed to largely resist his own terror. He wouldn't let his second chance be torn away, not without a fight, and that meant putting one foot in front of the other.

Another vision would help, too, although Tommy dreaded what his next vision would reveal.

# GRIDLOCKED

## Chapter 15

Death watches with interest as the vans roll past, remembering what it was like to walk among them.

Many seasons have traversed since Death was trapped in that form, yet still he remains one of the youngest envoys. He knows he has much to learn before the perfect X can be drawn.

Perhaps, when his own army rises, the seas will turn red and that infallible X will welter across the land in blood.

# KEVIN FLANDERS

## Part III: Lower

## Chapter 1

In the tunnels of the MSR, dark but for the evenly spaced emergency exit signs, travelers scrambled about, their phones and shifters lighting the way, their voices panicked. Children cried. Questions went unanswered. Fights erupted as everyone funneled toward the exits. For one young lovemaking couple in a van, with the music turned up loud and retractable window screens engaged to block out the world, panic was postponed.

Above ground, where the stall of the grid was scarcely less congested, fires raged. There was looting, violence, depravity. Laws and freedoms ceased to exist. Countless individuals seeking valiantly to preserve and protect were killed; others ran for miles in search of loved ones, until finally exhaustion reduced them to a gasping stagger. Some families huddled together and tried to ride it out like a hurricane, wondering often if the worst had passed. Most families had been split apart.

At Tantasqua High School – where school buses had punctually departed at 2:20 that Friday afternoon, where tests had been administered and science experiments had been conducted – the process of survival now carried on.

Normally, in the world of law, firearms on school grounds would have translated into sirens and coppers. Now, though, with the sun gone and a new world rising, guns were everywhere. Men were packing. Women were packing. Even kids as young as thirteen were packing.

Xeke knew he had to get out of this place, the school turned into a powder keg. Just one fight and everyone would be shooting. Yet even if they didn't turn on each other, the Gridhacks/Gridlocks, as people called them, were probably regrouping. They'd attack again soon, Xeke sensed, and this time they wouldn't take prisoners.

# GRIDLOCKED

"I'm gonna kill that motherfucker," the first man growled – the one Virgil had invited to leave the camp if he dared. With his palm he slammed the fence spanning banks of lockers, prisoners scattering on the other side. "I'm gonna kill that bastard and take this place over, that's what."

Xeke drifted from the group, their hatred of Virgil serving as the perfect distraction. When none of them were looking, Xeke ducked into an alcove that brought him to a door.

He tugged it open, lights coming on automatically to reveal a storage room, its shelves stacked with pool maintenance equipment. The smell of chlorine was even stronger in here, but Xeke wouldn't have to stay for long.

There was another door at the opposite end, which opened to a hallway. Locked.

"Dammit."

Xeke pacmanned through rows of racks, until he came to a side door that took him to the pool. The lights were dim, the water a sheet of glass. The air was warm and frenny.

Xeke ran the length of the pool and stood for a while at the far door, the Glock in his right hand. Seeing no one out there in the hallway, he pushed the door open and braced himself for Virgil's appearance.

Surely Virgil would be there, waiting for him. He was always there. He was everywhere.

Xeke stepped into the hallway. It was empty.

Carmen Valenzuela made contact with a number of people during the thirty minutes they waited for Amie's father and grandfather to return.

# KEVIN FLANDERS

From Sgt. Percival Stoughts, of the Colorado State Patrol, to Reverend Andy Allenberg, of St. Thomas Episcopal Church in Bethlehem, PA, to Rudy Heller, Chicago's oldest resident at 106, to Ricardo Rodriguez, a firefighter at the southeastern tip of the nation in Key West, FL, the hand of ham radio reached across the country.

The reports varied, but everyone essentially reported the same thing. The U.S. was under attack, not from another country but everyday Americans: men, women, and teenagers of every race. Their only commonality was their black uniform – the uniform Amie currently wore, bloodstained and stinking of something worse than death.

"I still can't believe it," Mom said, setting down the transceiver and looking Amie over once more. "My baby, my little girl – you're so much braver than I could ever be."

Between radio conversations, Jazzi had recounted their ordeal in surprising detail, even remembering how the guard at the facility had called Amie "Captain" and referred to Jazzi as a deportee. Sgt. Stoughts, who'd ambushed and imprisoned two attackers outside Denver, had also heard them describing deportees. He'd even mentioned the possibility that the entire thing was government-sanctioned, a plot straight out of an undiscovered Orwell manuscript hidden beneath the tomes of time.

Jazzi pointed again to the golden eagle pin on the collar of Amie's uniform – its only distinctive accoutrement – setting her uniform apart from the monochromatic black tide of the others.

"Whoever that guard was," Jazzi said, "she was pretty important."

Mom looked wide-eyed at Jazzi, as stunned as Amie was by the girl's equanimity amidst chaos.

"You should get that uniform cleaned up," Grammy advised. "If we run into trouble, it could save our lives."

# GRIDLOCKED

"But that was just one guard I tricked. He was hurt, not thinking straight. It'll never work again," Amie protested, wanting to be done with the uniform forever.

Grammy shook a gnarled finger. "You're an actress, Amelia. You can fool the world if you want to."

Amie smiled thinly in resignation. "Fine, you win. We'll wash it."

Rather than head back the way he'd come and be subjected to questions from the Freedom Riders, Xeke instead ran to the east end of the school. He passed trophy cases and plaques and photos of sports teams on the walls, vaguely remembering the handful of youth league basketball games he'd played in this building years ago. The school had been greatly enhanced since then (many public school facilities were now about as impressive as prep school complexes, the grid having saved billions).

Xeke glanced sharply behind him, aware of gaining footsteps, but the hallway was still empty.

*Great. Now I'm hearing things.*

Almost to a set of double-doors, Xeke wondered what he should do. He hated being in here while his family and Amie were somewhere out there, beyond the barricades the Freedom Riders had set up. For the majority of the motorcycle ride, clinging to Virgil, Xeke had glimpsed the devastation as a blur of wreckage and fire. People had been running, limping, fighting – all of them seemingly at a standstill – like seeing dots of traffic from an airplane.

But when the Harley had slowed at intersections, Xeke had seen the horrors with clarity: a fireman swinging a knife at two attackers; an old woman writhing in the street outside a church, blood pouring from her stomach; a group of wounded kids waving for the Freedom Riders to stop; a mob torching a flag and smashing storefront windows; an overturned stroller, the toddler screaming on the sidewalk.

Hell. That was what awaited Xeke beyond the barricades, yet still he was dominated by an urge to leave.

They climbed the basement stairs, both Amie and her mother armed with Smith and Wesson 9mm pistols (Dad's trusty standbys).

The creak of the door as Mom pushed it open was utterly foreign sounding, as if Amie were in a stranger's house. Grammy, also armed, pulled the door shut behind them and retreated to the station, where she and Jazzi would wait in safety.

"Probably just someone looking for shelter," Mom said when Amie reminded her of the hooded man who'd stared at the house and somehow eluded – jumped? – the SUV.

"No, definitely not," Amie murmured. "The way he was standing, it's like he came here for a reason. Maybe we should wait in the basement for Dad and Grandpa."

Mom waved off the suggestion. "I'm a better shot than both of them. Your father learned everything he knows from me."

They hurried upstairs, but not before clearing rooms as their firearms instructor had taught them a few years ago in drills that seemed ridiculous. But now they were in it – a world tossed on its side and sent for a roll, its contents like shaken soda.

And some idiot had cracked open the can too soon.

The house was empty, both floors. Amie stripped out of the uniform and gathered new clothes from her room, convincing herself a handful of times that she'd heard something downstairs.

# GRIDLOCKED

Her mother opened the washer and tossed in the bloody mess. Amie listened carefully beyond the filling water. Nothing.

"Let's get back downstairs," Mom said at last.

They were almost to the basement door when the house was plunged into darkness, the shock like that of a jump into an icy pool. But if the electricity hadn't been cut in that precise moment, if the house hadn't been brought to perfect black, Amie wouldn't have seen the face straight ahead, peering through the living room window, silhouetted in the lesser dark outside, where solar lamps lit the back walkway.

It was him. The hooded man from the street. And he was staring right at her.

## Chapter 2

They ran for a time without speaking. Even if words had been shared, they would have been insufficient to articulate fears not fully formed – fears that were like the frame of a malefic puzzle. Even without the middle pieces in place, Paul and Steel somehow knew that whatever image was destined to invent itself before them would transcend the very definition of terror.

Twigs snapped beneath them. Leaves flew up and absquatulated, reminding Paul of autumn raking with his son and how Maze loved jumping into piles of leaves. Had Paul still been without his vision, had he asked his guide to paint for him in that moment a picture, Steel might have described the sentinel trees and their narrow height. He might have mentioned something about the climbing sun and the strange-angled light and shadows it deflected through the wilderness. He surely would have noted the little stream ahead to their left…and the cabin.

It wouldn't have been foreboding on another morning. It would have been just a dilapidated cabin in the woods, with a crumbling stone chimney and a roof blanketed in leaves and pine needles. The porch had a slight bow to it, the windows smashed to varying degrees, some completely, others with baseball-size holes.

Paul would have avoided the cabin, but he was drawn curiously to the porch by something gleaming upon it.

"Follow me. There's something over there." Paul led Steel off what had been a rocky yet agreeable path, and together they navigated the sprawled remains of a stone wall. The smell of the place came fiercely over them, a damp, rotten ill – the stench of death and forever. Up in the trees, a vulture took flight from a nest practically worthy of an address. The stream glinted with morning brilliance. The wind, not ready to call it quits just yet, hugged them coolly.

# GRIDLOCKED

Paul scooped up the silver pocketknife from the sodden porch. Examining it, he felt the cabin – perhaps the entire woods – shift subtly around him, the scene not the same when he looked up again, none of it, the cabin shadowed, the sky suddenly overcast. The stream was darker now, more reflective. Faster than before? A little more turbulent?

Unseen in the trees, the vultures began to caw. Steel could hear their wings beating with agitation…or dark interest. "What the hell is going on with these weapons we keep finding?" he said, watching as Paul observed the knife.

"Jesus Lord!" Dropping the knife, Paul recoiled as if his hand had been burned.

"What? What is it?" Steel felt like he'd swallowed something jagged.

Paul glanced back at the knife with disgust. "Damn spider popped out of that thing." He pointed at Steel. "Now don't you get started on me. You don't know what it's like for a blind man with even the mildest case of arachnophobia. You feel something crawling around – you don't got the luxury of checking it. Every ant, fly, damn ladybug turns into a little tarantula, you hear what I'm saying?"

"Loud and clear, brother – though I'd take a spider over those stinky ass ladybugs any day." Steel turned back to the path, thinking they'd be on their way, but Paul pushed open the cabin door.

Paul knew not what he was searching for, but something had called to him just now. He sensed they'd find something of use in this place.

"Give me the strength," Paul whispered once inside.

With gathering dread Steel watched his friend kneel upon the littered floor and clasp his hands together. One horror at a time, it felt like they were slowly losing themselves, drifting ever nearer to the edge of human endurance.

"I think this is bigger than we could ever imagine." Paul looked up at Steel, who was frowning worriedly, his shoulders slumped.

Not once during their countless times together on the road, hot days and thundery evenings and nights of laughter and exhaustion, had Paul envisioned his guide as a man with sagging shoulders. But the man before him was different. Paul, himself, was different. They would never be the same, he feared.

"These woods – they're making us crazy, don't you see it, Steel? When you can't look past it and there's nothing but death all around, the woods play tricks on you. They mess with your mind."

Steel took him by the shoulders. "Just breathe." Steel tried to steady him, but Paul's eyes were widening, a moment's reflection within them – that phantasm wisp of a face from before, misty and leering.

"What's that?" Paul gasped, his eyes flashing to the far corner. "Tell me it ain't there, man, tell me I'm seeing things!"

Steel whirled around, saw only the fireplace and a forgotten rocking chair amidst the clutter of nature's debris. But there was more. Beneath the chair rested a stack of books – thin like children's books – barely visible past a quilt of leaves and pine needles that had blown in through the broken windows. Atop the seat of the lonely, decrepit chair waited a coffee mug. And wrapped around that chair was an orange windbreaker which almost positively hadn't been there before. It was seemingly the only thing of color in the shadow-choked cabin, sunlight pouring in strongly at the windows but languishing as it proceeded toward the center of the structure, as if there were an invisible funnel that drained most of the light.

It really was an awful place, Steel felt, beginning with the smell and ending with the strange items surrounding the shadow hearth.

# GRIDLOCKED

*We're too close to the edge. Gotta pull it together.*

"We should get out of here," Steel said, teeming with the need to find the road again.

"No, please, not yet!" Paul resisted, almost in a shout. "Let's just take a little while longer to get ourselves right. We've been scarred by what we've seen. This whole thing is clearly" – his voice came down considerably – "beyond our limits of understanding. And so we need to pray on it. We need to stay inside from those terrible woods and use to our advantage the respite our Lord has provisioned."

Steel was quiet, too depleted to argue. Leaving Paul to his prayers, he came to the chair and dragged it aside, then grabbed the first book, its once yellow cover now a faded, dusty brown. He swept away a layer of dirt, but no letters peeked out to reveal a title or an author, the first few pages blank as well.

Then Steel saw it. A few pages in, the drawing had been done by hand. This wasn't a children's book, in fact, but a sketchbook. The simple drawing was of a house; tall and leaning, the windows disproportionate from floor to floor, the image had been made by a child using a black marker.

But the writing below the house – *You can check out any time you like...* – flowed with the elegance of a poet's hand.

Steel flipped to the next page, where he found stick figures spilling over a cliff, razor-toothed creatures – sharks? – awaiting their fall in red waters beneath. The next page was red and orange with flames, additional stick figures burning.

"What the fuck is this?"

Paul's eyes lifted, his mind torn free of prayer. Without speaking, he stared at the book in Steel's hands, wondering what his friend had seen. Riding a burst of wind, leaves swirled through the broken windows and settled scrapingly against the floorboards. Birds cawed from high branches. The sun receded behind a new rank of clouds, the cabin darkening.

Steel tossed the book in Paul's direction. It hit the floor with a heavy clap. "There's more drawings, just like the ones we found before."

When Paul pored through the book, then progressed to the others, he became wholly convinced that this was indeed the Great Tribulation. Of all the years in time, of all the souls that had inhabited God's lands, Paul Shannon and Sherman Sparks, in this moment and place, were enduring what had for others been limited to prophecy.

Soon millions more would suffer.

"It can't be," Paul murmured, but he knew this was real, inescapable. The worst world war yet was underway, Paul's vision restored perhaps so that he might have a fighting chance against the tribulations reserved for them. "It's almost like they're trying to communicate with us." Paul remembered the images from before, back at the first house they'd searched. (**THE END. JESUS SAVES.**)

"*Who's* trying to communicate with us?"

"I'm not sure. Angels? Demons? I don't know what to make of it, any of it. Are they trying to warn us of something, maybe? Or are they only toying with us, threatening us?"

Paul opened his pack and tugged out the threadbare little stuffed pony. He gave it a squeeze, despair raking through him, and returned it to his pack. He felt as though he were falling from a high place.

"Those drawings aren't the only things we keep finding, and it's no coincidence," Steel said. "Weapons. First, the sword, and now" – he nodded to the porch – "that pocketknife. Are we supposed to take them, you think?"

# GRIDLOCKED

Steel couldn't get his thoughts straight. He felt impaired by the poisons of what he'd seen, his heart electrified with terror. Wherever they went, the ceaseless massacre had already been there. Wherever they looked, the dead stared back at them. For a moment nothing seemed real, as if he were on a tremendous high. The next moment found him cursing and pacing, then firing the books at the rocking chair.

"Where's the goddamn road?" he shouted. "We have to get back to the road!"

Steel hurtled out of the cabin and, with a leap, cleared the porch steps. Paul, for a few breathless moments, feared his friend would put the pistol in his mouth and pull the trigger, unable to withstand the totality of their torment.

Paul listened. Waited. Dreaded the next sound.

The sun came back out then, and Paul, fears dazzling, took a few steps toward the door.

He stopped upon hearing the whispered voice directly above him. "Warmer," it announced, followed swiftly by gunshots outside.

## Chapter 3

Tommy didn't know how long they'd been walking. Fifteen minutes? Thirty? They'd gone through the woods, then cut diagonally across to the next street, passing groups of frantic residents and houses aflame. They'd helped an old lady track down two of her fussily dressed lapdogs, one of them cowering beneath her pool deck. They'd then moved on to her next-door neighbor's yard and carried a wounded man to his shed to take shelter with family, his legs badly burned. Later, they'd told two wailing preteen girls that they hadn't seen their parents; Tommy had tried to provide further help, but the girls had gone careening down the street, screaming for their parents.

All around them had been chaos, most people trying to account for their families, the rest trying to hide from the next wave of attackers. A bloodied middle-aged man, meanwhile, had shoveled pills into his mouth and washed them down with alcohol, then shouted, "I'll die on my terms!"

That image lingered longer than the rest for Tommy. Even as the other memories faded into a clustered haze, he couldn't wrest free of the man's defeated eyes.

The Sims brothers were on the next street now. The smell was crushing, exceedingly smoky but something more, something worse – the stench of suffering and loss. Windows exploded. Walls collapsed. Passing one house, Tommy thought he heard screams from within, though they were impossible to differentiate from other screams, everything muddled by the fire's relentless roar.

Exhausted, they rounded a curve and made it to a cul-de-sac, stunned to find that one house had been spared from the flames. Observing the black wrought iron fences lining the property – set aglow by the flaming homes to the immediate left and right – Dom was steeped with suspicion.

"Why didn't they light that house up?" he said.

# GRIDLOCKED

Tommy stared up at the big house, entirely dark beyond the fences. Drawing closer, he noticed a sign posted to the front gate: **KEEP BACK FROM FENCE! VIOLATORS WILL BE SHOT!**

"Them evil sonsabitches knew this would happen!" came a voice to their right, rising above the fire.

A hooded man ducked out from behind a tree twenty feet away, his face heavily shadowed. Tommy might have assumed the guy was a kid if he hadn't first heard his voice. He was diminutive, barely five-five, with spindly legs that seemed to constitute three quarters of his frame.

The man pushed back his hood, revealing a bald pate that carried on long past where it should have stopped, then extended some more like a deformed potato. Coming closer, the man shook a knobby finger at the house. "They built that fence just last year, you know. Clearly they were preparing for this!"

"Where do you live?" Dom asked.

The stranger shook his head. "Don't live anywhere now. My house is up in flames just like everyone else's." He waved at the untouched house. "Except that one. Next thing you know, they've got a sign warning people to keep back from the goddamn fence. Tell you what we should do – bust down that stupid fence and torch the place!"

"You'll get your head blown off before you even get close," a woman said dispassionately.

She'd crept up on them like a deadline. Muscular and freckled, blonde hair pulled into a ponytail and tinted amber by the devilish light, she wore tight jeans and high leather boots – and she had a shotgun slung over her shoulder.

*She's gorgeous*, Tommy thought, feeling exceptionally unsafe in her presence but not fearful.

"I'm Beatrice. That's my parents' house down there – *was* my parents' house." She pointed to one of the houses along the last curve. "We've got a group down at the church, maybe thirty people. I came up here to get weapons from my parents' place, but" – she made a circling gaze – "it looks like Dad's guns are toast."

"They probably burned the church, too," Dom said. "They burned everything."

"Except *that* goddamn house," the old man cranked, stomping a foot. He'd receded from the conversation and now stood at an awkward distance like a child peering up and trying to understand the adults.

"Not everything," Beatrice said. "We have a bunker under the church, and there's room for more if you boys are interested. All those community preservation grants we got after the grid went up – Pastor Thorne decided it'd be a good idea to set up a shelter, just in case of a rainy or radioactive day."

They were briefly speechless. Then, turning, Beatrice glanced over her shoulder and said, "Well, you boys coming or not?"

Dom and Tommy exchanged glances. Down the street, blue headlights swept around the curve. A tanker truck was fast approaching.

The four of them ran for the woods. Hidden now, they watched as the truck came to a groaning stop outside the burning house to the left of the one that had been spared. Men in firefighting gear jumped off the truck and prepared hoses. Soon arcs of water combated the flames.

Three more tanker units arrived, the cul-de-sac a sea of blue. The trucks themselves were black, with instrument panels between the cabs and tanks. At the back of each truck, armed guards watched from platforms as the firemen did their work.

"Motherfuckers," the old man murmured while the firefighters extinguished the two blazes nearest the chosen house. "They're protecting it. With the wind, they knew the flames would spread quick."

"Just keep it down, will you?" Tommy closed his eyes, tried to conjure up something from the middle. Somehow he'd seen all of this happen in the middle, the future coming to him during his coma, but how? He'd heard of bizarre miracles (people emerging from comas and speaking foreign languages), but this was well beyond a miracle. God had given him a purpose, but now what? The cars had been cleared from the road, the houses burned, and *now what*?

What was he supposed to do? Regardless, he would need more than just glimpses to make any progress.

The firefighters worked their way backward, away from the cul-de-sac, putting out blazes as they went. When one truck was spent and departed, another arrived with a full tank of water. Again Tommy was dismayed by the scale of the plot that was well underway, as layered as a millionaire's wedding cake, the intricacies defined all the way down to the colors of the headlights.

*But what's next? What color? Come on, think! You've seen it. You must have seen it.*

Yellow flashed across Tommy's mind, and something was briefly there, the interior of a house, maybe. No, not a house. Something else, an expansive room at its center, and there was blood, death, a creeping form, a twisted, shadowy, eyeless face beyond a foggy mask.

Tommy tried to hold the image firm in his head, but the details faded until they were gone altogether.

*Dammit!*

"Let's go," Beatrice said. "We need to get back to the church."

"How far is it?" Dom asked, wondering if they should go with Beatrice or continue on to Tantasqua High School, where Rock had said a camp was set up. They'd promised to rejoin Gene there (and maybe Cyri and their parents had gone there as well), but what if the school had already been torched? A bunker might be the best option for now, Dom thought, at least until the authorities could finally begin to subdue an enemy far larger than he'd initially assumed.

"About twenty minutes on foot," Beatrice said.

"Okay, we'll go with you, maybe stay for the night. It's too dangerous out here right now."

Beatrice's flashlight guiding the way, they descended further into the woods, the old man (whose name was Larry Knight) lagging behind.

"You kids go on ahead," Larry said after a while, panting. "Just give me the address. I'll make it eventually – don't wanna slow you down."

Beatrice stopped. Angling the light up the hill at Larry, she said, "We'll wait. We're not leaving you out here alone."

"You got family around, Larry?" Dom asked.

He shook his head. "Divorced. My only son died ten years back – car accident. With everything that's happened tonight, I'm glad he didn't live to see it. They're killing people, man, *killing* 'em!"

# GRIDLOCKED

Indeed, they were neck-deep now, but where there were positives Tommy would unfalteringly reach. For a man whose last five years had been nothingness, even the heaviest darkness was better than nonexistence.

*Every night must end*, he thought, but it was a thought that hadn't come from within. He'd heard it before, and now the yellow lights were bursting back into his head, taking him once more to that place, the details sweeping in with heightened clarity. The faces were...their own. The yellow headlights belonged to sedans parked outside a house, no...the church.

*The gasmen.*

Somehow Tommy knew what they were called.

"We have to get everyone out of that bunker! Come on, there isn't much time!"

# KEVIN FLANDERS

## Chapter 4

Amie let out a choked yelp. Seeing the hooded man just outside the living room window had pushed the air from her lungs. He'd been watching them, but for how long?

By the time Amie described what she'd seen, his face was gone from the window. Amie hadn't gotten a detailed look, but there'd been something about his eyes, something unnatural.

They stood there in the darkness, momentarily paralyzed. Then Mom said, "Come on, we have to–"

The front door cranked open.

Amie and her mother turned, directed their weapons at the foyer, ready to shoot if the voice recognition locks had somehow been breached – but there was no hooded intruder, only bobbing flashlights and the voices of Amie's father and Grandpa Joe.

"There's someone out there!" Mom warned. "Amie just saw him through the window – the same guy from before."

Dad and Grandpa already had their pistols out. For a while they all listened, waited, flashlights in constant sweeping search, but they heard only the washer going through its cycle upstairs.

"The generator," Dad said. "It should have gotten the lights on by now. Is Grammy down in the station?"

Mom nodded. "She went back down there after we came upstairs."

Grandpa sighed with relief. "That guy Amie saw could have broken in earlier and messed up the system. We'll check the house…and shoot anyone we catch inside!" he hollered.

# GRIDLOCKED

"No, you won't." Mom started toward the basement. "We're all going downstairs where it's safe."

With minimal protest, Dad and Grandpa lighted the way to the basement, where they were met by the bluish glow of the station's battery-powered emergency lights. If they could get the generator working (it was supposed to fire up automatically following power outages), it would allow for full lighting and running water.

But even if the generator failed, at least they were secure for the moment. Amie felt like she could breathe again once they were locked away in the station, her immediate family together again. But what about Xeke? Had he escaped the facility? Was he out there looking for her?

Jazzi greeted Amie with a lengthy embrace. It was the first of several hugs, Amie reduced to tears by the presence of her family.

They rattled through their experiences, Amie's father hugging her again after she recounted her ordeal. Meanwhile, a former electrical engineer, Grandpa got the generator running by the time Amie finished describing their escape. He reported a small glitch with the transfer switch as the culprit (which probably meant a fairly complicated issue no one else could have solved). With the rest of the lights now back in service, the room was bright and hopeful, the mood instantly lifted.

"We'll get through this," Dad said, taking Amie's hand. "With God's help, we'll all get through this. We just have to stay together."

When Amie told her father about everything Jazzi had been through, and not just tonight, her family's expressions took on a collectively deep pity.

"You poor, poor thing," Grammy said, hugging the girl.

"Don't worry – once this is all over, we'll get you back to Sena," Dad said with his unfailing optimism.

Mom frowned. "From what we've heard on the radio, no one's doing much to stop these people. Whoever they are, they've caught everyone completely unprepared."

"What do they want?" Dad said. "Are they just trying to kill as many people as they can? If so, why imprison people and put them on trains?"

"I expected to see a heavy military force out there getting a handle on things." Grandpa shrugged. "But there's just…no one. No order. It's chaos."

His words made Amie shiver. *No one. Chaos.* Even with her family surrounding her, she suddenly felt isolated and thin of hope, reminded that many people had died and countless more wouldn't survive the night. With hospitals likely overfilled or under attack, even unremarkable injuries might prove deadly due to infection, never mind critical wounds.

After a few more minutes of terrified conversation, Dad grabbed the transceiver and resumed communications. It wasn't long before he made contact with a high school kid in Santa Barbara, California; then a young woman who'd been traveling with her family just south of Wichita, Kansas, on their way to her cousin's wedding rehearsal; then a handful of others who all confirmed the same thing (reiterated by several transmissions from across the country they heard between their talks with contacts, including one transmission from an emergency operations frequency based in Taunton). Apparently the enemy was shipping people south on trains. Those who refused to board the trains were shot. In many places people were being forced into warehouses and burned to death.

# GRIDLOCKED

"What about the police? Why aren't they doing anything to stop this?" Mom said between bursts of communications. "They must know about what's happening in other places, right?"

Dad shook his head. "Maybe not. Most police radio systems use repeaters placed at high locations. But assuming they've been taken out along with other communications, radios by themselves are very limited in range. Vehicle and base radios will transmit farther, five miles, I'd say – but portable radios will only give you about a mile or two. Much of it depends on terrain. Higher up you are, the farther you can reach, but most police departments still rely on the local ham guys when things go south. They never thought this would happen after Satellite Awakening, but someone's controlling everything."

Mom's face was twisted with fear. "What if this goes for days, weeks, before they get it under control?"

Dad took her hand. "Let's pray it ends soon."

Xeke stopped and backed away from the door, knowing whose face he would see when he turned. He'd been about to push open that door and leave the school when Virgil had called his name.

"The momentum of one is great, kid," Virgil said, stepping closer, hands shoved into his jacket pockets, "but the strength of unity is unstoppable."

Xeke handed his weapon to Virgil. "I can't stay. Not with my family out there."

Holstering the gun, Virgil rubbed his beard and stared inexpressively at Xeke for a time. Had a menu been placed in his hands, he could have been a man deciding what to order for dinner.

"You remind me somewhat of myself, kid," Virgil eventually said. "I never listened to no one. When my daddy told me not to take out the car in that April nor'easter junior year, I'll give you one guess as to how many tow trucks it took to haul me out of the ditch. It's what we do, guys like me and you. Even if we see the shitstorm coming, we'd rather eat crap than go inside on somebody else's call."

Xeke grimaced, wanting to get away but held captive by the senseless need to hear more.

Virgil started into a pace. "My folks told me to steer clear of the war, said there's defending freedom and then there's wasting time. Freedom never lived in that place, and it never will – but damn if I didn't feel compelled to serve." He shook his head. "Seeing those towers go down gets me every time, kid – one minute they're standing tall, and the next…" He expanded his pace, from wall to wall in front of Xeke. "Despite what my folks said, I wanted to serve. I wanted justice – hell, we all wanted justice, but sometimes what you search for and what you find are night and day, kid. And after too much blood and nights that don't end, you start to forget what you were searching for in the first place."

"What are you talking about? And why do you keep following me? Stop giving me a bunch of poodyloose already!"

"*Poodyloose?*" A strange rictus dominated Virgil's face. "Is that what they call horseshit these days? You kids and your dumb new words – it's like a bad version of *A Clockwork Orange*."

"What do you want from me?" Xeke blurted, but it came out sounding pitifully petulant.

Virgil shrugged. "To stay alive," he said plainly. "You leave this place – I give you maybe an hour. You seem resourceful, though, so maybe a couple hours. I'd be shocked if you lasted till sunup."

"It'd be better than dying in here when they blow the shit out of this place."

# GRIDLOCKED

"Not gonna happen." This time, Virgil spoke with emotion.

"How do you know?"

The calm returned to his voice. "The strength of unity. We're all pulling hard on that rope, kid, and the enemy is weakening. Only reason they got so strong in the first place was our concession of freedom. You hand over the reins, and you've got no idea who's gonna take 'em. But tonight we're taking freedom back!"

## Chapter 5

Paul stumbled out of the cabin, echoes slamming his eardrums. "Jesus, Steel, put it down! Put the gun down!"

Steel pivoted, directed the gun briefly at Paul, then up to the trees, desperation stampeding in his eyes – the eyes of a cornered animal.

"Put the gun down!" Paul repeated, ducking when his friend flashed the gun around again, waving it at shadows.

Steel eventually focused his aim on the bushes huddled against the cabin. He thought he'd heard it moving down there. Then he'd seen the phantasm again, higher, climbing the trees with those impossibly disjointed movements, looking at him the whole time.

"It's following us," Steel said, dropping the weapon, bafflement and terror mixing toxically in his heart.

"We're just seeing things, Steel. All that death – it snapped us, man. Snapped us good." Paul recovered the pistol, wondered if they should abandon the weapons.

*No, we're not hallucinating! Something's making us see all of this. It's controlling everything.*

Steel's expression was as inscrutable as a night river. Paul didn't know what lurked in those depths, his friend's instability scaring him badly because it reflected his own. A part of him wanted to go back inside and see if anything had been drawn in that sketchbook at all.

Paul stepped carefully toward his friend, arms outstretched. "We're gonna make it through this, man. It might look like God's left us behind, but He'll never abandon us." Steel turned, started to walk away, but Paul kept pace. "You hear what I'm saying, friend? No matter how bad it gets, no matter how long the war lasts, we'll find a way through these tribulations. The woods will end somewhere, and the demons will be forced back. We just have to prove ourselves, keep fighting, don't give up."

Momentarily thoughtless, it was as if Steel had just awakened. He was disoriented and a little dizzy, absently checking his compass. "There's something real fucked up about these woods," he said in a low voice, stopping at the edge of a short, rocky drop. "This thing – it's…everywhere."

Paul hated what emerged in Steel's eyes – a blend of despair and desolation. To be lost was tolerable, but to lose oneself…Paul knew they had to fight it until their fingernails bled.

"Let's keep going," Paul said. Lightly, he patted Steel's shoulder. "We've got a long day ahead."

The drop was maybe eight feet, the ground below jagged with spearing rocks. The underbrush was thick and uninviting.

They decided to go around, Paul leading the way, Steel tottering clumsily behind him like a drunkard. Exhaustion had come heavily and suddenly at Steel, his legs crampy, his lower back pinched sharply. Every step was brutal, like the first few hangover moments before popping a Xanax.

After briefly following another winding stream, they climbed a short hill and came achingly down the other side, no carnage to greet them this time, only a pair of gently rocking nightmares. It was as if those nooses had been there forever, waiting for Paul Shannon and Sherman Sparks since their births, patiently enduring the storms and seasons, hanging from the same branch ten feet apart, a pair of tall stools beneath them.

Yet Paul knew the nooses had just been arranged there by whatever they kept hearing and glimpsing, its pursuit like the moon following you down the road. No matter how fast you went, it rode along with you.

*It mocks and torments...Pestilence blackens these woods...We are at war for our souls now...*

For a pulse-pounding moment, the woods took on the gray-black of a photo negative, Paul blinking it away. He listened closely. Waited for the whispered voice that would surely return.

Warmer?

Colder?

But there was only a tepid wind and the stream's distant babble.

Steel gazed up at the nooses, frozen. "It's messing with us. It won't let us leave. This really is the–"

"Keep moving," Paul urged.

There was nothing more to say, not without falling into hopelessness, their heels already backed up to the plank's edge. Paul dared not even glance over his shoulder again, for he knew it was there, watching.

# GRIDLOCKED

## Chapter 6

First Baptist Church of Sturbridge was an almost thirty-minute northeasterly trek through the woods. The church towered darkly at the top of a steep hill, where a dozen vehicles remained wherever they'd been when the grid went down, some parked, some on their way up the entry drive, one SUV about to pull onto Grove Street.

The SUV was abandoned. Two doors left open, it patiently awaited its owner's return. Beatrice snapped one door shut on the way by, Tommy taking care of the other. It didn't matter if the doors were open or closed, not anymore, but they'd both nonetheless felt an urge to restore things to how they should have been.

"They didn't burn the church or wreck the cars," Dom said, surprised.

"Give it time," Larry huffed. "Another ten minutes and this place'll be torched like the rest of 'em."

Tommy had warned Beatrice about his latest vision – *yellow lights, the gasmen* – but they hadn't been able to move quickly. No one had wanted to leave Larry behind, even with the old man insisting that they drop the dead weight he added.

A few stops had delayed the walk maybe ten minutes, but they still had time, Tommy sensed. They could still get everyone out…if the other parishioners heeded his warnings. Beatrice had said she believed what Tommy and Dom told her about his visions and how they'd saved their lives, but the others might think he was insane. There didn't seem to be a way to describe it sanely, though, and so they would have to either believe him or die by their disbelief.

*Hopefully it's wrong. Please let this vision be wrong for once.*

Beatrice led them through the side door of the church, then down a flight of stairs to a basement cluttered with boxes and pews and stacks of old books. The power had gone out, forcing them to navigate by Beatrice's flashlight.

"There's another bunker access in the woods out back," she said, passing the elevator entrance and lifting a trapdoor hidden in the cement floor.

Tommy and Dom peered down from either side of the black square that had formed in the floor. A long fold-down ramp descended into darkness, a sweet chemical smell rising up at them.

"Christ, what the hell is that?" Larry said, coughing.

Tommy, a little lightheaded, experienced another layer of the vision. There were men with suits and canisters and bubble helmets. Vaguely resembling astronauts, they ran toward the church and through the doors, down into the basement.

"We shouldn't go down there," Tommy warned. "They might have beaten us here and pumped in the gas."

Larry was already retreating to the basement door. "Kid, you couldn't pay me to go into that shithole."

"We'll try the other entrance," Beatrice said, tears burgeoning. "If they only used the gas from out here, the bunker won't be affected."

"I don't feel right," Dom said once they were back outside. "Head hurts. Nauseous, too."

"Same here," Larry added. "Smelled like liquid adhesive."

They formed a circle in the parking lot. With the cold wind tossing about, they gradually felt a little better.

Larry crossed his arms. "Tell ya what, people, that shelter at the high school sounds pretty good right now."

Dom turned to Beatrice. "We should get to the shelter. There's no telling if it's safe down there. Your family and the others might have already moved on to Tantasqua."

"No, they wouldn't have left! My parents are down there!"

"She's right," Tommy agreed. "We can't leave them."

Dom's stomach dropped, the nausea returning. "Are you serious, Tommy? Just opening the door and that stuff messed us up. How are we gonna make it all the way down?"

"The other entrance," Beatrice insisted, starting toward the woods before turning back. "They have airtight doors down there."

Larry waved a hand and snapped the hood back over his misshapen head. "You're on your own, lady. I'll start ahead and you guys can catch up to me, assuming you don't drop dead in that toxic chamber." He grabbed Tommy's forearm. "Come on, pal, you can't be stupid enough to ignore what you saw. You said it got you this far, didn't you?"

"He's right," Dom said. "It's too big a risk."

Tommy's eyes shifted uncertainly between Dom and Beatrice. "Go with Larry to the school," he told his brother. "I need to help her do this."

Dom cemented his feet. "I'm not going anywhere without you, Tommy. For five years you were gone, kid. Don't ask me to leave you."

Tommy watched as Larry began hobbling down the hill toward the road. Maybe he'd get to Tantasqua by sunrise.

Maybe he wouldn't get there at all.

"Dom, he's gonna die if you don't go with him."

"I go where you go." Dom put an arm around Tommy's shoulders. "Live or die, we're sticking together."

The wind clattered against the church and rushed down the hill. For a moment Tommy thought he had a new vision trembling into form, but like an elusive fish it was gone with the bait.

Had there been a truck in that fleeting scrap of a vision? Suddenly Tommy couldn't separate his visions from imagination, and there was a stab of terrified self-loathing as he and Dom followed Beatrice into the woods, for he knew his decision might get his brother killed.

But the alternative, leaving Beatrice on her own to search the bunker for her parents, was intolerable. She was beautiful and immensely brave, but there was something infinitely more. It weakened and strengthened Tommy, lifted him up but simultaneously pulled him down. He thought of those marrow-melting scenes in movies where ropes are attached to four horses, each rope then tied to a victim's limb – and off the horses thundered in sprays of blood. Attempting to help Beatrice was like tying the first rope around his ankle, Tommy realized.

On they walked.

Dom tried to fight off fear that death would catch up to them this time. You can only steal so many bags before the catcher finally guns you down, he'd learned during an above average high school baseball career (which, in Massachusetts, pretty much meant you were terrible).

But once more they were getting their collective lead, studying the pitcher's moves, readying for another run, a new attempt, and that bastard catcher would come up firing. The fears were piling up like a heap of fisher cats on his back, Dom feeling slower beneath their weight. He could use a bottle of water…or vodka. And a shower. And Cyri lying in his arms.

*Where is she? What happened to her?*

"Pastor Thorne knew something like this would happen," Beatrice said. She held branches for them and warned of upcoming tripping hazards. The bouncing path of her flashlight made Tommy think of campouts and ghost stories and coyotes deciding whether to rip you apart or hunt an easier victim. "That's why he was so determined to get the funds for this bunker."

"How will we find it in the dark?" Tommy said, noticing for the first time a new sound above the wind: distant clinking.

"You follow the chimes," Beatrice replied, picking up the pace. A minute later, when the wind chimes became an orchestra above them and Beatrice's flashlight was shining upon a manhole cover, she said, "I can't thank you guys enough for staying with me."

Her fear-shaken voice sent a shudder through Tommy's chest. He experienced simultaneous urges, one to kiss her and the other to run from the woods with Dom. Ignoring both urges, he said, "It's no problem, really," as Beatrice kicked up leaves at the base of a tree and recovered a crowbar.

In a moment they were descending a fold-down ramp, sweat trickling coldly down Tommy's back. Below, the flashlight sprayed shadows about.

The gently declining ramp led them to a wide metal door. Overhead, a bank of lights clicked on automatically. Beatrice punched numbers into a recessed keypad and, with a whooshing jolt, the door slid open, revealing a brightly lit corridor.

There were no suspicious odors at this end of the bunker, the air as warm and lifeless as that of a parking garage.

"Jesus, how big is this thing?" Dom said.

"Pretty massive...and expensive." Beatrice leading the way, they ran through the slightly curving corridor. Tommy had expected perfunctory construction – images of earthen walls, scaffolding, and dim lamps coming to mind – but the concrete floor, walls, and ceiling testified to an endeavor of careful design and extensive funding. The lights were strong and evenly spaced. Further along, through another sliding door, the tunnel was ventilated with cool air, a motor humming distantly.

"This place must have cost millions," Tommy guessed.

"I'm telling you," Beatrice said, panting, "Pastor Thorne was convinced we'd need it one day. For a while the construction was so heavy we had to go to Brimfield for church."

She brought them through yet another passcode protected door, where a group of people occupied a well-furnished living space. It reminded Tommy of submarine movies, with tri-level bunks fastened to the walls and a bathroom at the far end, everything confined and claustrophobic. Off a wing to their left, a kitchenette was partially visible, and beyond it Tommy could see darkened opposing rooms, the doors propped open.

Beatrice raced across the main room and hugged a man and woman who were obviously her parents. They sat around a small circular table, her father in a wheelchair.

"Thank God you're okay, Bea!" Her mother clutched and rocked her. "What took you so long? We were about to send people to look for you."

"You never should have left," her father said. "Where's Matthias?"

# GRIDLOCKED

"He took off, told me he had to get to his sister," Bea said, then waved over Tommy and Dom, who'd been nodding uncomfortably at the less than inviting inhabitants of the bunker. As chary as Marco Polo participants in a small pool, none of them had taken a step toward the newcomers or maintained eye contact.

"This is Tommy and Dominick," Bea told her parents. "I met them in your neighborhood. The houses were all on fire – your house, too, it's just…gone. They're destroying everything."

Her parents recoiled as if slapped. Others murmured and whispered.

"It's like another world out there," Tommy said, shaking her parents' hands, the father's hand like a limp, clammy creation of clay. "They came with vans and shot Molotov cocktails into all the houses, but about twenty minutes later they put out the fires. This whole thing has been coordinated into detailed steps."

"Indeed. Indeed," came a spirited voice from behind them. A lanky, long-haired man emerged from the wing that opened to the kitchenette. He was smiling, eyes locked on Tommy. "Welcome, gentlemen. Thanks be given to Our Lord Jesus for your presence among us. You are safe now." He extended his hand to the Sims brothers. "I'm Timothy Thorne – *Reverend* Timothy Thorne, proud servant of this fine congregation of survivors. Please accept my invitation to join our humble house. Can I get you gentlemen some water, maybe a couple Cokes? There's enough food and water to last us all a week."

"Not enough weapons, though," Bea said, setting the shotgun on a bunk and slumping into a chair to the left of her mother. "Tommy, if your visions are right and we have to leave soon, we'll need way more weapons."

"What visions?" her mother said.

Tommy offered a condensed recap of the night, trying to inspire urgency by focusing on his latest sights from the middle. As he carried on, an uncanny familiarity crept over him, as if he'd given this very warning to this very group of people in his dreams. Even the room was suddenly familiar, and for a moment he thought he might remember the exact layout of the place like a guy stepping into his old high school.

Had this been the room from his vision? Yes, he was fairly certain it had been.

"There was a *chemical* smell at the other end of the bunker?" Thorne questioned.

Dom nodded. "It was real bad, made us lightheaded and nauseous. Somehow they knew you people were down here and tried to gas you. Clearly they haven't figured out how far the bunker goes, or how complex it is."

Thorne's eyebrows lifted. His slate-gray eyes flashed. "And what makes you so sure of that?"

"Because you're alive," Dom said. "But if you don't listen to my brother, it won't be for much longer." He turned to address the group. "Listen, everyone, they've got a shelter set up at Tantasqua. The authorities are getting families back together there, and we need to get to that school. Believe it or don't believe it, but right now my little brother's the best chance we've got. If we wait any longer here, this place will be our coffin."

# GRIDLOCKED

## Chapter 7

Death grins.

He can hear them on the other side of the door. They're telling each other to keep the faith, that things will get better – the predictable line of platitudes journeying on. Hearing such fear-driven remarks makes Death's tongue crave sweet blood. It makes his wings twitch with the need to soar into the night. He owns them all. He could kill them this second…break down the door and split their heads like watermelons, then chew on the seeds as they spill out.

Though Death cannot kill the child, an X of blood would taste lovely on her face, so much exposed skin to work with on this little creature, yes, yes, a canvas primed and ready for the rendering of the very first perfect X. She can already feel Death upon her, this child, more so than the others, an invisible X branded with every treatment and setback. The fear is already there, the seeds sown, and how riveting it would be to amplify her fear exponentially, to obliterate them all and leave the girl swimming in their blood.

Death drags his scythe down the length of the door, lightly, with the expert subtlety of another of his kind, the demon Kaad which now patrols the woods.

Kaad. What a pity it must be to never fly but instead to crawl-drag-twist-lurch. To each his own.

Death smiles at the door a moment longer. He aches to do it, to quench his thirst with their blood.

He steps back, still smiling, still facing the door as he backwardly climbs the stairs. He waits another moment, deciding.

"Not yet. Let's see them squirm," he whispers, chuckling at what he has discovered throughout the course of this observation, so much pain, so much blood, enough to satisfy the full range of his palate. "You're already dead, already mine."

## Chapter 8

"What was that?" Amie jolted up from her chair and faced the door.

"What?" her mother said.

"I heard something. It was scraping the door."

Her father stood, his face pinched with fear. "You think it's–?"

"The guy we saw." Jazzi spoke with quiet dread. "There's something wrong with him, really wrong."

"There's something wrong with everyone tonight," Grandpa Joe muttered. "Never thought I'd see a night gone this far to Hell."

Readying his gun, Dad took a few steps toward the door.

"Dad, don't," Amie urged.

"Listen to her, David," Mom agreed. "We're safe in here. You open that door and we're all exposed."

They were quiet for a long time. Amie was about to break the silence when, from the top of the stairs, they heard the cellar door slam shut.

Xeke studied the prisoners, wondering why Virgil had brought him back to the locker room. Every time Xeke turned, it seemed like Virgil was right there, watching him, measuring him.

Why? What did one kid matter, a grain of sand in the desert?

Virgil had left ten minutes ago, leaving Xeke and the others to watch the prisoners. Time passed at a torturous crawl. At the head of the room near the door, leaning back in a leather swivel chair, the old dustlord tasked with distributing the weapons was half asleep, his eyes fluttering open occasionally, accompanied by a snort. His hands were folded across his Grateful Dead T-shirt. At his feet, a collection of toothpicks had been discarded from his cracked lips.

To the dustlord's right, most of the locker doors were open; inside, a few rifles hung by their slings, the pistols stored in crates below. The lockers themselves were old and dinged, one of them spray-painted, a group of defunct units perhaps hauled up from the basement. Again Xeke wondered how Virgil and his people had managed to get everything coordinated so quickly. How long had it been since the grid went down? Five hours, maybe?

"This was bound to happen, if you ask me," came a new voice many minutes later.

Xeke's eyes shot open. Slumped against the wall, he couldn't believe he'd almost fallen asleep, himself.

A tall guy was standing over him. He wore jeans and a black leather jacket, a blue-collared shirt poking out beneath.

Xeke got to his feet, readied himself for a reprimand. He was fully prepared to tell the guy to fuck off, that he had no right to order him around, but there was no trouble forthcoming, only an offered stick of gum.

"I hate gum," Xeke said blandly, and the guy shrugged.

"Suit yourself, kid. I'm Randy, by the way. I'm a sergeant with the Brimfield Police Department." He glanced back toward the others, who were talking quietly or napping or staring blankly at the prisoners; deprived of torture as an option, it seemed all they could do was wait.

Randy nodded at Xeke. "Looks like you took a decent pop or two."

"It's nothing. I'll be fine."

# GRIDLOCKED

The prisoners, meanwhile, kept their heads low and their voices lower. Occasionally they glanced out at their captors, then went back to whispering, plotting. If Xeke were in charge, the bastards might well be back in the showers choking on water and fists, but Virgil had said no torture.

Xeke told his story after a little prodding, Randy offering obligatory remarks of sympathy before tracing back through his own night from Hell.

"Was going to my ex's house to pick up the kids, but halfway there my truck stopped dead in the road. By the time I got there on foot, my kids and their mother were gone."

Randy chewed his gum noisily, popping it like Xeke's mother did, a sound that always disgusted him, especially when he was trying to eat.

"Grid's a goddamn joke, kid. My chief drank the Kool-Aid just like the rest of them – said what they wanted him to say, statistics exploding out of his ass, for Christ's sake. But what about the night the grid gets hacked like everyone knew it would? All it takes is that one time and we're all screwed."

Randy sighed, took a breath. "*Now* look at the statistics," he said with gathering defeat. "My kids could be dead." A whispery quiet came into his voice. "Twelve and ten years old."

Xeke opened his mouth, but Randy would not be interrupted, his voice starting to break, his eyes misting. "I thought maybe my kids would be here, searched every inch of this place. These people keep barking out their commands – they want us to get in line and do our jobs like fucking communists." He moved in close. "Let me tell you something, kid, me and you should get out of here right now. What do you say? We both have family out there." He took a glance back. "I tried talking to some of these other guys, but half of them are fucktards, the other half too scared to leave. What do you say? You seem like a smart kid – can you use that weapon, or are you just holding it?"

Xeke felt like he was being pushed against a wall. Now that Randy was urging him to leave, it suddenly seemed like a terrible idea. "No…I mean, yeah. I can use it," he blundered. "I'm good with guns."

"Perfect," Randy snapped. "We could help each other out."

"What do you mean?"

"I mean, if someone tries to shoot you, I'll shoot him first. And the other way around. Our department's too small for me to have a partner – I'm used to working alone, but tonight four eyes are sure as hell better than two, right?"

"Right," Xeke heard himself say, but then his attention was rocketed away from Randy.

Handcuffed, three new prisoners were being led through the door, the dustpan old dude in the Grateful Dead T-shirt coming awake with the loudest snort yet.

The first prisoner was a Hispanic teenager who swore every other word. The second man was fortyish and fat, his face bloodied and dress shirt torn. The third person, initially unrecognizable behind the hood of his sweatshirt, was Dalton Rose, Xeke getting a look at his hockey teammate's face when Dalton glanced fearfully in his direction.

"I know that kid," Xeke whispered to Randy. "He goes to my school."

"Really? Then what the hell are they locking him up for?"

# GRIDLOCKED

Virgil joined the procession of men leading the latest prisoners toward the enclosure.

"Get back! Get back!" the first two tattooed gunmen shouted at those already in captivity behind the fences. The prisoners scrambled to the back wall like frightened chickens stacking up and suffocating themselves in the corner of their coop.

With arms as thick as firewood, the first pair of gunmen slid aside the makeshift fence sections, and the second pair shoved Dalton and the others in. The fences were then dragged back in place, followed by the issuance of warnings.

"There are no locks on these gates," Virgil said, his face iron. "Due to the suddenness of your attempted takeover, we weren't able to arrange proper prisons."

"Screw you!" shouted the oldest of the three new prisoners. (*Is that Dalton's uncle?*) His eyes were wide and shifting, his face flushed with rage. Behind him, Dalton was exceedingly pale, perhaps ready to piss through his paint-on jeans.

*Fucking toolbag.*

Xeke clenched the gun, remembering that December night sophomore year, wind-lashed snow spraying into his face, moonlight and shadows spilling across the driveway, hatred tightening its hold on his heart, Christmas lights painting a cheery picture for all who might have driven past. Xeke could have blasted Dalton away that night, could have made sure he bragged no more about hurting Amie, but the next morning he'd been weak again, tolerant, abiding of Dalton's bragfests, always bragging, that kid. He bragged about how many girls he banged. He bragged about his soccer successes. He bragged about his uncle's Hellcat, which Dalton claimed to drive on Route 49 late at night. (*Dude, I blazed the fucking grid at 150 – made cars look like they were in a parking lot!*)

Xeke hated Dalton, though the two had never said a disagreeable word to each other. And now here they were, on opposite sides of the fence.

"You'd be wise to refrain from acting on thoughts of escape," Virgil elaborated, pacing, his eyes wandering from one prisoner to the next. "My people are teeming with the need to blow your heads off. Believe me, I feel like a guy with ten psycho dogs and only eight leashes." Shrugging, he tapped the fences lightly. "These bars are keeping you boys alive. Try to break out, and my people are not only authorized but encouraged to open your heads up like Halloween jack-o-lanterns."

On his way out, Virgil nodded at Xeke and said, "Recognize someone?"

Xeke met him at the door. "How do you know?" he whispered.

Virgil's eyes brightened enigmatically. The faintest smile appeared as he patted Xeke's shoulder. "You really ought to read more, kid." Then he turned and strode off, Xeke resisting an urge to follow. He shook with the need to learn how Virgil knew him – he had to be one of Dad's friends, but how could someone Xeke had never seen before know so much about his life?

*Come on, think! A neighbor? A coworker?*

"Question that kid you know," Randy urged when Xeke returned. He pointed to the jail, where Dalton was sitting against the lockers and looking sullen, not a sliver different from how he usually looked in class or before hockey practice, constantly staring into his shifter, the hoodie keeping the world at bay.

"Is he your friend, or do you just know him?" Randy said. "This could be a chance to find out what's happening."

"We play on the same hockey team. He's a douche."

# GRIDLOCKED

"You think you can get something out of him?"

Xeke shrugged. "I can try."

"Yes, do it. Right now. Then we're getting out of here."

Xeke walked over to the fences – escorted by Randy through a group of guards – and stood in front of Dalton until he looked up.

"Xeke!" He stood, eyes drifting to Xeke's weapon. There was a scared half-smile then, Dalton's lips stretched into a wince. "You have to get us out of here. Tell them we have nothing to do with this."

"With what? What's going on?"

Dalton turned to the other guy. His uncle? Dalton lived with his uncle, not his parents; Xeke knew that much, thinking that maybe he'd seen the uncle a few times after practice, one of those Level Two business classer/flash passer dirtbags who paid to go faster than everyone else. With the grid you always knew the wealthy people and the politicians – the ones passing you, though recent legislative attempts had been made to include senior citizens and veterans in Level Two at no charge.

"Uncle Ed, this is Xeke Hamilton," Dalton said. "He's on my hockey team. Maybe he can help us get out of here."

Blood continued to leak from a gash on the uncle's left cheek, the sight of which made Xeke's own injuries briefly hurt a little worse.

"Dalton, why did they put you in here?" Xeke pressed.

"We didn't do anything. We were just–"

Dalton's uncle grabbed him by the shoulder. "Not another word," he warned, spinning Dalton away from the fence.

"But he can help us. He can tell them we didn't do anything." Dalton's voice was fragile and desperate.

"I said, not another word."

Behind Xeke, Randy and the others were getting impatient.

"He knows something."

"Yeah, he knows exactly what's going on."

"I say we beat it out of him. Virgil won't come back for a while."

"Yeah, do it, but not him. Take the kid. Then he'll talk."

This last voice belonged to Randy. Before Xeke could say another word to Dalton, the fences were dragged open again and guns were pointed in faces. The prisoners held up their hands and begged.

"Let me go, you fucking defects!" Dalton erupted as he was hauled up, the uncle smacked away by two gunmen.

Outside the jail, they shoved Dalton down hard, Randy the first to pounce on him. He pulled Dalton's sweatshirt over his head and let him flail for a moment, then kicked him in the stomach, inducing a groan but surprisingly not the salvo of tears Xeke greedily expected.

Randy tore off Dalton's sweatshirt and grabbed him by the hair, the others surrounding him like dogs intent on getting their pieces of meat.

"My kids could be dead because of you people!" Randy glared at Dalton's uncle. "You hear me, motherfucker? My kids could be dead, and now your kid's gonna get it! You better start talking!" The uncle was silent and sneering.

"You think I'm joking?" Randy slapped Dalton's cheek, then slapped him again, this time a quick backhand, still holding him by the hair. A third slap, and a fourth, Dalton's head wrenched in the direction of each blow.

Xeke felt a half-sick, half-sweet swell in his chest. A part of him pitied Dalton and wished an end to his abuse. A far greater part of him wanted to see Dalton pounded until the tears flooded – revenge long delayed.

"Do I need to start breaking fingers?" Randy threatened.

"Fine. You win." Dalton's uncle put both hands up. "Just let him go. I'll tell you everything."

# KEVIN FLANDERS

## Chapter 9

In a second floor classroom at Tantasqua High School, Gene watched people come and go.

He was hollowed out by what he'd seen. Crying this much had strained his chest and made his head and nose hurt.

He wondered if his grandmother was dead. So much blood after she was shot – and there'd been an emptiness in her eyes that had crushed Gene, made him feel like one of the pennies he and his father set on the railroad tracks each Saturday, returning on Sundays to search the rocks for glinting pancake slivers.

Gene wondered where his parents were, feeling a little sicker each time at the thought of them. Grandma had stayed with him while they worked late. Mom had promised to take him to the movies tomorrow. He wanted to see that scary movie his older cousins talked about, *House of Doom and Prosper*, but that was rated R and Gene was only eight. He would have to wait forever to see a movie that scary, but nothing in the movies could surpass the fear that was his custodian tonight.

The man. Shuddering, Gene touched his bandaged forehead, the pain much less now. The nice lady, Mikaela, had fixed him up and given him medicine, and Rock had brought food for him.

Gene pulled from his pocket the cross necklace Tommy had given him. He clutched it, remembering. Tommy and Dom and Rock were nice – Gene was glad they'd found him out there and not the man. The idea of him flying about the night – swooping out of darkened woods and rising up to rooftops, landing with a sound scarcely louder than a fallen leaf – brought a sharp pinch to Gene's bowels.

From a creaky cot outfitted with one pillow, sheets, and a thin blanket, Gene watched more people coming and going, many of them kids accompanied by grownups. There were a lot of kids in this room,

# GRIDLOCKED

and even a few babies, too. Gene settled back against the pillow. He was tired, but he knew he couldn't sleep, not with so many people around and fear looming over him like a nightmare fiend. What if the man came in and found him? Everyone had said he'd be safe, but the man had said he would find him anywhere – and he could fly.

No one here could fly.

Waiting for Rock to return (he'd promised to be back soon), Gene kept his eyes on the door and thought a little about how a man could fly. Those wingsuit guys were all over TV, but this man hadn't been wearing a suit, only a robe and hood. And he hadn't jumped from a high place and soared but instead launched himself like a rocket.

Gene bit his fingernails. Mom said it was bad to bite your nails, but Gene couldn't stop himself. It was all he could do to keep from crying again.

"He tried to get in, but he can't," Jazzi said, the slamming of the door upstairs still rattling in her bones. She was as terrified as she'd ever been, even when she was told she had leukemia, even during the worst nights when she'd wondered if there would be no sunrise for her the next day but instead…whatever there is before you're born…Heaven, Sena said, a perfect place where people live before and after their journeys in this world.

Jazzi fought the tears. Sena had been dragged away by the uniformed men and put into another car, probably taken to another jail. Was she in Heaven now?

Jazzi tried to focus on what Amie and her family were saying, something scary about the radio which Jazzi didn't understand – a weird transmission that kept repeating the same emergency broadcast about radiation and needing to seek shelter immediately. Amie's dad said the transmission had been interrupted on three occasions by a new voice rising above the static fuzz and dentist drill whine, a strange rasping voice that in no way resembled the robotic emergency transmission voice. Amie's dad was confident that the intruding voice had demanded the same thing all three times, enunciating each word into its own sentence: "Give. Me. The. Girl."

But when Mr. Valenzuela had taken his headphones off and turned up the volume, the rest of them had only heard the emergency notifications and static.

SEEK UNDERGROUND SHELTER IMMEDIATELY. THIS IS NOT A DRILL. RADIATION LEVELS CONTINUE TO INCREASE. AT GREATEST RISK ARE RESIDENTS OF MISSOURI, ILLINOIS, ARKANSAS, KENTUCKY, AND TENNESSEE...

Fear pounded in Jazzi's head and twisted tighter in her chest, a fear deep enough to drown in.

*Where are you, Sena?*

They'd been on their way home from a treatment, Sena trying to distract Jazzi with talk of their shopping day tomorrow.

Jazzi looked briefly to the ceiling. *Are you with God?*

They were arguing now, Amie's family, making the fear even deeper and darker for Jazzi.

"We can't stay here," Amie's father said. "There's countless reports of them burning houses. Plus, that guy knows we're down here – he'll bring more people and they'll come for us."

"And what do you suggest?" Mrs. Valenzuela said, almost yelling. "We'll be killed if we go out there."

Amie came to Jazzi's side and took her hand. She offered a little smile that shallowed the fear somehow. "We'll get through this," Amie said, squeezing her hand, and Jazzi could no longer keep back the tears.

# GRIDLOCKED

When the arguing stopped, a brief silence was interrupted by the thudding of footsteps upstairs. With four words lodged in her head, words that had insisted over the radio, Jazzi knew with near certainty what had inspired the intruder's search.

The man. He had come for her!

## Chapter 10

Paul felt cold and vacant.

With Steel to his right, he patiently followed what had become a steady trail, the nooses hanging somewhere behind them, the sun indecisive on whether it wanted to peek through the clouds or hide.

Paul sought shelter in the stories as he walked. But many of those stories, he now realized, had been harbingers of a storm.

"Of course it's not a damn surprise!" Mr. Lefebvre had railed one fresh spring day, Steel later advising Paul to get his jacket washed at the next host's house, for Mr. Lefebvre had been a bona fide saliva spewer.

The question that had elicited Mr. Lefebvre's impassioned response, asked sincerely – not from a deceitful angle intended to produce a certain answer – had been, "Did it surprise you that AVA was passed so quickly?"

Mr. Lefebvre had proceeded to describe a government as stable as a pen balancing on a finger. The latest shutdown had endured as the water wars flared up across the southwest…and then AVA had been pushed through, nothing but positive news forthcoming, money infused into the system like a shot of adrenaline when people prepaid for Level Two travel.

Following AVA's passage, water had been delivered to the thirsty almost overnight, the wars temporarily put down, Providence Devlin extolled as a hero. Tunnels had been dug with the speed and tenacity of ant colonies, each state with its own planned SR network. Government approval ratings had soared. Grant monies had been disbursed as readily as change tossed into a fountain. Promises had been made of highway trips cut in half.

But…

# GRIDLOCKED

"Never trust politicians who turn their backs on the people who elected them," Mr. Lefebvre had said, a rather surprising statement at a time when AVA was thriving, people free to do whatever they wanted while their vehicles safely transported them: catch up on work, eat, sleep, watch movies, shoot video game zombies and build video game kingdoms, form their fantasy football rosters, eat some more, and, in the casket-dark tunnels of the SR systems, engage in other forms of entertainment, all while, on a glowing screen up front, a red dot inched along a green line.

For a blind man, it had all been impossibly tantalizing, Paul wanting desperately to see what the country had done with itself. Shifters that could be "maximized" nearly to the length of a tennis racket and then "minimized" to wallet size? Printers that could provide you with a new wardrobe overnight? Paul had touched and even sniffed a few of the innovations, but sight was the ultimate proof, damn it. Otherwise it could all be a joke, a cruel joke.

Paul went on remembering the stories people had shared with him. So many stories of inspiration and tragedy and triumph…a man with stage-four colon cancer forsaken by his insurance company, forced to live out of his car. The community had raised $60,000 for him in a month. A stranger had offered her guest house to him.

…An elderly woman who, with the help of a few benevolent backers, had turned a decades-defunct psychiatric hospital into a leading veterinary clinic and rescue center, with dozens of acres dedicated to equine rehab and two new buildings constructed for emergency care.

…A child who'd known only the reflection of deformity, and yet her singing and laughter had been like Heaven's music, Steel describing a smile as bright as a summer afternoon.

…A grandmother who'd lost her house to a fire, her entire neighborhood coming out the next week to build her a new one.

There were people who said the country was crumbling. There were people who painted everything black and, when they were in a good mood, brushed in a few strokes of gray. But there was so much good out there, Paul had discovered, persistence and kindness and selflessness, all of these colors to be revealed if you turned off the news channels and went street by street to learn how it really was.

Tonight, however, the nation's strength had met its ultimate test. Tonight, even the stoutest walls of fortitude might fall.

Paul was just about to stop to rest when they topped another hill – and there it was down below, Route 49, a sign right there to prove it.

Steel, desperate to free himself from the woods, had started down toward the road when he glanced left and saw a fleet of eighteen-wheelers coming.

"Back, get back!" Steel and Paul ducked behind a tree and watched as the first five trucks, all flatbeds, ripped northbound, stacks of mangled vehicles piled up high.

Multiple car carriers followed, each with a full load of damaged yet salvageable vehicles. Then came an empty flatbed, which pulled into the northbound shoulder down below, just ahead of a cluster of ruined vehicles.

The operator, a burly, bearded guy in a flannel shirt (some things never change), climbed out of his truck and came around front. "Got a fine smashup, boys. Podunk Pike North, mile 4.1," he said over the radio.

Paul, with his superb hearing, didn't miss a word. Steel heard none of it over the rumbling engine.

The trucker was laughing now. "Yes, sir, gotta love this brave new world. Sounds like a nice little setup you got there. I'm not quite that fancy – they've got us lined up for Minnesota in the summers, South Carolina in the winters. Could do worse, right?"

"What's he saying? Can you hear it?" Steel asked.

"Tell you later."

Quick as a cat after a squirrel, the trucker yanked a gun out of his belt and pointed it in their general direction. Had he somehow heard them all the way up here? Paul receded instinctively, then realized they hadn't been seen, the trucker resuming his conversation.

Steel pulled two pistols from his backpack, Paul arming himself as well. "Motherfucker," Steel whispered. "I should end him and take his truck – it could be a manual!"

Paul shook his head. "There's more trucks coming," he said, afraid of the intensity in Steel's eyes, almost grateful for the onrushing procession of car carriers and flatbeds, an SUV with fully tinted windows sprinkled in.

A flatbed rigged with a crane arrived a short time later, and the process of lifting vehicles onto the first truck commenced. Two men in dress suits who'd gotten out of the crane truck were now talking with the bearded operator of the first truck. Paperwork was exchanged. There was a small cooler involved, and soon they all had a can of Coke. Pull tabs were cracked. Swigs were had. The three of them nodded curtly at each other once the cans were crunched underfoot, the work progressing around them.

After the massacred vehicles were carefully stacked onto the flatbed, the entourage continued north, now joined by two black humvees with gunners poking through the rooftops.

"What the fuck is going on?" Steel kicked a rock against the tree. "I swear, the next truck that comes by I'm commandeering. No more walking – I'm done with this shit."

Paul fished a bottle of water out of his pack. He tried to think of something that would change Steel's mind, but there was nothing, only the cold realization that the enemy was getting stronger.

*It's controlling these people. They're all driverless.*

Paul drew in a deep, shaky breath, knowing they couldn't survive by hiding and scuttling. There was no hope of evading their way back to Chicago. They would only get home if they stopped dodging and fought.

## GRIDLOCKED

### Chapter 11

Even when Reverend Timothy Thorne directed the pistol at them, Tommy didn't register the danger. In fact, he thought the guy was delivering a bizarre joke.

"I'm afraid I can't let you leave," Thorne said, unsmiling, and then it hit Tommy like waves crashing over a seawall. The pastor was serious. If they tried to leave, he'd shoot them.

Thorne wagged the gun at them, even his parishioners. "Stay exactly where you are, all of you! Move an inch and you're toast, got it?" He chuckled thinly. "You don't want to make me nervous with this thing. I'll end up kneecapping someone, and then you'll wish I'd shot you in the head."

Beatrice was speechless. Gaping, she could only stare at her pastor with dark incredulity as he hurried over and confiscated her shotgun from the bunk.

"Any other weapons?" he demanded, returning to the center of the room after recovering two more firearms.

Rage boiled through Dominick, directed not only at Thorne but Beatrice. She'd brought them down here, and now this long-haired, sunken-eyed psycho was lining them up. The guy was like a broomstick with clothes draped over it, a methlord transvestite doppelganger of Howard Stern. If not for the gun, Dom would break him in half.

"Tim, what are you doing?" Beatrice finally said, some of the others questioning him as well.

Thorne looked in all directions with the wariness of a pre-grid elderly lady reversing out of a parking space. "Now, let's all just calm down and let me explain," he said.

"How about you explain why you're pointing a gun at us?" Dom countered.

Thorne stumbled over a chair when he took a few backward steps, recovering with a sweep of the arm that got everyone ducking and shouting.

"Better put that gun away before you kill someone, Tim!" an old guy hollered. "What're you doing with that thing anyhow? You just let these fellas be on their way now."

Thorne shook his head adamantly. "I can't do that. If they leave, that puts us all at risk. Someone could see them and figure out where they came from. Next thing you know, everyone will be trying to get at us."

"They already know we're down here," Tommy said.

"No. You're lying."

"Why would I lie about that?"

"Just stay back, man!"

Tommy hadn't been aware of his approach. He'd drawn to within twenty feet of his captor.

Thorne brought both hands to his head, the gun pointed toward the ceiling. He seemed about as sure of himself as a chipmunk on the double-yellow line. There was an urge to rush him, but Tommy let it taper away, far too risky.

Instead, he backed away from Thorne. "Just think this through, guy. Why would you want two more mouths to feed?"

"We'll be fine at least a week."

"But the shelter at Tantasqua," Dom said. "We'll all be safer there."

Thorne stomped a black leather boot down hard. "We're not going to the shelter!"

Tommy whispered in his brother's ear. "We'll get out of here – just don't do anything crazy."

"Hey! Hey! What are you saying?" Gripping the pistol with both hands, Thorne trained it on them as best he could, though it shook wildly and probably wouldn't shoot straight if God's own hands tightened around the pastor's hands.

"Just let 'em go, damn it!" the old guy chimed. "I didn't come down here for this, Tim. We're better off out there if this is gonna be a dictatorship."

Others murmured in agreement. Sensing a possible mutiny, Thorne ordered everyone to their bunks. "I *will* shoot you," he warned after the initial group refusal. "This is about the survival of the congregation. As the guardian of this bunker, I am responsible for the group at large. If pruning a branch or two saves the tree, Lord as my witness, I'll do it."

That got people moving. They grumbled and huffed as they took their bunks, a few of them standing near the bunks in a mild act of disobedience. There were about a dozen children in the bunker, and most of them were crying. A teenage girl was in tears as well. Two teenage boys, meanwhile, stared forth with scared amazement.

Thorne nodded twitchingly at the Sims brothers, then pointed to a pair of unoccupied bunks in the far left corner. Beatrice and her parents protested, but Thorne put his palm up and shook his head like an umpire ready to eject someone from a game. "Enough already! How can I think with everyone badgering me?"

Tommy studied Thorne as he paced. The way his eyes shifted and his head jittered, the way he seemed to be engaged in a silent strife with himself – it was almost as if he were being tugged in opposite directions by invisible forces. Clearly he was afraid of something far greater than Tommy and Dom giving them away by leaving.

"I think Thorne knows what's going on out there," Tommy whispered a while later, after Thorne had left his fat, greasy-haired teenage son, Logan, in charge of the pistol and then disappeared into one of the back rooms.

Logan was a typical techno-teen, unable to keep a firm eye on anything but his devices, the kind of kid who would use texting abbreviations in his English essays. The kind of kid who, in a few years, would saddle his parents with paying off his college loans while he spent nonemployed days gaming and talking politics on social media, his diploma gathering dust on a shelf somewhere, evidence of the tireless work he put into attaining a philosophy/creative writing/Thai cuisine degree.

At the moment Logan was peering into his shifter, the gun in his lap, though he looked up every few seconds to make sure no one was coming at him.

"We need to get out of here," Dom urged. "Now's our chance, before Thorne gets back. I say we charge the kid – he doesn't look like he could shoot anything but his load."

Logan looked over at them, suspicious. There were words ready on his tongue, but they didn't fall, his eyes returning to his device.

"Let's wait," Tommy insisted, sensing an imminent vision. It had been building these last few minutes, flashing things too quickly into his head. If he could just slow it down, then maybe…but now Beatrice was coming over, looking miserable.

# GRIDLOCKED

She took Tommy's hand. "I'm so, so sorry. I don't know what's wrong with him—"

"Hey!" Logan snapped, his face scrunched into a petulant scowl. "You're not supposed to leave your bunk." "Shut the fuck up, kid."

Spurts of chuckling across the room. Murmurs. Whispers. Sniffles. A few more tears from the children.

Bea's words had iced Logan over, and now he could only blink, stunned, searching for a retort that wouldn't come. Sulkily, he returned to his shifter.

"We're getting out of here," Bea whispered. "All of us. I just talked to my parents – they have a plan."

## Chapter 12

"I think all of these wall sections we keep hearing about are eventually gonna be connected," Amie's father said, removing his headset.

Despite multiple reports of entire neighborhoods burning, they'd decided to stay in the basement a while longer, too fearful of who might be waiting for them upstairs or outside. Manning the radio, Dad had made contact with dozens of people over the last hour while Amie, her mother, and Jazzi played cards with a Red Sox-themed deck they'd found in one of the drawers.

Exhausted, Amie's grandparents were seated on the old sofa in the corner, a blanket spread over them, Grandpa's legs resting on a hassock.

Everyone's attention latched onto Dad when he elaborated on the subject of the wall.

"People in Arizona, New Mexico, Kansas, Alabama, and Arkansas have all seen walls going up," Dad said. "They're already up to twenty feet in some places, and things are only getting worse." He made his hands into a pyramid, elbows on the chair's armrests, and brought his chin down against his fingertips. "I don't know how much longer I can listen to this before it drives me insane."

"A wall," Mom murmured. "Is that because of the water wars, you think?"

Dad shook his head. "I think it goes well beyond that. There've been more reports of heavy train traffic, most of it southbound. People are being loaded up and brought to states south of the wall, and everyone else they're just killing. But what would possess them to transport certain people down there?"

Dad showed them a map of the country, dots marking the locations from which reports of wall construction had come, a curving black marker having connected them. The result was a parabola, the low points in Alabama and Arizona, the approximate vertex situated at a little town in central Kansas. There were allegedly gunmen guarding every wall under construction, keeping people in and out like a scene from Berlin.

With each of her father's reports, Amie felt jolts of rage and disbelief and fear. Yet even after everything she'd endured, there was an unreal, movielike quality to the night that kept her from fully accepting that such a catastrophe could happen in the U.S. Safe for now at home with her family, an appreciable layer of insulation from the chaos had formed – to the extent that it seemed like the man she'd shot had been the inhabitant of a nightmare.

But whenever her thoughts turned back to Xeke, reality came crashing down on her like a doomed gantry. Xeke was out there, and she was in here. It wasn't fair. What if he was…no, she wouldn't even think it. Just the idea stole her breath.

But what if he really was gone? Even if he'd made it, what if they never saw each other again?

Xeke stood in the shower block, pistol in hand. Dalton was kneeling on the tiles before him, bloodied yet still not stripped of a smirk. His hands were cuffed, his ankles bound with rope, his eyes a strangely translucent green which betrayed his fear but also something else. It was almost as if some maddened part of his mind was enjoying this.

Randy had taken Xeke aside and given him instructions. "Tell him all he has to do is be honest and no further harm will come to him," Randy had said. "Meanwhile, I'll work the uncle and we'll see if we get the same story."

A moment later they'd hauled Dalton up, Randy splitting his lip, but still Dalton hadn't broken down and cried, Xeke wanting very much to see him cry, an inexplicable desire creeping closer to a thirst.

"He's all yours, Xeke," Randy had said, and the others had gotten raucous, dragging Dalton by the legs and shouting: "Fuck him up, kid," and "Kneecap him if you have to," and "Give me a go at him – I'll make him talk."

"Xeke, get me out of these cuffs, man! Give me a fair fight – I'll knock those defects out!" Dalton's beseeching stare made initial progress, but Xeke's fleeting pity shifted to a darkling joy. It jittered beneath his skin, in his bones, made him even more thirsty for Dalton's tears.

Xeke said nothing, concentrated on not smiling, not yet, but how could he force back a smile when Dalton Rose was on his knees and begging him? Dalton, who always bragged; Dalton, who was beyond reproach, even when he showed up late to practice; Dalton, who claimed he made thousands by 3D-printing and selling drugs; Dalton, who'd gloated about boofing Lexi Underwood while she was blackout drunk at a summer party and then pissing on her, most guys laughing him off as a bullshitter, but then Lexi had switched schools in the fall of sophomore year, rumors circulating about her going to Leicester High on school choice, other rumors filing in about her being homeschooled. Dalton, who'd later made claims about Amie, his words leaving Xeke sleepless on a frigid December night. Shaking and near septic, food turning acidly in his stomach, Xeke had been shattered almost to tears for the girl who was his childhood friend, and there'd been no one to tell because the pain was too much and all the others had done was laugh, laugh, laugh at her.

The hatred came steadily over Xeke like a sickness, and suddenly he was taken back to that night with Dad's gun in the driveway. He could have killed Dalton that night, could have shot him in the head and murdered him, maybe could have shot himself as punishment for his weakness, or scraped himself skinless on the salt-crusted driveway, preferable to hearing Amie's name torn and trampled and left to the vultures again. But now everything was different, so much different. Dalton really was at his mercy, not a dream, not a fantasy.

This was real. Xeke had a gun. Dalton was defenseless.

"You're a piece of shit," Xeke heard himself say, his eyes widening, his skin icing over.

Fear shined wildly into Dalton's eyes. "W..*what*?" His voice was small, kiddish.

"You heard me."

Dalton spat blood onto the tiles and put his cuffed hands out in front of him, as if he were a panhandler and Xeke had a few coins of mercy ready to toss. "Please, man," he rasped, his eyes gleaming with tears that refused to fall. "Are you really gonna be their bitch?"

For a surreal moment Xeke was lost in an entirely new headspace, feeling briefly detached from his body and yet trapped within it at the same time. The lights dimmed a little, shadows edging in along the walls. Xeke detected the gentlest of nudges from behind and an invisible hand upon his own, guiding him, and then he was steadying the gun, pointing it at Dalton, not thinking anymore, vacuous with hatred, revenge a trigger pull away, but he wasn't even thinking about revenge, just staring, leaning in closer, smiling mindlessly, lifting away from himself, sound and sight losing clarity.

The next few moments were a blur of shadows and distant voices, but with a lurch it all came frantically and confusedly back to Xeke. The muzzle was in Dalton's bloody mouth, wiggling, Xeke's finger on the trigger. Too much time had been lost. Things were different, too different. What the hell was this?!!? He'd forced his teammate into a corner, Dalton gurgling and shaking, his hands held up in futile defense.

Xeke ripped the weapon away with crimson drips, feeling a scrape-clack of resistance as it left Dalton's mouth. Xeke took a few stunned steps back. It was like he'd been sleepwalking, vestiges of a dream still lingering like embers – *Do it! Shoot him! Give him a good piss shower, too!* the first voice had urged. Xeke remembered these words unreliably, in the way that one might remember words spoken to him during a somnolent early morning state, but nevertheless they were present. *Your pretty mouth doesn't look so good, Dollface, but look, his hands are as fine as ever,* another voice had clanged. *Better call the dentist – you've been blitzed!* came a third voice.

Moaning, glued to the corner, Dalton spewed blood and fragmented teeth, rich streams running down his chin. His eyes were a sickeningly dilated portrait of horror and misery.

*Jesus, what did I do?*

Xeke checked the gun, its muzzle still dripping, his left index finger slicked red as well.

*Do you like it in the mouth, Dollface? Do you want a Coke to make it all better?* a new voice taunted, counterpointed with screams.

"Fuck you!" Xeke thought he heard Dalton shout, blood and tooth chips gushing, but the words were as gurgly and meaningless as those of an underwater conversation.

And still there were no tears.

Dumbstruck, Xeke allowed Randy to escort him from the shower block. "What the hell happened, kid? Christ, what did you do to him?"

"I...I don't know, I just lost it." Xeke handed off the gun, needing to free himself of it.

# GRIDLOCKED

In a moment Dalton was dragged back in, his uncle raging against the fences when he saw his nephew's condition.

"Shut yo ass up, or I'll rip yo ears off, boy," a guard threatened, and the uncle went abruptly quiet. "That shit ain't nothing compared to what I'd do."

Randy, meanwhile, produced a pocketknife and asked two men to hold Dalton still, for he was thrashing like a sheep in a coyote's jaws, his watery bleats grinding in Xeke's heart like ingredients subjected to mortar and pestle.

"Fuckin-A, Xeke, this isn't Gitmo. I should have done this myself," Randy complained, then came behind a kneeling Dalton and secured his neck in the crux of an elbow. "Start talking!" he ordered the prisoners. "Otherwise I'm gonna cut off his fingers until I hear something that sounds like the truth."

Xeke staggered into a corner and finished off the alcohol in his possession. But his hands couldn't be stilled, and he kept getting little bursts of memory, his treatment of Dalton making him feel cold with guilt.

*I almost killed him. Fuck, I almost goddamn killed him! I'm a psycho, a scrambler – I should be the one behind bars.*

"That's all I know, okay? You've gotta believe me," Dalton's uncle was saying. "I'm not with these guys. I've never seen them before in my life."

"Horseshit," one of the prisoners mumbled.

"Try again," Randy said with vitriolic calm, and he took Dalton's right hand and snapped back one of the fingers with a brutal crack, unleashing a dry shriek.

"I'm telling the truth, I swear on my life! Please, just stop, leave him alone!"

Another crack, Dalton's shredded mouth flapping into an agonized rictus. But still no tears, Xeke discovering in that moment the depth of his teammate's fortitude.

*Shit, why can't they break him?*

"We paid for protection," one of the oldest prisoners finally admitted, emerging from the group. Several men tried to push him back, warned him to shut up, but he stepped through. "We knew this was coming, okay? You win. Just don't hurt that poor kid any more."

"Now was that so hard?" Randy nodded to his men. "Bring him out, guys. If anyone tries to stop you, shoot them."

# GRIDLOCKED

## Chapter 13

Death plummets beneath the overpass, then lifts back up to the tracks, where he glides a few feet above the rails.

Accelerating, rising higher, swinging back around to the lake, fires outlining the shore, the little houses ablaze. Indeed, it is a joy to witness, but for the first time Death senses the window beginning to close as this great war sees a decided advantage taken.

Time to finish the job.

## Chapter 14

"You sure this isn't the best way imaginable to get ourselves killed?" Paul said.

They were hidden beyond the northbound shoulder of Route 49, behind a tree, waiting. A few more trucks had lumbered past, their operators unaware of the plan developed by two men who'd inhaled the toxic air of desperation for far too long.

"It's the only way." Steel was feeling better now, like he was in control of himself again. "I'd rather fight than spend another second in there." He glanced back into the deeper woods, half-expecting another glimpse of darting, unnatural movement. "Whatever's in these woods, it's a hell of a lot worse than anything they could throw at us."

Paul peeked out from behind the tree and looked down the road, searching for an unaccompanied vehicle to emerge from the horizon so they could actuate their half-baked plan.

The waiting nearly made Paul sick. He'd said his prayers and tried to ready himself, but it was like trying to prepare for an NBA game when you've never made a basket outside intramurals and adult leagues. There was no preparation for this. When teetering on the edge of suicide, it's best to not have any thoughts at all, he decided, wishing he could shut off his brain.

As if God Himself were offering a warning, Route 49 remained empty for several minutes. Paul wondered if they'd been forsaken, left to plod along the road like lost pets – or was this God's way of protecting them from their own stupidity?

The carousel making another rotation, Paul thought of all they'd endured and once again arrived at **TRIBULATIONS**. But hadn't his life since high school been a series of tribulations?

# GRIDLOCKED

*Why us, Lord?*

Paul heard the whisper just then, distant yet direct, the wind perfectly still. "Colder," it said, dark clouds sweeping over the treetops like a stage curtain, moving at a speed that defied nature, as if the sky were a rapids river and the clouds were rafts tumbling helplessly along.

Steel saw the northbound truck first. At the edge of vision, it appeared to be standing still. "We've got a drone landing," he said, Paul going cold.

It was like they'd been teleported into a war zone but worse, a surreal place whose creator had selected them as the subjects of an experiment. In the woods waited a pair of nooses, among other evils – Options? Exits on this terrible highway? – and out here the road had transformed hideously into a battlefield.

The truck shimmered with the mirage-like quality of distance, impossible for a few moments to tell what came behind it. Paul felt as though a fireplace poker, glowing hot, had been thrust through his chest. He focused on each leaden step, tried to remember the specifics of the plan, but suddenly he couldn't think, could hardly even move, too scared with the truck accelerating and enlarging.

"Down! Stay low!" Steel reminded, and Paul angled out behind him toward the road.

Soon they stood abreast, Steel leveling his weapons on the truck, an eighteen-wheeler closing fast, the hum of its motor a death promise.

"Ready?" Steel shouted. "Remember, aim and focus!"

The truck slowed considerably. "What's that?" Paul said, but he wasn't watching the road, his head lifted.

Steel heard the rumbling a few moments later, the truck continuing to brake ahead of them. He was ready to shoot, but this latest threat sent him into panic. "Get off the road!"

They'd barely made it back to the woods when the helicopter's shadow crossed over them, as black as a midnight corridor. A torrent of bullets shredded into the woods with the sound of birds departing a cornfield. Five feet to their right, a rock exploded into dust.

Steel pulled Paul down against a tree and they huddled there, crouching as the gunfire faded, the chopper's roar subsiding, but then it swung back around, so low that they could feel the cold air funneled down by the rotors.

The helicopter hovered almost directly above them, Steel thinking maybe they would attempt a landing.

Paul squeezed his eyes shut and prayed. There was no additional gunfire, but the thought of the gunners tracking their heat signatures through the trees scrambled Paul enough to leave him mumbling: "Jesus, save us."

Finally, like a wasp with better things to do than continue harassing its target, the pilot decided they weren't worth more time and ammunition. The helicopter banked north and did not return, Paul so relieved that he forgot about the truck.

Steel was pointing his gun through the trees at the stopped truck, an empty flatbed. It had advanced much closer, and Paul could hear people creeping through the woods with the stealth of hunters, slowly approaching.

*Jesus, we're dead! They're gonna shoot us dead!*

# GRIDLOCKED

Paul didn't even think to grab the weapon at his feet, paralyzed by a fear as absolute as that of a freefaller accelerating toward death. He kept his head down, prayers abounding.

Just out of sight, the truckers steadily progressed, pushing through branches and underbrush. One of them took a series of shots, clearing the woods of winged creatures and causing Paul to lurch back against the tree.

But then the truckers turned south, away from them, crunchy footsteps betraying their movements.

There were more people out there, though, new footsteps rustling the leaves and heading in the direction of the others.

*How many more? Five? Ten? They won't stop until–*

Another burst of gunfire echoed in waves that crashed against the trees and skittered dutifully back to the point of origin. Paul glanced at Steel, and realized with breathless incredulity that he was alone, his guide having left him.

*No. He wouldn't. He'd never leave.*

More crunching footsteps a minute later, this time quickly approaching from the north.

Risking a backward glance beyond the tree, Paul was stunned by what he discovered. Like a victorious western hero passing through the saloon doors following a shootout, Steel shoved through the young pines with a grinning swagger.

"Looks like we just got ourselves a ride," Steel said.

Paul's mouth fell open. "W…*what?*"

Steel shrugged. "I finished them. And it felt fucking great."

## Chapter 15

Xeke sat in the far corner of the locker room, his head against the wall. In quieter times, as now, the constriction of fear brought pain to his chest and stomach. His parents and Amie dominated these fears, but everyone took a little piece of the pie...his cousins and uncles and aunts, his friends at school, his dog, even dusty old Grandma Hilly, who always forced him to eat the plungelick foods she brought for holidays (Dad occasionally recounted a story predating Xeke's existence of how Grandma had accidentally mixed cat food into her chicken salad, then screamed for everyone to stop eating midway through their Thanksgiving meal, though this was a story for straighter times, not when people were massacred and life was beyond scrambled – blendered).

"Fucking blendered."

Xeke's words were flat and fraught with disbelief, induced not only by the night in general but how it had changed him. He couldn't get Dalton's bloody, ruined mouth out of his head, the kid's once perfect teeth now resembling a smashed piano keyboard – and then Dalton had been hauled away screaming by two of the thug guards, his uncle begging.

And what was being done to Dalton Rose now?

Xeke told himself it was deserved. *Karma*, he thought. *Not my problem.* Dalton was a dick – evil, really, the things he did to girls, treating them like inanimate objects he could use for whatever he wanted and then discarding them. Dalton didn't care about who he hurt or how, and it didn't seem to matter to anyone else that he hurt people with impunity.

But now, finally, it was Dalton's turn to pay. He was obviously involved with the people responsible for all of this, or else he wouldn't have been apprehended along with his uncle in the first place. He deserved this, damn it…but why did the thought of Dalton being dragged out of the locker room make Xeke nauseous?

*He's evil, but so am I. I'm just as bad as him.*

Xeke gritted his teeth. He felt overwhelmed, possibly on the verge of a breakdown. He didn't understand what was happening and why it was happening and who the hell these people were. He didn't understand what would drive them to tank the grid and take prisoners and send the country to shit. He didn't even understand his own heart and what had blackened it when he was alone with Dalton, a gun in hand and that feeling creeping over him, returning him to that night in the driveway.

There was an urge to slam his fists into the lockers, rage the only recourse by which he could temporarily escape his torment.

Reports from the four ends of the country and in between quickly began to reflect others. Accounts were corroborated. The grid had been intentionally shut down. The nation had been set on fire and then partially extinguished. A wall was going up. People were being loaded in boxcars and autoracks, crammed in until the doors barely shut. Those who refused to board the trains were shot. Children and the elderly and the sick and the disabled were tossed in rivers, sometimes burned alive. Suicides were soaring.

These were the most prominent diamonds on the fabric, but what about the little stitches that connected them, uniting a million insanities and atrocities into a single tapestry?

Several facilities nationwide had been surrounded by guards for reasons that apparently did not include imprisonment, a stream of buses and limousines and armored vehicles permitted to enter. The majority of these vehicles, sources said, had been seen arriving at the facilities a few hours before the grid shut down. Moreover, multiple people had been spotted with luggage.

"Somehow these people knew about what would happen – an elite few – and they were prepared for it," Dad said.

Mom threw her hands up. "So, what, the millionaires get together one day and decide they want to burn down the country, go underground for a while, and start fresh?"

Dad gulped down water and tossed the bottle aside. "Maybe they view the rest of us as a threat to their continued luxury. Or maybe they got brainwashed into thinking a mass deportation will make them safer."

"Maybe they finally got tired of increased taxes," Grandpa said with a hopeless smile, Amie recoiling because she'd never seen her grandfather in such a frenzied state. He'd gotten up from the sofa a while ago to stretch his legs and had been pacing ever since, Mom trying unsuccessfully to calm him, Grammy shouting at him to sit because he was making her nervous.

"Or maybe there's too many junkies out there," Grandpa added, nodding at Amie. "They need to kill off some people so the jails and hospitals don't overflow."

"This isn't helping, Joe," Grammy complained.

Grandpa shook a finger at her. "And what the hell do you think will help us? This might be what's left of our family, Julia, stuffed in here like goddamn sardines. Who knows where the others are – they could be anywhere out there!"

Tears shining, Grandpa returned to the sofa and covered his face, a sight somehow worse than everything else for Amie, even the murdered masses and their blank, unseeing eyes, even the man whose life she herself had ended.

Because if Grandpa was defeated, how would any of them go on?

## GRIDLOCKED

Xeke watched as Randy interrogated the old man for round two.

The duster was probably feeding Randy a bunch of pudding – chocolate, stinking, poodyloose pudding – but wouldn't a copper like Randy know if he was being bullshitted?

"I didn't ask for this to happen. I didn't organize it. I paid only to protect my family once I knew it was unavoidable," the old guy was saying, his face pasty with fear.

Randy maintained a cold, impassive look. "Why not call the cops if you knew this attack would happen?"

The dustmaestro let out an acidic, almost musically cadenced laugh, rising and falling devilishly as if practiced before a fire-ringed mirror in some dim, smoky room. His eyes smoldered like wreckage. His grin was that of a corrupt politician. "The *cops*?" he said, and the awful laughter skated through the room once more, eyes of hatred fixed firmly on Randy. "The authorities are responsible for this, you idiot."

Xeke eyed the pistol in hand, wishing Randy hadn't returned it to him. The situation was steepening precipitously, only a matter of time, Xeke feared, before a trigger was pulled.

# KEVIN FLANDERS

## Part IV: Darker

## Chapter 1

Dalton Rose's towering pain was rivaled in strength only by exhaustion. He gasped and choked, struggling for air as though attempting to tread stormy ocean swells, plunged at last into the depths.

For a time there was nothingness, and then, waking, Dalton was still submerged, though not in water but blood. It was warm and fetid and bubbling, Dalton fighting up to the surface, where two headless corpses hung upside down directly above him, blood dripping steadily as if from a shower faucet.

The hazy yellow sky was clouded by an approaching silhouette. The bloody sea slowly drained away, leaving Dalton on an elevated little island in the middle of a corridor. Rubbing his eyes (but how had he escaped the cuffs, and how had his broken fingers been healed?), wringing crimson from his hair, scared beyond fear, Dalton at first assumed the thing's face to be an illusion – a product of blood-blurred vision.

But this hooded stranger, drawing nearer, arms outstretched, was precisely as it appeared, Dalton realized. Where there should have been skin was blistered, raw ruin, pinkish and oozing with pustules. The eyes were portals to nowhere, twitching with the need to fill their emptiness.

Looming over Dalton now, the scrambled, wicked thing produced two heads from its robe. Dangling from the hair, tendriled gristle ribboning out at the necks, the severed spheres were gripped by hands hooked and razored like vultures' claws.

The victims' eyes were clamped open, as grotesquely wide as those of caricatures, bulging, cartoonish, unreal. The foreheads were stitched red like baseballs.

# GRIDLOCKED

Only when Dalton lurched to puke did the totality of his pain come fiercely back to him, though his fingers were no longer limp and useless but somehow normal again – a meager solace.

Beside him, the heads fell from the thing's grip, Dalton enduring the explosive splash of inner matter against his face, almost the exact color of a watermelon. But the bits of brain did not smell much like watermelon.

"Recognize those faces?" came a voice deader than shredded winter leaves spat out by a snowblower.

Feebly, Dalton tried to drag himself backward, but his hands slipped in sanguine puddles, his island sinking in like a giant sponge – and all he could do now was be helpless again, terrified and helpless, just as he'd been so many times before, most recently when Xeke Hamilton had turned his mouth into a pencil sharpener and laughed at him and told him he deserved it.

Like broken bits of a licked-white candy cane, Dalton could feel the remains of his front teeth clicking around in his mouth, his jaw throbbing and busted, his throat burning from the gun's repeated destruction.

Now there was a blade slowly forcing him down, onto his back. It trailed icily across his forehead.

"Recognize the faces?" The thing was kneeling now, patting Dalton's head and then slashing him twice with what looked like a key.

Blood spilled hotly from his forehead. At first there was no new pain, only shock – and then a memory. He had recognized those faces. They had dragged him out of the locker room, those now mutilated men, and one of them had thrown him into a wall and reached for his belt.

## KEVIN FLANDERS

That was all Dalton could remember.

The thing stood, stepped back, Dalton covering his face with his hands, the bloody shower still leaking down on him from overhead, where the bodies dribbled themselves dry.

"They wanted to hurt you, but I hurt them first," the thing said, smiling – the black, sagging smile of a Halloween pumpkin beneath a November moon. "Join me. I sense something inside you, boy. You will do well at my side, and then you will lead. You are destined to lead."

Dalton, starting into a useless inching crawl, stopped and turned when the thing said, "Join me, and together we'll make Xeke feel your pain. And your father, too."

A short time later, Dalton Rose was dressed in someone else's clothes and armed with someone else's semiautomatic rifle, the heavily accessorized AR-15 slung over his shoulder.

He stared deeply and hatefully into the gymnasium locker room mirror, producing the kind of reflection that can make even a saint see a demon's eyes in his own if he examines them at length. Blood was still crusted around his lips, even after a lukewarm shower that had stung him worse than a thousand bees, and a trace of a lunatic smile arrived in response to his near toothless, irreparable reflection, his cheeks bruised into an eclectic palette, his forehead still dripping blood, an X gouged at its center.

Impossibly, he was feeling mildly better after the shower, the pain suddenly not as total. The worst agony, in fact, was the echo of laughter in his head – the echo of a bell tolled often by his father and sounded again by Xeke Hamilton tonight.

Still hearing that laughter as he turned slowly from the mirror, Dalton was plunged back into his childhood, when his father had laughed drunkenly after beating him and his mother. It had happened more

# GRIDLOCKED

frequently as Dalton aged, the smell of alcohol always preceding that of iron, Dalton and his mother cowering as the laughter rained down on them.

*Stupid cunt! Little twat!*

Dalton hadn't known his mother was dead when the police came that Christmas Eve, two coppers finding him hiding in his room, where Mom had told him to go and lock the door after Dad flung him into the kitchen countertop. His injuries had been notable that snowy night, though not worse than many of the other nights, his split lip, broken tooth, and sore arm failing to induce a single tear.

*Look what you made me do, kid! This is all your fault, you little shit! You think you can disrespect me? This is my house!*

Dalton had trembled in the closet as his bedroom door was repeatedly slammed that final night of his former life, afraid of being hurt even worse but mostly afraid for his mother. He'd felt like he was choking on his fear, for the shouts hadn't belonged to his father but instead the menace his father became when he drank, a devil whose face twisted unrecognizably with rage. *He's not the same when he drinks*, Mom had said, warning Dalton to never intervene.

His name hadn't been Dalton Rose then. When questioned that night, he'd truthfully told the police that he was homeschooled, and they'd proceeded to ask about when he'd last seen a doctor. Years, he'd replied, a nine-year-old boy soon to be extracted from a home painted with blood and lorded by a tolling bell.

A bell whose echo never ceased.

Dalton crumpled down before the sink, his legs kicked out in front of him, boots far too big for him like anchors on his feet. He set the gun down by his side, and the tears torrented with memories of his mother…so many nights spent together, usually with the bedroom door locked, Mom holding him and singing him to sleep after Dad rattled into the basement, where he usually disappeared after giving them something to cry about, either that or Uncle Troy's bar across town. If Dalton or Mom heard the rumble of Dad's truck at the end of the driveway following a beatdown, or if they saw his tail lights streaking off into the night, they knew they could go downstairs for a few hours and watch a movie. They were safe then, and with that safety was relief. Sometimes Mom would make popcorn. Other nights she'd bake cookies. They liked comedy movies the best. It felt better to go to bed after a few sniffly laughs; comedy helped get the shakes out, helped make the pain less.

Mom had often said it would be all right, that they'd get through it together, that Dad was just going through a bad stretch after Grandpa died or he got fired from work or he hurt his back or he couldn't find a new job. It was always worse in the winter. At least when Dalton was doing well at baseball, he could make Dad happy and proud. Dad would take them out to dinner on those nights and celebrate and pat Dalton on the head and call him "slugger." Things were good on those nights. Dalton's parents never fought after he did well in sports, but the police told Dalton his mother was dead that Christmas Eve, and he knew right then, like a knife to the back and yet still half-disbelieving, that it was his fault.

It would never be good again, never all right.

There had been Christmas lights blinking at the emergency room reception desk that night, the ER unusually busy for such a late hour, Dalton briefly forgotten by the nurses and cops, left alone with his anguish and his fear and his desperate, fading denial, one person expecting the next to be watching him as the paperwork was filled out and the phone calls were made.

An ailing woman had occupied the ER cubicle to Dalton's right, faceless beyond the curtain, and every now and again she'd erupted into tortured moans, eerie sounds that Dalton, torn between sickened grief and numb incredulity, had envisioned as issuing from his mother. She couldn't really be dead. They were wrong – they were lying! She was right there behind that curtain. She would get better – she just needed to get away from Dad.

Dalton's ruined mouth began to throb even stronger. *I should have helped her. She needed me. I was weak, always weak.*

For a time that Christmas Eve, alone, listening closely, his knees pulled up to his chin on the ER bed, shivery and scared, Dalton had been sure he heard his mother calling to him from the other side of the curtain.

"Mom?" he'd managed, the air drained from his lungs.

Sniffling, dabbing his eyes, his arm still hurting despite the painkillers, Dalton padded gingerly out of his cubicle and very nearly pulled back the curtain to the next section. But what if it wasn't his mother? What if it was just an old woman lying gauntly on the bed?

Continuing through the ER, unsupervised and invisible, Dalton remembered how Mom and Dad had said just yesterday that it would be the best Christmas ever. They'd even given him a few early gifts, among them the Exceed Smartwatch currently around his wrist, its sensors confirming an unusually fast heart rate.

Snow drifted lightly that night, the flakes impossibly huge. No one saw Dalton at the waiting room window, hands pressed against the glass, until his sobbing betrayed him.

Later, when his uncle arrived to pick him up, one of the officers gave Dalton a stuffed bear, its T-shirt displaying a message of encouragement. The bear came with a card written by a local girl scout troop, a service project that had seen the scouts deliver dozens of stuffed animals to area police departments, each to be handed out to a distraught child the cops encountered during emergency responses.

## KEVIN FLANDERS

Riding in the passenger seat of his uncle's car, Dalton shredded the card into snowflakes and tried to rip the bear's eyes out.

*I wasn't there. I let her die.*

Dalton stood, fought through the pain, noticing another mild improvement. He held his jaw firm. With his other hand he wiped the tears away, hating them worse than his reflection, worse than Xeke's laughter, worse than Dad's laughter, worse than thoughts of Xeke railing him with the gun, worse than memories of Dad knocking him to the floor again and again, choking him, slapping him, breaking him, throwing him into the trunk, and all he'd wanted to do was protect Mom, fully aware of the price of intervention.

*Your father has a bad temper, sweetie, but he loves you very much. He had a difficult childhood. He never learned how to control his temper. Promise me you'll stay out of it when we fight – you know that only makes him madder.*

Dalton gathered the rifle, eased it back over his shoulder.

Readied himself, flexed his fingers.

Spat out another fragment of tooth, prepared to silence the bell forever.

The hooded thing had asked Dalton if he wanted to make them pay, all of them.

Now the thing was back, a robed monstrosity with a face that had seemingly been burned a thousand times over. It tossed a bulky mask to Dalton – the golden head of a lion, eerily inexpressive, the mouth closed, the mane rough like carpet.

Dalton parted his lips to speak, but pain slashed through his jaw.

# GRIDLOCKED

"Wear it," the thing commanded, nodding at the mask in Dalton's hands. "Go on. You can't be seen, boy, not until later."

Arms sore and heavy, Dalton lifted the mask and settled it over his head, a sour rubbery smell taking over.

The thing's dead squid lips stretched into a smile. "Good. Very good. Are you ready for death?"

Dalton nodded, the urge dazzling over him again, the one that had first come to him in the quietude of his uncle's house the day after his move to central Massachusetts – the urge to hurt. Charlie the cat had almost enjoyed his final dinner that night, almost, but something had stopped Dalton at the last second, knife in hand…a thought of Mom and…something else, a flash of what it felt like to be helpless and scared and looking up at that which scared you. There had been a simultaneous desire in that moment to never author the same agonies that had been forced upon him, no matter how strong the urge became.

But now, seven years later, Dalton wore the mask, the AR-15 slung over his shoulder and the revenant urge in his gut.

In spite of the pain, Dalton Rose grinned.

## Chapter 2

Tommy, pretending to sleep on the stiff lower level of the bunks, was instead reliving his latest vision.

There were two men, both of them tall. Tommy saw them striding down an indigo-tinted road, the moon barely more than a sliver at the horizon, a shadowed sign in the distance:

## NORTH
# 49

Tommy's eyes fluttered open, his heart accelerating at the sound of the men's thudding boots in his head…but then he was back, the vision fading. The room was mostly dark, Timothy Thorne still standing guard at its center, the pistol on the desk beside him. He was staring down at the floor, lost in thought, Tommy wondering for a moment if rushing him could actually work.

*No, you can't. Trust Beatrice's plan. This will work.*

Tommy closed his eyes again and conjured the images. The men were shouting something, but he couldn't understand. The sky seemed to shimmer, the moon disappearing. The Route 49 sign was swallowed by darkness.

One level higher, on a bunk as narrow as that of a submarine, Dom listened to apprehensive rustling and whispering and shifting. In the opposite corner, an old man was snoring loudly, only the Lord Himself understanding how one could sleep at such a time.

Dom hurt with fear for Cyri and his family. His muscles had become tight and achy, to the point that he'd needed to descend the ladder a few minutes ago and pace, Timothy Thorne glaring at him from his position at the center of the room. Dom had flipped him off and received in return an arrogant shake of the head.

Dom couldn't wait for 2:30. Showtime.

# GRIDLOCKED

## Chapter 3

Bruce Harrelson waited impatiently behind the wheel of the Kenworth. He checked his mirrors often. He checked his watch even more often. He told himself he could shoot a man if he had to, just like sniping targets at the gun range.

Bruce couldn't believe Keene and Drayson had gone off chasing those bastards like idiot dogs after rabbits, gunfire erupting in the woods a few moments ago as they put down whoever was out there. "Orders are orders," Drayson had said before they left, reminding Bruce that priority one was to eliminate all combatants.

Bruce, having lowered the window, thought he heard footsteps coming up on the driver's side. "Ready to roll, boys?"

No response.

Panicking, he shoved his 9 mm out the window and waved it a little. "Back off – I'll shoot!"

A two-note whistle issued from below – the sound to which dogs answer.

Bruce, pale with terror, poked his head out the window and trained his gun on the pavement. No one there. A look in the mirrors confirmed an empty road behind the truck.

Bruce receded into the cab, fear latching coldly to his neck. He squawked words of alarm over the radio.

"Where the fuck are you guys? Someone's here – I think he might attack the truck!" He checked the mirrors again, a poisonous fear delving deeper. If his guys had wasted the bastards, then why weren't they back yet? And who had whistled?

## KEVIN FLANDERS

Bruce wondered if it had only been the wind.

*No, someone's out there. He wants the truck!*

Desperate, Bruce tried the radio once more. "Get your asses back here! You left me out to dry! Hey, you hear me? Answer, goddammit!"

The whistling came again, indisputable. Bruce lurched out the window but did not aim his weapon this time, for a single round left him slumping through the window, a red perforation center-cut in his forehead.

Steel climbed the truck's steps and completed the defenestration his bullet had begun, then hopped down and recovered the driver's gun.

Steel had leaned out just far enough from his position in front of the left headlight to take the kill shot, Paul watching it all unfold from the edge of the woods, triumph met with disgust.

After Steel waved him over, Paul watched as his friend dragged the driver's body behind the truck, a streak of blood left in its wake.

"Let's ride. We need to get moving before someone else comes," Steel said, dumping the body in the breakdown lane like a tattered old sofa.

Inside the cab, which smelled of cigarettes and diesel, Paul made a quick search for anything useful while Steel shifted the rig back out onto 49 North. The glove box was clean, the sleeper compartment seemingly unused, and not a single receipt or gum wrapper lingered beneath the passenger seat.

"Anything?" Steel said when Paul returned from the sleeper.

"Nothing. Neater than the first glimpse of a hotel room."

# GRIDLOCKED

They passed a convoy of eighteen wheelers and military vehicles heading south. Dread grabbed at Paul as the fleet rumbled past, but none of the vehicles so much as braked.

They'd done it, overtaking a truck without detection. But where would they go now?

"They stripped the Q out of this thing," Steel noted, indicating a recess in the center control panel occupied by dime-size holes for wiring. "Then they restored the manual controls."

Using the side mirror, Paul sized up the road behind them, another truck in the distance. "Where we heading, y'ole gunslinger?"

"Anywhere that's far from these woods. Gotta ride this thing out and eventually turn west."

Like a poorly made boat destined to sink, their plan's holes were easily visible now that it had been launched. "What if they've got checkpoints set up?"

"Then I guess we'll see who's the better shot. If the rest of 'em are as useless as those last three, I like our chances." Feeling oddly relaxed, Steel leaned back and settled a hand comfortably over the wheel, the truck purring now that he had it geared up higher. He sure could use a smoke.

Paul swallowed with a catch. He felt as if he were buckled into a roller coaster, and now the damn thing was shooting up the chain hill, its passengers compelled to endure every rise, fall, and curve, too late to get off and run back to mommy. Yet somehow he wasn't as panicked as before – was he already acclimating to survival mode?

When the road straightened out before them again after a bend, Steel ramped the speed up to seventy. Most of the ruined vehicles had been cleared from the breakdown lanes, and the sun was getting the better of gray-tinged clouds. For the moment, the road looked like countless previous roads that had led them here, their journeys like chapters, one flowing into another as the overall story played out. Steel figured their tale would end with bullets, lots of them, a fitting end for himself, he supposed – a grand finale of violence for a violent life – but not for Paul.

Paul was the one with a wife and son, the one who needed to make it home, and Steel, not merely as his guide but his friend, vowed in silence – one hand spread casually over the wheel – to get Paul back to Chicago, even if it meant he got there alone.

Paul cringed when another convoy passed southbound, this one flanked by black SUVs, forcing Steel to angle into the breakdown lane and chase a stranded pair into the woods. The sight of those people, an elderly couple, reminded Paul of the early days of the grid, when citizens had been informed that taking to the road for any purpose other than AVA-sanctioned travel was illegal. Dog walkers, joggers, high school cross country teams, vagrants, bicyclists – all of it illegal.

Amidst widespread protests, the government had announced a massive sidewalk restoration/aerial crosswalk implementation project. The goal, Providence Devlin had said, was to ensure that every major road in the nation featured sidewalks and aerial crosswalks by 2040. Meanwhile, anyone wishing to continue using roadways for non-automotive purposes had been required to go through the dreaded process of applying for an exemption, each application sent not to town or state agencies but the Department of Homeland Security.

As such, in the fall of 2026, government men in a black SUV like the ones they'd recently passed on 49 had arrived at Paul's house. They'd worn suits and sunglasses, Maddie had reported.

"Good afternoon, sir. We're Agents Berenguer and Lyons, Department of Homeland Security, Illinois COMPLEX Office

# GRIDLOCKED

[Autonomous **Compl**iance and **Ex**emptions]," they'd identified with the warmth of a January wind. "We're here to discuss the application you filed with this office on July 7, 2026."

Paul had gone against Steel's advice in filing for the exemption. Steel, indignant, had told him to keep on walking and to Hell with a government that prohibited pedestrians, even on private ways and dirt roads. Following the grid's launch, town parade vehicles were sent into the Q's PARADE SEQUENCE; the Amish were permitted quarantined "safe zones" that didn't interfere with Grid traffic; and anyone who dared to defy the system was hit with heavy fines, even imprisonment.

*If mentalities like yours, sir, had existed in previous generations, we'd still be riding horses to our destinations,* Devlin had told a senator in opposition to AVA.

It had all been thought of, it seemed, and if there was ever a question, the COMPLEX agents were there to answer it. *AVA will create hundreds of thousands of jobs,* Devlin had touted, jobs for people like Agents Berenguer and Lyons, who'd sampled Maddie's cheesecake in the living room and voiced their approval with tepid friendliness.

"Mr. Shannon, we're pleased to inform you that your application has been approved," Agent Lyons had announced. "This exemption permit, good for one year and renewable for a small fee, will allow you to travel by foot on all roads below Class 1. Due to your most unfortunate circumstances, this permit will also enable not more than two guides to accompany you at any given time. Should you have any further questions, Mr. Shannon, we will provide you with a copy of the AVA regulations handbook and the *Don't Drive, Stay Alive* audiobook."

Paul had wondered if his stature as a bestselling author had aided in the seemingly expedient approval of his permit. But regardless of how it had happened, he'd managed to accomplish what, according to a *New York Times* report, less than two percent of the population achieved. He'd been granted the right to walk on American roads.

After Agents Berenguer and Lyons had departed, the scent of rain hanging in the air, Paul had sat on the porch swing with Maddie and let his shame and disgust pour out.

"Our forefathers," he'd said, taking her hand, "would they have stood for this? Would they have given away their freedom to drive for a promise of making people safer?"

"Don't beat yourself up," she'd said. "Sometimes you have to make sacrifices to save lives."

But hadn't Devlin spoken those very words? Yes, Paul was almost sure of it. Devlin – a man who'd also said the price of refused transcendence is paid not with money but lives.

They rumbled into Spencer and, just after crossing the Sevenmile River, took a left onto Route 9. Surrounded by woods, Route 49 had sheltered them from the widespread horrors, but now, proceeding west on 9, they passed one smoking ruin after another.

The buildings had been reduced to blackened shells and rubble. Shops and a restaurant and a church – everything black and curling with smoke. Up ahead on the right, a recharge station had collapsed, vehicular skeletons crushed beneath the canopy. They looked like the blown out ruins of vehicles seen on the news following a mortar attack in the Gaza Strip.

Farther along, the golden McDonald's *M* had been severed from the sign pole and now rested on the sidewalk. The restaurant itself was blasted and burnt. Behind it, trees were still on fire, sending up columns of smoke that amalgamated into a sinister mushroom.

# GRIDLOCKED

"Jesus, they destroyed everything," Paul managed, the tears in his eyes not only for Spencer, Massachusetts, but Chicago, Illinois, where his wife and son might be trying to survive a similar scene.

*How far does the suffering go?*

When they slowed behind a cavalcade of trucks and SUVs, Paul descried bodies amidst the burnt ruins, many of them heaped together. Some were still alive, clutching their wounds and dragging themselves through the disaster, no hope of a hospital for them.

"Annihilation," Paul murmured when they passed a parking lot turned graveyard. He could hardly stand to look, even after everything they'd already seen…and the smell was infinitely worse than the sights. It penetrated the shut windows, driving straight down to their viscera.

Overhead, the clouds were thickening once more, Steel crushed by the helplessness. They couldn't help any of these people lying dead and hurt, nor could they tell people that things would get better because they sure as shit appeared to be getting worse.

To see enemy vehicles continuing to rush past made something in Paul snap, a cable of trust, perhaps. Where were the men and women charged with protecting their nation? Why wasn't anyone fighting this? How could this constant procession of trucks and armored vehicles be allowed to carry on undisturbed?

And what the fuck was this "brave new world", as the man on Route 49 had called it?

"You think the residents were all killed in their houses?" Paul said.

Steel glanced grimly over at him. "The ones who survived are probably hiding in the woods like we were. Either that, or they tried to leave town."

"They wouldn't have gotten far."

"No, not unless they had a vehicle off grid."

Rain spattered against the windshield. The sky had turned even angrier, though the sun was breaking through in the distance, ethereal shafts of light angling down across the western hills. When Steel switched on the windshield wipers, they made dull thumps that grated in Paul's bones.

He checked the mirrors, still no vehicles racing up at them.

"Grab my map," Steel said. "What's the next town?"

Paul gathered the map from Steel's pack and unfolded it, the sight of their planned route like a kick to the stomach. Highlighted in orange, it accentuated the utter wrongness of the turn life had taken last night, veering off the path of normalcy and careening an insane course through increasingly hopeless destinations. They'd been walking Route 49 just last night, hurried but content, Paul trapped in a world of darkness yet undisturbed by his imprisonment because life was good, blessed, predictable. His family was back home, safe.

Now Paul was free of the dark, his vision restored, but he was condemned to endure a darkness far more oppressive than that of blindness – the absolute darkness of destruction and suffering.

# GRIDLOCKED

## Chapter 4

Xeke glared into the dark, wildly shifting eyes behind the mask. "Fuck you!"

The mask, a wolf's head, was detailed enough to have once belonged to a living animal – the mouth stretched back into a snarl, pearly razor teeth daggering down from pinkish-black gums.

The masked men, led by a robed-hooded psycho who could fight like he was in the movies, had overtaken the locker room prison without firing a shot. Randy and the other guys Virgil had chosen as "guards", including Xeke, had fired liberally at the attackers. They'd been effective only at hitting each other, though, none of the attackers falling.

Even with a face dripping blood, the guy in the robe and hood had destroyed Randy and three other men. He'd broken arms, caved in knees, snapped a neck, and administered a vicious kick that had made a three-hundred-pounder squeal like a piglet.

It had been quick but not painless.

"What did you say?" came hoarse, whispery words from behind the mask. The man was armed, as were his masked cohorts, but Xeke was strangely unafraid (perhaps because the masked men hadn't actually done anything to help their leader during the fight).

"You heard me," Xeke said, sensing weakness behind the mask. He stood about five feet from the man, close enough to detect something soft in those shifting eyes.

After liberating the prisoners, the guy in the robe/hood had departed, leaving Wolfman in charge of the room. Scraggly gray hair spilled out the back of his mask, body odor pouring from him in waves.

Weakness confirmed, the man did not shoot or even strike Xeke. For a time they stared wordlessly at each other, and then the guy directed Dalton's uncle and another man to "toss the little shit into the cage."

When David Valenzuela turned to face Amie, his expression brightened considerably.

"There's definitely a shelter at Tantasqua – I confirmed it through three contacts," he reported, pulling off his headset. "I guess the Freedom Riders have it sealed off, and they're still taking people in."

The debate ensued – the same one they'd been having since Dad arrived. Should they remain hidden in the basement bunker, or should they attempt to reach a shelter?

"Apparently they've got fences set up around the school – and weapons." Dad glanced about the room he'd begun constructing years ago, long before the first commercials endorsing AVA were introduced, with pop stars and athletes and politicians urging people to "be the change"; long before the SR system was fast-tracked and letters arrived explaining that the government would be supplying vehicle owners with AVA-compatible exchanges.

"But this is our home, David," Mom said. "If we leave, it could be destroyed."

"It could be destroyed anyhow." Grandpa had taken to pacing again. "The fires are getting worse, right?" He turned to Dad, who'd relayed multiple reports of area neighborhoods set ablaze.

Nodding, Dad inhaled deeply. He'd already reminded them that the station wasn't fireproof, featuring an emergency hatchway in case they were forced out by flames.

"I'm surprised they haven't torched this place already," added Grandpa, a man whose bumper bore a withered **THINK POSITIVE** sticker.

# GRIDLOCKED

Amie squeezed Jazzi's hand. Watching her family and her newest friend, slowly looking each of them over, there was an icy thought that she would rather die than see these people hurt.

And what about Xeke? She wondered how badly he was hurt. She wondered if he'd made it out of the prison. For a moment of distilled terror, she wondered if she would ever see him again.

She absently looked up at the clock. It was almost one a.m.

On the wrong side of the cage, Xeke checked on Randy and the others. Randy was wheezing and sputtering, the victim of a demolition derby courtesy of the lunatic in the robe and hood. Randy's nose was bloody, most likely broken, and he gritted his teeth and clutched his left arm as if it, too, was broken.

The others who'd dared to fight were in similarly bad shape, one man unconscious. The rest of them – the ones who'd shot at the intruders but hadn't gone man-to-man – were quiet and cowering, heads drooped. Three of Virgil's men had been killed by friendly fire, and therefore were not in the cage with them but stacked in the far corner like hockey bags waiting to be hauled onto the team bus. One of them seemed to be staring straight at Xeke, his eyes like a portal to Hell.

When the storm had quieted and the guard-prisoner status had found itself reversed, Xeke had been singled out by Dalton's uncle. As the robed bastard was leaving, the uncle screamed at Xeke to tell him where Dalton had been taken. When Xeke refused to answer, Wolfman launched questions and fists at him, Xeke telling the attackers to take a southernmost trip.

Now, behind the cage, battered and bleeding, the pent up fear came shuddering through and Xeke realized just how afraid he was.

*We're all gonna die.*

*No, Virgil will come back. He'll get us out of this.*

Xeke could practically hear Virgil's advice, quick and enigmatically apt. Just hold on, kid, he might say. Keep your trap shut and check your pride at the door (older dudes were always telling you to check things at the door, it seemed, or cautioning you against trying things at home).

"I'm gonna waste that bastard," Randy growled, using Xeke's extended arm to steady himself into a sitting position.

"I wouldn't recommend it. Dude had some dire moves," Xeke said quietly, convinced that he'd shot at least two attackers…but they hadn't even been fazed. This whole thing was like a trip to Leapland, too fast and chaotic.

Randy coughed, wiped blood from his nose. "He sucker-punched me, caught me off guard, that's all. Can't believe none of these idiots could hit the guy's head – they kept shooting his vest."

Xeke pressed his lips together, enduring the sting of failure. "Yeah, they were all shooting like dusters. I thought I had the guy harrowed, though, but he just…dodged it somehow."

A thick, brooding quiet overtook the station – the sort of baleful silence that, beneath blackened skies, precedes a tornado.

Amie and Jazzi were drawing pictures together, a beach and a rainbow and a house standing tall and peaceful in the serene world of imagination.

Dad, headset on, was recording information. He'd recently heard the same demand – Give. Me. The. Girl. – on another frequency, whereupon he'd gathered them in a circle of prayer.

# GRIDLOCKED

Mom was staring into an old paperback, though Amie hadn't heard a page turn in a while, her mother's expression fixed and relentlessly dour.

Grandpa, having been forced by Grammy to sit, was staring almost vacuously ahead, Grammy beside him on the sofa with her eyes closed.

No one said anything for a few minutes, the silence strengthening, enfolding them, too heavy, suffocating…finally broken by a frightened yelp.

Jazzi. She was looking past Amie, to the far wall, which had gone up in flames.

## Chapter 5

They weren't able to launch their plan.

With the clock nudging up against two a.m., Pastor Timothy Thorne flipped on the lights and ordered everyone up. He and Logan, a father-son duo about as appealing as a pair of used band-aids, waved their guns at people and shouted, "Form a line! Everyone form a line!"

Panic weltered in Thorne's eyes, almost as if he'd sensed the imminent attack and was rushing to preempt it. Tommy frowned at his brother as they stood, his eyes then sliding over to Beatrice and her parents, their faces mottled with fear and dismay.

Like dogs torn from sleep by a doorbell, people were barking and glaring at the Thornes, a few of them remaining in their bunks. Two little girls were crying. The older kids were quiet and horrified, sheltered behind their parents.

"Get up! Come on, right now! We have to go!" Timothy Thorne shouted, pointing the pistol at his parishioners. "Form a line at the center of the room!"

Dom had strong thoughts of refusal. Thorne was no sniper, just an obnoxious motherfucking squirrel with a gun. And his son, the little puke, Dom wanted to rearrange his face.

Tommy met Bea at the center of the room, took her hand, a quiet strength coursing between them – a mutual intuition that they were in this together, no matter what.

"We're leaving," Thorne said once everyone was in line. "This place isn't safe. Not anymore."

Dom shook his head, stepped out from the line. "That's what I told you hours ago, asshole. We should be at the shelter by now."

# GRIDLOCKED

Thorne poured acid into his glare and shot it across the room at them, where they stood at the back of the line.

"We're not going anywhere with you, Tim!" the old guy hollered, the same one who'd stood up to Thorne earlier. "You're out of your mind!"

Thorne marched over to the guy and wagged the gun in his face. "As the leader of this group, I make the decisions, you hear? I cannot abide one or two people jeopardizing the safety of the group." He walked the line, keeping a safe distance, staring at his parishioners appraisingly. Tommy didn't dare attack him, not now...*He's crazy enough to shoot us. Jesus, I think he'd actually do it.*

"I shouldn't even need a gun," Thorne complained. "You people should listen to me. Why don't you trust me?"

"Because you're pointing a gun at us," Bea said, each word a spear of disgust.

Thorne recoiled, his lips moving but not producing words, and then there was an eerie inaction on the pastor's part, his body stilling all at once as if clapped by ice rings from Mr. Freeze's gun. His mouth hung partly open. His gun leveled steady. His head remained strangely tilted, like a kindergartener posing for a photo. His eyes went glassy, unblinking, fastened upon Bea.

Moments later, he was back from wherever he'd gone, shaking his head repeatedly, a half-dazed, almost searching glaze to his eyes. It looked like he'd undergone a round of moderate electroshock therapy, his faculties slowly returning.

Logan noticed it, too. How could he not? "Dad, are you all right?"

Thorne nodded irritably. "Fine, fine, everyone stay in the goddamn line! We're moving!" He turned to his son. "Stand behind them. Make sure they all leave. If someone refuses, shoot them."

With that, Thorne waved them on, making little circles with his arms like a pre-grid traffic cop guiding a line of vehicles through a construction zone. "Everyone out! We're all going outside. This place isn't safe anymore."

Heading back the way they'd come, Dom was surprised to find the doors open and the dropdown ramp already lowered, a handful of armed men awaiting their arrival. They all wore police uniforms belonging to various departments (one was a state trooper, campaign hat and all).

Fear barreled through Dom. If they'd been lucky and caught the Thornes off guard, they might have been able to take the guns…but five more men? The scale was badly tipped now, the seesaw rattling down hard, Dom and Tommy and the rest of them hanging up in the air.

"Get your hands off, you bastard!" Bea's father shouted when one of the uniforms pushed his wheelchair up the ramp. Dom wondered if any of them was actually a cop.

Outside again, Tommy shivered, the night having dipped ten degrees. The trees stirred in a rejuvenated breeze. The air was thinly redolent with smoke, as if they were standing downwind of a chimney.

A ring of construction spotlights beamed down on them. Fixed to trailers, the units had been brought in while the Sims brothers were held underground in Thorne's bunker. But why? What was the plan now?

The Thornes briefly conferred with their reinforcements, softly spoken conversations masked by their hands.

# GRIDLOCKED

"I've never seen these people before," Bea said, sliding in at Tommy's side. "What do you think they're planning?"

"No clue. It seems like if they wanted us dead, they would have done it by now."

She took his hand, her fingers like slips of ice in his. Dom and Bea's parents gathered around them, everyone waiting for a decision, too afraid to run. The state trooper had warned that there were others guarding the woods – escapees would be shot.

"This is a matter of national security," he'd said. "We don't know who is behind this act of terror."

For a while longer they watched as Thorne gestured and nodded, Logan a few feet from his father, kicking at the dirt. Whenever one of the parishioners uttered an objectionable comment, a gun was pointed in the general direction of the offending voice.

When the conversation broke up a few minutes later, the trooper came over to them and tried to speak conciliatorily.

"We apologize for all of this," he said, holstering his gun. "But we can't be careful enough on a night like this. Our nation, our *freedom*, is under attack, ladies and gentlemen."

"Damn straight our freedom's under attack!" Bea's father hollered, shaking a fist from his wheelchair. "It's under attack from you people!"

"Sir, this isn't the time to be adversarial." The trooper's voice remained calm, but Dom could see the rage streaking into his eyes, barely visible in the shadows beneath the brim of his hat. Behind him, Thorne and the others kept their weapons pointed downward, but as surely as Tuesday follows Monday, they were ready to initiate target practice on the First Baptist Church of Sturbridge congregation if somebody decided to roll the dice.

Dom kept his mouth shut. If it'd been just him, this would have been different, much different – *You're shooting or I'm walking* – but with his brother and a bunch of women and children to protect, Dom knew he had to keep it below a boil.

"We have to get you all to safety," the trooper said. "Once you're in a secure location, there will be plenty of time for questions. Believe me, I've got a ton of questions myself. We're all in the dark here."

"How do we know *you're* not the terrorists?" Tommy flinched, unable to believe Beatrice had actually said it. But there she stood at his side, arms crossed, staring at the burly trooper.

The trooper said nothing, his eyes smoldering like coals.

Thorne stepped forward. "We should get moving. It's a long walk."

Nodding, the trooper grunted his approval and led the way, Thorne and Logan right behind him, the other four men prodding the cattle.

Before anyone knew a shot had been fired, their captors swiftly joined the ranks of the dead, the sounds of their collective demise no louder than the splattering of water balloons. They did not suffer. They didn't even gurgle out a few dying breaths, all seven souls instantly departed via headshots.

It wouldn't be until later that Tommy realized exactly what had happened. For now he could only react. When he saw the men fall, he dragged Bea down and threw himself atop her, Dominick doing the same for him, the mothers and fathers around them doing the same for their children.

# GRIDLOCKED

There had been no visions this time, no advanced warning whatsoever, the camouflaged men emerging from behind the trees a complete and horrifying shock.

## Chapter 6

Paul and Steel had continued west, crossing briefly back into East Brookfield ten minutes ago, greeted by the smoldering remains of a courthouse on a hill.

The vehicles parked outside the courthouse had looked like they were fresh off the grill, charbroiled and ready for serving. The grocery store had been torched as well, a few brave souls raiding it for whatever usable food and supplies lingered. There'd been a melee in the grocery store parking lot, ten or fifteen people kicking and swinging at each other, one man thrusting a knife at anyone who came near him, another man lying in a pool of blood. Paul had wanted to make it stop, desperate to bring order, but they were only two men passing by in a truck. They weren't an army. They weren't the police. They weren't even security guards. Now that society had disintegrated overnight, what could two men possibly do?

They were rolling out of East Brookfield now, well past Lake Lashaway, and entering Brookfield, Route 9 still teeming with convoys, the scenes of destruction the same. Above them, a flaming scanner gantry could have served as the gateway to Hell; to their right, a pair of COMPLEX cars had been bashed and burned.

"This road will take us all the way to Pittsfield, almost to the New York border," Paul informed, studying the map. "I'm guessing you want to stay off the SR and the turnpike."

"Definitely," Steel said, checking the rearview mirror. "Last thing we need is to get ourselves stuck underground, and the Pike will be heavily monitored. I think our only option is to keep heading west on roads like this and stay under the radar as long as we can. Luckily this bad boy's got almost a full tank."

"Who knows, maybe it won't be as bad once we get past Albany. A lot of farmland through New York – they might not have such a strong presence out there yet. They can't be everywhere."

# GRIDLOCKED

Steel nodded. "Good point. I imagine New York City's their main focus right now, but they're mobilizing quick. Hopefully they haven't hit Chicago yet."

The thought made Paul's stomach lurch. By avoiding the highways, it would take them several days to reach Chicago, and what would be left of the Windy City when they got there?

"The woods," Paul said after a while. "I still can't believe any of that was real. We were being tormented, man. Tormented by…only God Himself knows."

"This whole thing's crazy," Steel murmured, trying not to let his mind wander. "Right now all I care about is the next mile. The past is done, nothing we can do to change it. We're living in a war zone now, and we've gotta keep fighting."

Paul began to respond, but his attention was stolen by a fast approaching vehicle from behind, then another: a pair of vans shooting around a corner.

Black vans with something projecting from the roofs. Gunmen.

"Shit, Steel, we've got big trouble!"

The vans raced up nearly to the bumper of the flatbed trailer, leaning off to each side, one van straddling the double-yellow line, the other in the breakdown lane.

"Pull over immediately!" boomed the megaphone voice, the leftward van creeping up alongside the truck, then ducking back into the lane behind them when oncoming traffic appeared around an approaching curve.

Clutching the wheel with both hands, Steel resisted urges to gun the accelerator. This was an eighteen-wheeler, not a motorcycle. No matter how fast he went, the vans could outrun him.

"What are we gonna do? They've got heavy weapons, man!" In the side mirror, Paul saw the other van advancing on their right, the gunner poking out through the roof as if he were in a humvee. He wore a gray helmet and goggles, his machine gun swiveling back and forth on a makeshift mount.

"Pull over immediately! This is your final chance!"

"He's passing on our right!" Paul warned.

Even at a moderate speed, Steel still felt like he might roll the truck around the curve. Without any oncoming traffic, he crossed into the eastbound lane to ease the severity of the radius, then returned between the lines, the trailer seeming to swing a little as they came out of the curve.

The pursuing vans fell back. Navigating a series of sharp S-curves that rose and dipped, downshifting and then bringing the gear back up, Steel wondered if the attackers were waiting for reinforcements.

But when the road straightened again, the vans were back on them, venturing alongside the truck again, no warnings this time, only the flash-roar of gunfire.

Windows shattered, the truck hissing as rounds shredded through the engine, steam billowing against the windshield.

Steel could barely steady the wheel. His hands were hot with stinging pain. "Get down!"

Bullets rattled and whined through the cab. The truck thudded on a ruined tire, sparks careening, the trailer tilting to the right with a grinding crank.

# GRIDLOCKED

Steel rode the brakes and, glimpsing in the fragmented remains of mirror the godforsaken van trying to pass again on his right, he expended what little control he had left of the truck and veered into the breakdown lane.

The collision sent the van rolling but also caused the truck to lock and slew, the cab jackknifing to a stop, the trailer breaking off and overturning with a thunderous clout.

The chorus of gunfire became a symphony. Steel, heeding his own advice, crouched as low as he could, his back screaming in protest.

"Holy Mary, Mother of Jesus, save us!" Paul shouted, hardly able to hear his own voice.

The gunstorm raged even higher, rocking the truck like an earthquake. Steel braced for the blackness, the nothingness, the end.

But the cab seemed to be sustaining fewer shots now, the majority of tinks and clanks echoing off the trailer, which rested on its side about fifty feet away. It took Steel a paralyzed moment to understand what was happening, and then the picture was at least translucent for him, though not fully clear just yet.

A secondary battle of some sort had broken out, their attackers coming under attack. Peeking into the largest shard of the left mirror, Steel could see a handful of black-uniformed men hiding behind the downed trailer, occasionally extending their guns past it to shoot into the woods. Two of them were bleeding profusely. A third alternated between firing blindly and shouting into a radio.

A dozen other men lied dead near four additional vans that had pulled up, two of the vehicles on fire.

"I don't believe it!" Steel rasped, releasing a long-held breath. "Someone's saving our asses!"

The truck was no longer taking hits whatsoever, the enemy now focused entirely on self-preservation.

Steel lowered his head out of sight, then craned his neck in Paul's direction. "Are you hit?"

"No, I'm good…for now. What about you?"

"A few cuts from flying glass."

"Your hands are bleeding bad."

"It's nothing, really – paper cuts hurt worse."

The symphony gradually tapered, until all that remained was the drumming of gunfire in the woods.

Then, with the simplicity of a shut-off valve, there was silence.

When Steel looked back at the trailer, the five besieged combatants were swimming in pools of their own blood, deader than the truck in which Steel and Paul took shelter. It was a miracle, among others, that the diesel tanks hadn't ignited.

"Hey, buddy, you all right in there?" echoed a voice to Steel's left.

Several men emerged from the woods, led by a bearded man with an AK-47. He wore a black leather jacket and fedora, not merely walking but striding.

"Come on out of there, man," the guy called. "You're about as safe here as a liberal at an NRA convention."

Realizing they would already be dead if these guys had wanted them dead, Steel staggered out of the truck and called Paul out as well. By the time they hit the asphalt of Route 9, twenty more men had appeared. About two hundred feet down the road in both directions, rows of rumbling motorcycles and their armed riders formed a blockade.

Stumbling in front of the truck, amazed that they were alive, Paul took in the scene with disbelieving dread. Vehicles destroyed, men massacred, fires ravaging – it looked like a snapshot from somewhere in the Middle East. Chaos like this didn't happen in America. "Lawlessness," Paul murmured. "Utter anarchy."

"Welcome to the new world," the bearded man commented with a strange flippancy. "I'm Virgil, by the way." He took a moment to look over the men around him. "Myself, as well as these fine gentlemen, are the Freedom Riders."

A cold gust barreled into their faces. Riding along it was music, wafting fuzzily in from the nearest black van. The song was "Hotel California"…almost to the best part…*You can check out any time you like*…and a bloodied attacker was crawling out from the wreckage, dragging himself weakly toward oblivion, his hands scraping across glittering glass. Paul briefly thought he saw phantoms gathering around the man, leering and beckoning, shimmering up from the pavement and seeping back within it.

The doomed man tried to reach back for a weapon in his belt, but Virgil put a bullet in his forehead, shooting with a sidelong glance as though the guy posed no greater threat than a mannequin, all while "Hotel California" spirited on. At the wind's behest, the music eased in and out of clarity – and when the Eagles' masterpiece was finally finished, there was a strange stillness to the air, charged with expectation like a stormy sky before the first streak of lightning.

"You guys want to go it alone, or would you like to help us?" Virgil said after an assessment of the scene, his men seemingly unbothered by the carnage, waiting patiently for instructions.

Steel and Paul exchanged the briefest of glances, though their decision had already been made.

## Chapter 7

Dalton was eventually summoned to the school's natatorium, a white-haired duster informing him that his work was soon to begin. At first Dalton was reluctant and very still – almost cemented – but then the duster whispered, "To inflict the greatest pain, boy, you must be able to act without thought."

Walking with tiny shuffling steps, the man led Dalton into an office behind the bleachers in the natatorium, a little side room where some gym teacher probably porned up during breaks.

Inside that stuffy, chlorine-scented office, a shifter was waiting on the gym teacher's desk, the virtvoice app pulled up, reminding Dalton of the defect in his science class who used the app to communicate. It had been good times that day in the bathroom, taking the shifter from the little defect and writing, *I'm a defect* and *My name is Ballsack* and *My mom sucks huge dick.*

That kid was surely dead by now. No way he survived this shit.

"Try it out. Go ahead," the old man invited, smiling, Dalton resisting an urge to smack him down and make him bleed.

Dalton snatched up the shifter and typed, *Fuck off duster,* eliciting harsh, grating laughter from the old man.

*I don't need this thing.*

A glimmer traced into Dusty's eyes. "But Master begs to differ, young man. With that busted jaw of yours, speaking won't be very enjoyable."

Dalton began to type, but the man held up a hand. "I seem to recall Master rescuing you." He took a step closer, his breath a natural emetic, explicitly hellish. "Do you know what those men planned to do to you?" Dusty made a tittering sound and leaped back with a grin.

# GRIDLOCKED

"They think you're a very lovely boy, with your slender hands and your terribly haunted eyes. But Master would never have such things done to you. He's been watching you for a long time, indeed, and now it's your turn to lead."

Dalton tore off the mask and fired it at him, Dusty catching it with one hand and windmilling it like a hockey goalie. As the old man backed past a mirror and shuffled forth once more, Dalton was frigidly aware of a lack of reflection…and what about Dusty's face, which had just now become different somehow? The eyes – something deep and dark behind them? No, the mouth – a little more wrinkled? No, it was the ears, had they been that sharply pointed before?

"Take the device." The man's eyes were impossibly wide, preternatural, his whisper like a river of sand over rocks, grainy, sliding, scorched, stinging, to the extent that Dalton could almost feel the grit in his endlessly bloody mouth, sloshing around along with bits of teeth that still crumbled, crumbled, crumbled away. If only he could stop the bleeding, get that taste out of his mouth, spit out the last of what was ruined.

"You deserve this," Dalton thought he heard the man whisper, memories whisking him back to that moment with Xeke, just before the gun had been shoved into his mouth.

***

Gradually their captors left the locker room, trickling out until only Wolfman remained.

*He's an old guy*, Xeke thought from behind the cage. *A duster. Even with his gun, I can take him if I need to. He probably can't even shoot.*

Wolfman paced the room like a boy left home alone for the first time. He glanced often to the door.

Xeke, even in his dire situation, couldn't get Dalton out of his head. Guilt kept stabbing at him, and still he didn't understand what had happened during the fugue spell. How had Dalton ended up like that? Where had Xeke gone, lost in hatred so absolute that it had consumed him to the point of virtual sleepwalking?

He feared it would happen again. *I'm messed up, explicitly scrambled.*

Eventually Xeke's thoughts roamed back to the night's beginning. They'd been on their way to Friendly's for ice cream cones, so many stars lighting the way.

But now Xeke was apart from everyone he loved, and it was all infinitely worse because he knew he wasn't fully in control of himself. Maybe he hadn't been in control for some time now. That night with the AR-15 in the driveway – the hatred of that night had festered within him, and given the opportunity tonight with society having gone to shit and Dalton at his mercy, the hatred had ruled, not merely manifesting but overtaking.

Xeke banged his head against the lockers, beginning to feel like he might lose his mind.

***

Just as Amie's father extinguished the flames on the first wall, two additional fires spontaneously assailed the bunker, one spanning the ceiling.

Resigned to the inevitable, the six of them escaped through the soundproof hatchway, choking on heavy smoke.

# GRIDLOCKED

The house was almost fully engulfed, Amie left motionless by the sight of her home in flames. Heat charged in waves from the inferno, singeing their skin, the roar like a clattering train.

Glass burst outward. Inside, something collapsed with a protracted crash.

Amie would have remained there, tears running, if Dad hadn't taken her by the wrist, a gun in his other hand. "Come on! Everyone follow me!"

Their vehicles and the garage were also on fire. The rest of the houses on the street were on fire. Every vehicle in sight was on fire.

The air was toxic, Amie forced to pull the collar of her sweatshirt over her face, the others doing the same. Grandpa began to cough uncontrollably as they ran down the street, and luckily they slowed to match his speed when he fell behind – for an SUV parked streetside ahead of them exploded and launched debris, a large projectile shearing a mailbox post in half just to Amie's right.

"We have to get off the road!" Dad shouted, banking left toward a patch of woods behind the Ruocco and Powell houses, which were nothing more than logs in a fireplace, flames leaping nightmarishly from the windows.

Running alongside the hedges that divided the houses, Amie thought she heard a scream rise above the blaze in the Powell house…and then she remembered the Powells had two dogs, a lab mix and a German shepherd. A sense of peace had slid over Amie lately whenever she saw Mr. Powell walking his dogs at dusk, like things were all right in their little corner of the universe, her life not the bane she'd once thought it to be, not something she needed to run from.

But now she was running. All of them were running, Amie momentarily torn, wondering if she should go back and try to help the Powells – *What if they're still inside?* – but she knew she had to keep going. To enter these houses would be to enter her coffin.

*Who's doing this? Why isn't anyone stopping them?*

They were panting by the time they reached the woods. Grandpa erupted with rattling wheezes, his hand pressed against his chest, Mom and Grammy at his sides.

"Deep breaths. Deep breaths," Mom reminded.

Amie, glancing down at Jazzi, came briefly free of her own fear and centered her focus on a girl who had it so much worse than any of them. "It's gonna be okay," Amie said, lowering herself to Jazzi's level and taking her hands.

Nodding, Jazzi bit her lip to force back the tears. Her face took on an ethereal radiance in the firelight, shadow branches sketched across her eyes and forehead.

"What if your grandpa dies?" Jazzi whispered, lips trembling.

Amie hugged her new friend, the night having made them sisters. "He's strong – we're all strong," she said, the hurt escalating for all that had been lost, powerful enough to stop her breath.

They took a few minutes to gather themselves. Impossibly, there were no sirens wailing in the distance, no firefighters coming to quell the conflagrations and rescue those in trouble, no paramedics to help the weak and wounded, no police to restore order.

They were on their own.

Peering through the trees at jagging orange tendrils, the utter desolation of the night was reaffirmed for Amie – yet still a locked chamber of her mind was incredulous, unable to reconcile the canyon that had been torn between the start and finish of this unspeakable night, two different worlds on either side. They had been on their way to Friendly's for ice cream cones, maybe a sundae if they were in the mood, lots of sprinkles to be had, and a cherry, too…and then a pop of whiskey to give them a true happy ending. Stars would have winked down at them on the way home, but now there was only smoke-lorded oblivion.

The word shot icily through Amie: *oblivion*. It was followed closely by: *apocalypse*.

"What do we do?" she said.

"We stay together," Dad answered. "We keep the faith."

Thanks, friends, for your constant support! We hope to see you back on the Grid soon, with the second book in the trilogy – *Blaze the Grid*.

## MEET THE AUTHOR

A lifelong resident of Massachusetts, Kevin Flanders has written over ten novels and multiple short stories. In 2010, he graduated from Franklin Pierce University with a degree in mass communications, then served as a reporter for several newspapers.

When he isn't writing, Flanders enjoys spending time with his family and two dogs, playing ice hockey, and traveling to a new baseball stadium with his father each summer. He also takes part in several functions and mentors student writers.

But no matter where Flanders travels or who he meets along the way, he is always searching for inspiration for the next project.

The author resides in Monson, MA.

For more information about upcoming works, visit www.kmflanders.wordpress.com.

Made in the USA
Middletown, DE
12 October 2021